THE SURVIVOR

DENNIS ARTHUR PARRY was born in 1912 and was educated at Rugby School. He read Classics at King's College, Cambridge and obtained a first class degree. He then read Law and qualified as a Chancery Barrister. In 1937, he married Kathleen Arona Forbes, with whom he had two children, Susan and Jonathan. He was rejected for service in the Second World War because of poor eyesight and instead joined the civil service, eventually rising to the post of Permanent Under-Secretary to the Minister for Coal Production. After the war, his marriage collapsed, and following a divorce, Parry married his second wife, Audrey Dockerill, with whom he had one son, Mark.

Parry published his first novel, *Attic Meteor* (1936) at age 24, and would go on to publish nine others. None of these books achieved large sales, though they generally earned good reviews. An obituary in the *Times* characterized Parry's works as "entertaining on the surface, and written in an easy, forceful prose . . . continuously witty rather than comic, and penetrating rather than profound. . . . All his books are enjoyable, and almost all successful within the limits which Parry set himself." His final book, *Sea of Glass* (1955), was probably his most successful, earning widespread critical acclaim and running into a second edition. Unfortunately, the book's modest success was overshadowed by Parry's death shortly after its publication; he was severely injured in a car accident in June 1955 and died two days later at age 42.

MARK VALENTINE is the author of several collections of short fiction and has published biographies of Arthur Machen and Sarban. He is the editor of *Wormwood*, a journal of the literature of the fantastic, supernatural, and decadent, and has previously written the introductions to editions of Walter de la Mare, Robert Louis Stevenson, L. P. Hartley, and others, and has introduced John Davidson's novel *Earl Lavender* (1895), Claude Houghton's *This Was Ivor Trent* (1935), Oliver Onions's *The Hand of Kornelius Voyt* (1939), and other novels, for Valancourt Books.

Cover: The cover of this edition reproduces Irving Miller's jacket art for the first American edition, published by Henry Holt and Company.

By Dennis Parry

Attic Meteor (1936)

The Bishop's Move (1938)

The Survivor (1940)

Atalanta's Case (1945)

Mooncalf (1947)

Outward Be Fair (1949)

Fair House of Joy (1950)

Going Up—Going Down (1953)

Horseman, Pass By (1954)

Sea of Glass (1955)

THE SURVIVOR

DENNIS PARRY

"Quisque suos potimur manes"

With a new introduction by
MARK VALENTINE

VALANCOURT BOOKS

The Survivor by Dennis Parry
First published London: Robert Hale, 1940
Reprinted from the 1st U.S. edition (New York: Holt, 1940)
First Valancourt Books edition 2014

Copyright © 1940 by Dennis Parry
Introduction © 2014 by Mark Valentine

All rights reserved. In accordance with the U.S. Copyright Act of 1976, the copying, scanning, uploading, and/or electronic sharing of any part of this book without the permission of the publisher constitutes unlawful piracy and theft of the author's intellectual property. If you would like to use material from the book (other than for review purposes), prior written permission must be obtained by contacting the publisher.

Published by Valancourt Books, Richmond, Virginia
http://www.valancourtbooks.com

ISBN 978-1-941147-36-8 (*trade paperback*)
Also available as an electronic book.

All Valancourt Books publications are printed on acid free paper that meets all ANSI standards for archival quality paper.

Set in Dante MT 11/13.2

INTRODUCTION

WHEN Walter Allen published his important study of mid-20th century British (and American) literature, *Tradition and Dream* (1964), he was willing to consider some aspects of the fantastic in literature, a field which the more fastidious amongst literary critics tended to shun altogether. Realism was in the ascendant, and any breath of the marvellous was enough to curl the lips and quiver the nostrils of the panjandrums.

But Allen's slightly more open approach only went so far. Those he considered included David Garnett, a Bloomsburyite, and so still within the literary pale; T. F. Powys, who had already been singled out for muted praise by F. R. and Queenie Leavis, the Cambridge arbitrators of distinction in fiction; and Ronald Firbank, whose elliptical and arch wit was rather warily celebrated, though chiefly for his influence upon Evelyn Waugh and others of eminence.

It was a measured, tentative selection. Missing were the seven supernatural thrillers of Charles Williams, which tussled with profound theology under the guise of rather breathless yarns, and the modernist, mystical novels of inner Bohemia by Mary Butts. Also overlooked were the elaborate epics of E.R. Eddison, told in majestic Jacobean prose, the stormy metaphysical dramas of Claude Houghton, and the delicate meditations on other realities in the novels of Ronald Fraser. There was no place either for the stories of independent young women finding metaphors of their own development in the worlds of magic and myth, as in Sylvia Townsend Warner's *Lolly Willowes*, or Stella Benson's *Living Alone*. These, we may suspect, were all a little too outré for the sober commentator.

Yet Walter Allen at least tried to look beyond the boundaries of the accepted canon. For there will always be authors whose works evade attention. Perhaps one fairly certain way to make it difficult to gain a following among readers or critics is to write very variously. When confronted with a set of books that fit into no obvious category, they are apt to shy away. What are we to make of an author who one moment has us among the glories and intrigues of the Byzantine Empire and the next amid the dreary frost-ridden fens, in the middle of a deadly 'flu epidemic?

That last is the setting for *The Survivor* (1940), and it is surprising that it has not gained a greater reputation among enthusiasts of supernatural fiction. It is true that the near-omniscient E. F. Bleiler does give it qualified praise, noting the book's "many good touches and flashes of wit" though he is less impressed by the plot and the attempt to convey real wickedness in the main character (*The Guide to Supernatural Fiction*, 1983). But it has otherwise been largely overlooked in the field.

This is curious, because the book in fact achieves a number of difficult things. Firstly, it is a successful full-length ghost story. Most notable supernatural tales are short stories: the antiquarian hauntings of M. R. James, the dreamlike reveries of Walter de la Mare, the pagan spells of Arthur Machen. There are a few good examples of ghostly novels, but not many: and even those, such as Henry James's *The Turn of the Screw*, have their doubters. Can the finely shaded ambiguities of the really effective spectral tale be sustained over the longer form? Parry tackles this dilemma breezily, by avoiding it altogether. In *The Survivor* we are soon left in no doubt about the haunting. His is not a stealthy spirit seen in half-light, but an arrogant, boisterous, and highly cunning force.

Secondly, he has written a modern and ironic ghost story. He has the nerve to use his characters to point out the distinction between his approach and those of convention. When they meet to discuss what is happening to them, they rather doubtfully consider, and reject, what they know from "tales and legends of the supernatural". One character, evolving a theory, admits it may not be "any higher than Dracula". Another "would greatly have preferred that the supernatural, if it must impinge on her life, should do so in a familiar, old-fashioned style, dressed in a white shroud and accompanied by clanking chains". This is a knowing, new style of ghost story, blithely acknowledging, but distancing itself from, the stock properties of the past.

Thirdly, Dennis Parry suggests a form of the supernatural which turns out to be predominantly a continuation of everyday reality. In the traditional ghost story, the frisson most often comes from an encounter with the unearthly. In M. R. James it is often graveyard relics, in de la Mare a shimmering suggestion of other realities, in Machen the survival of ancient gods. But Parry's book explores instead the effect on a small circle of family and friends if a revenant were to carry on in almost exactly the same ruthless and unwelcome way it had in life, using whatever vessel it may to extend its domineering and powerful personality. In this, he is pursuing a similar trend of thought that led certain interwar writers to depict the afterlife as the same grey existence, but intensified and endless, as their characters had known when mortal: examples include Claude Houghton's *Julian Grant Loses His Way* (1933) and Wyndham Lewis's *Childermass* sequence (1928 and later). If the term isn't too odd, this is a realist ghost story.

And fourthly there is another force at work in the novel's world, adding a further dimension of the sinister and merciless. Behind all the sometimes even slightly comic supernatural masquerade in the book lies the macabre spectre of a deadly disease, which the authorities have agreed to call influenza, though its exact pathology is not known. At times it seems to strike randomly: some who are unhealthy generally may still survive, the fittest may not. It is probable that Parry had in mind here the so-called "Spanish 'flu" epidemic of 1918 and after, which was so virulent that it caused more casualties even than the First World War. Parry would have been young (five years old) when it began but its shadow fell over many succeeding years. He conveys this modern plague austerely, with matter-of-fact precision, and this restraint makes it all the more disturbing. Here we are in the terrain of the ghost story, taken alongside other terrors, as dystopia.

These thoughtful innovations in the form suggest a formidable intelligence at work. Born on 7th November 1912, Dennis Parry had started his writing career after a conventional education at Rugby public school and King's College, Cambridge, where he gained a First Class degree in Classics. He then began studying to practice law. But alongside this, he published his first books. Perhaps there were divided loyalties here. From an already prosperous family, he may have hoped that literature would provide an outlet for the creative elements in his character while he more dutifully earned well from his legal profession. To judge from some aspects of his books, Parry also seems to have mixed in artistic and bohemian circles, enjoying the vivid characters and colourful lives he found there, but perhaps always something of an outsider, an observer. He married, in 1937, Kathleen Forbes, and the couple soon began a family, with the birth of their daughter Susan in December 1938. Their son Jonathan followed in September 1943

The Survivor was his third book, written in his mid-twenties. It was quite different from his two earlier books. The first, *Attic Meteor* (1936), now very hard to find, is a Buchanesque adventure set in Greece during a Fascist uprising. William Plomer, reviewing it in *The Spectator* (23 October 1936), was inclined to doubt the confidence of its invented politics and international chicanery. But he praised his prose, "when he is more devoted to the particular than the general", citing a descriptive passage as worth more than "pages and pages of the diffuse intrigue and adventure of the later part of the book."

The second, elaborately entitled *The Bishop's Move, Being the Autobiography of Dio Lord Bishop of Melitene, Freely Translated from the Lost Original* (1938), written in collaboration with H.W. Champness, is a historical picaresque set in Byzantine times, with scenes of sorcery and religious intrigue. Parry scholar Phil Cole suggests "Robert Graves is a possible inspiration here, from *Count Belisarius* and the Claudius books, but the pace and humour helps it stand out."

As if marking a deliberate break from these two books, *The Survivor* is a far more insular and sombre work. Its setting in the fenland of Cambridgeshire, around Ely, some of the bleakest landscape in England, must have been known to Parry from explorations while at college. The book conveys well the desolation of the country, where the huddled village hardly rises higher than the land and winter frost descends like white iron. This environment helps to build the sense of remorselessness in the story. One character speculates that in such flat and far-horizoned terrain, a forceful man's will might be able to stretch itself out, to extend its power. The suggestion is that the possession that is the focus of the book draws in part from its austere setting.

Parry's characters are also much more constrained than the

colourful reprobates of his earlier books. His precise delineation of the limited existences, petty squabbles and niggles of this family's life is full of hard-eyed observation. His writing here is reminiscent of the artful malice of the novels of Ivy Compton-Burnett, and sometimes a turn of phrase suggests the sardonic wit of 'Saki' (H. H. Munro).

During the war Parry was found unfit for military service due to poor eyesight. He joined the civil service and worked in the Ministry of Coal Production under the Labour politician and former miner Manny Shinwell. He stayed in the post after the war, was one of the authors of the official history of the war, and rose to become the Permanent Under-Secretary, the effective head of the department, answering directly to the Minister.

Alongside this demanding public service career, Dennis Parry was to go on to write seven more novels. They increasingly depict a protagonist with a background in law or bureaucracy, typically a solicitor or Whitehall civil servant, responding to various personal crises—overwork, an unhappy marriage, a yearning for a freer life. In *Going Up—Going Down* (1953), for example, about an official statistician and an impoverished young woman, the scene is, as *The Tablet* (9 May 1953) observed, "the frightened 'thirties and the warlike 'forties", adding "Mr. Parry's portrayal, not so much satirical as merciless, of the new-style Ministries and of the prickly relations between the expert and the mere administrator or politician holds the interest through quite a lengthy novel".

It's difficult to avoid the conclusion that this convincing-sounding intrigue was drawn from Parry's own experiences in the civil service, and that in turn raises the likelihood that some of the emotional upheavals in his books also reflect his personal difficulties. His first marriage ended around 1949, and he married again. His second wife was Audrey Dockerill, and their son Mark was born in February 1953.

They were not to have many years together. Dennis Parry was injured in a car accident in June 1955 and died two days later, on 21 June 1955, aged 42.

By a melancholy irony, his last book, the peculiar thriller *Sea of Glass* (1955, also available from Valancourt), was to prove one of his more successful. It was one of those chosen by Edward Gorey in an article for Antaeus magazine on neglected books, and it is this championing that has led others to look out for his books. In his *Observer* review of May 15, 1955, John Davenport, noting that this was Dennis Parry's tenth novel, also confessed that it was the first one he had read. This was a pity, he added, for Parry is "an uncommonly good writer", and "a bald recital of the plot . . . can only be misleading: you must read it for yourself."

Phil Cole has noticed that *Sea of Glass* represents a delicate return to the fantastic in Parry's work: "with its twin settings of a bizarre Aladdin's cave of a London townhouse and the remote oasis city of Doljuk (which the narrator only hears about when drugged or feverish), it often seems to have its feet slightly off the ground."

Dennis Parry's books suggest a man-of-the-world, with broad sympathies but an unillusioned knowledge of human motivations and frailties. We may sense that he sought out, relished and wanted to be a part of, a sphere of life different from his legal and official duties. Artistic, theatrical, bohemian and louche characters abound. He admires big and reckless personalities, while facing up to the havoc they can leave behind. He enjoys seeing the bursting of conventions, and being with those who are sure of themselves. But there is also a mood of weary futility even in this company, and we may sense that what this acutely intelligent author really thought, and what he wanted for himself, will always remain enigmatic.

MARK VALENTINE
August 12, 2014

THE SURVIVOR

CHAPTER ONE

THE iron rime lay over Bedford Level. From Spalding to Wicken Fen the roads rang hollow underfoot, and the grass stood up in brittle, jeweled tufts, and the still water in the dikes was crusted an inch thick. The hibernating moles were frozen in their underground burrows. The field mice went abroad all day searching food, and died at last of hunger and the bitter cold: their small, spare corpses lay upturned in mute atonement for the havoc they had wrought to growing crops.

The men who cultivated the earth died, too. Farmhouse or laborer's cottage shielded them from the pitiless moonlight and their bellies were not whitened with ice, but they perished under quilts in upper rooms, where the hot steam of gruel and the exhalations of human breath feebly combined against the outer atmosphere.

2

"Le chien aboie."
"Aboie," repeated Olive absently.
"Le lion rugit."
"Rugit."
"Le cheval hennit."
The dutiful echo failed. Olive was far away, perched on top of a flaming battlement, looking down into a chasm swept by alternate waves of yellow and crimson light.

Aunt Eva plucked irritably at her voluminous skirt.

"Le cheval hennit," she said again in tones of breaking patience.

Uncle James hurled his book to the floor.

"Et le poisson se tait, my dear Eva," he shouted. "Imitate the bon poisson, and for God's sake let's have a little quiet!"

The vibration of his powerful voice seemed to disturb the fine balance of half-consumed coals. The fire fell in with a crash and the feathery pinnacles of Olive's delight were razed to a hot, barren plain. Olive started.

"I'm sorry, auntie," she murmured.

But her offense had already been merged and lost in the greater one of Uncle James. Aunt Eva sat unconsciously following his advice. Whenever—and it was not an infrequent occurrence—she felt deeply indignant, she would sit silently opening and closing her mouth, not more than an inch at a time. The narrowness of her upper jaw and the long pinched lips which concealed her teeth increased her resemblance to a landed fish, mutely protesting against its plight. Auntie was wondering why she put up with such treatment from a mere half brother. Olive could have told her. Auntie had very little money and Uncle James had quite a lot. Moreover, Auntie was much concerned with an attribute of people called "their connection." She thought little of persons who could not glow with the reflected light of distinguished relationship. Birth was best, but achievement came a fair second, and Uncle James's fame, though a little obsolescent, had spread beyond the narrow circle of scientific men into the greater world. Olive had heard her say to Mrs. Aylmer, who sometimes drove out to tea from Ely and was the daughter of a bishop, that genius knows no law and that one must make allowances.

"Anyone would think," said Aunt Eva at last, "that it was a pleasure to me to spend my evenings trying to remedy the gaps in Olive's education."

"So it is," said Uncle James. "Immense satisfaction in teaching. Combines the illusion of superiority with that of usefulness."

His eyes sparkled frostily with the joy of battle. They were of a light, cold china blue, the color of the sky on a fine day in winter. They were ageless, fadeless eyes which seemed to disown their lined sockets and the white tangle of the brows above. Olive understood that Uncle James was a wicked old man: not quite in the same way as she understood that Aunt Eva was disappointed and mean and stupid and a proper object of compassion, for of these latter things she had abundant concrete evidence in her daily life, whereas the wickedness of Uncle James was an indefinable part of his personality. He did not need to forge a check or cut somebody's throat in order to substantiate it. It was true that he blasphemed against God: indeed, blaspheming against God was one of his chief recreations, and this had at one time seemed to Olive very terrible, but soon she came to see that the habit was altogether too common to account for Uncle James's peculiar and individual quality.

Olive did not think much about her surroundings, animate or otherwise. Despite her twenty years, she had an almost vegetable faculty for accepting the circumstances of her life and growth.

"It is scarcely my business," said Aunt Eva, after another series of minute gasps, "but it is obvious that you are overworking yourself, James. This violent irritability is a bad sign at your age."

Olive's palms tingled with the expectation of another outburst. Aunt Eva might have been "feeding" Uncle James, like the funny little man at the Variety show in Cambridge who gave the chief comedian the answers he required, and finally succeeded in stimulating him to such a pitch of indecency that Aunt Eva insisted on leaving in the middle of his act. Any reference to increasing years or failing powers was normally certain to send Uncle James into a paroxysm of truculence. This time, however, he inexplicably ignored the bait. Instead, he turned to Olive with his ironic smile.

"'... An evil plague throughout the host, and the people perished,'" he said. "The conditions bring one's old reading back to one, don't they, Olive?"

"I'm afraid I don't remember having read that, uncle," replied Olive timidly. "I expect I was taught it at school but my memory's so rotten."

Aunt Eva smiled acidly in agreement.

"No, no, my girl," said Uncle James, opening out his huge voice, "they didn't give you stuff like that at your academy for young ladies. They fed you a lot o' bloody pap on weekdays and tripe on Sundays. That was Homer—good stuff, a great comfort and example to me throughout my beastly and immoral life."

He broke off, then roared at Uncle Roger who was sitting, writing under the standard-lamp, swathed in waistcoats.

"Roger, you're a student of the Humanities. Don't you agree that the present situation has a Homeric quality?"

He had some excuse for yelling at Uncle Roger, who was completely deaf in one ear. It was generally agreed that this was very sad, and Eva had been known to say that if Roger could have heard more of the proceedings in court he would have gone further as a barrister. Olive, however, suspected that Uncle Roger looked kindly on his complaint, in that it had formerly hastened his retirement and now constituted a virtual alibi in family disputes.

"Ah," said Roger, looking up, "yes, indeed, James. Very apposite. The angry god plagues the Achaeans. *Iliad*, Book One, I think."

"And a fine, direct, unsissified god, too!" said James. "Apollo, the god of sudden death in pestilence: the god I've spent my life fighting, and can respect. When I've seen a city decimated by cholera, I've liked to think that it came from a deity who meant destruction, not one with a peculiar method of showing his love."

Aunt Eva stiffened and braced herself against the high back of her chair. It was her way of steeling herself to ignore the fit of prolonged and progressive blasphemy which all the signs appeared to promise. The thin, wire-drawn lines bit deeper into the base of her nose.

But tonight Uncle James seemed to have no regard for his own tradition. He forbore to develop his pagan ideas, he left his more familiar and ferocious aspersions on the Christian faith to be inferred. He seized the tasseled cord of the old-fashioned bellpull and wrenched it as though he were hauling on a ship's canvas. A brassy clamor returned from the kitchen. In all his actions Uncle James had an incurable tendency to be larger than life-size.

Dora peeped uncertainly round the door. She was not used to work abovestairs, but the absence of the more reliable and sophisticated Alice had made her temporary promotion unavoidable. Alice was miles away in Norwich, burying the rest of her family. The epidemic had killed them all within a week. Aunt Eva had lent her a prayer book before she left.

"Dora," said Uncle James, "bring me a bottle of rum and a jug of hot water. I'm going to attack this damned cold from the inside."

Dora suppressed the giggle that was never far from her loose pretty mouth. She was always fascinated by Uncle James, and in her eagerness to concentrate on his command she advanced farther into the room, allowing the door to swing wide behind her. Instantly the cold came sliding in, spreading thin tentacles through the warmed air, invading even the hearthstone.

"Wait a minute, girl," said James. "I said rum. Don't come back with whisky. D'you know the difference?"

"Oh, yes, sir," said Dora with an undisguised titter.

"That's good," said James. "Well brought up. I suppose your parents drink heavily?"

"Oh, no, sir," protested Dora happily. "Dad's reelly . . ."

"That will do, Dora," Aunt Eva interposed.

Uncle James picked up his book again and turned the pages, stroking his pointed beard. Although he ate with conspicuous disregard for convention, it was never soiled by the least spot. White and silky, its remotest hairs seemed ordered and immune from straying, as if they obeyed some centripetal force. Olive had never seen samite, but the word, occurring in poetry, invariably conjured up to her the beard of Uncle James.

Dora came back bearing a tray. The hot water steamed and the rum glowed opal against the firelight.

"Please, sir," she said, putting down her load in front of James, "I gone round by the back to get at the cellar and I found Teddy Fremlin ringing the doorbell. 'Is ma's bad, took sudden."

"Bloody hell!" said Uncle James. "They drop down like rabbits in a cornfield."

He picked up the bottle and tilted out half a tumbler of rum, to which he added the merest dash of hot water. He drank and rose to his feet, spryly enough, yet with that momentary delay for concentrating his strength, winding up his muscles, which alone betrayed his age.

"I shall have to go out," he said.

Aunt Eva remonstrated. "Really, James, you'll kill yourself. Can't you tell the boy what to do for his mother tonight, and visit her yourself in the morning? Surely it has been made clear to us that medical attention has little effect on the results of this illness."

For once Aunt Eva had turned the tables. The positions were reversed and she had blasphemed against Uncle James's creed. It would hardly be correct to represent him as conscientiously unwilling to spare any effort while there remained the least possibility of preserving life: for on the continued existence of individuals he certainly set no great value. Rather he conducted a bitter personal vendetta with disease and would have considered himself shamed if he had given away the least advantage to his ancient adversary. He smote microbes and bacilli because he enjoyed it: the cure of the patient was a mere incidental of victory.

"Tomorrow morning!" he said. "Tomorrow morning, my dear Eva, you can go round to Mrs. Fremlin with a little jelly wrapped in a tract, for all I care. Tonight's my business."

He paused at the door and chucked Dora under the chin.

"Ah," he said, "this is rotten weather for little girls like you, Dora, eh? Cold in the kitchen and impossible under the hedgerows!"

His great figure filled the doorway and his thick white hair twinkled for an instant against the frame of darkness. Soon he could be heard in the hall, cursing his gumboots.

"Ah, well," said Aunt Eva, "noblesse oblige!"

Much as she loathed Uncle James, she could never repress a certain satisfaction at his seigneurial gestures. When he stalked out from the Manor to succor the villagers she felt herself exalted, by inference, to the position of revered chatelaine, presiding over the well-being of those whom God had called to an inferior estate. The illusion ministered to her voracious sense of self-importance.

"Roger!" she said. Then more loudly: "Roger! Are you ready for your game of chess yet?"

The game of chess was always Roger's game, despite the fact that he had long ceased to propose it himself. Years ago he had indeed developed a transient enthusiasm for chess. It had waned quickly, but too late. Before its extinction Aunt Eva had learned to play and had, moreover, discovered a certain aptitude. Now poor Roger must sit nightly devising means to lose his pieces at a decent rate, with one eye on the clock lest the game end in time for another to be started.

Uncle Roger shuffled his notes.

"In just a moment, my dear. I've come across rather a quaint old report and I should like to copy down the reference."

"Perhaps, Olive, you will set the board for us," said Aunt Eva.

Olive rose apathetically and disentangled the box of chessmen from the cupboard under the bookcase. That part of the room was farthest from the fire and a zone of cold air clung about it. She came back shivering. She was like a little black cat in her love for large well-stoked fires.

Uncle Roger was taking a regretful farewell of a heavy volume with decayed binding and faded antique print. The pince-nez bobbed up and down on his nose as he rapidly raised and lowered his eyebrows in astonishment at the jewel which his researches had uncovered.

"My dear Eva," he said, "you must really listen to this. It's a report of the proceedings in the trial of one Andrew Burge indicted at the Norwich Assizes, Michaelmas, 1687, on a charge of grand larceny." He read: "'The prisoner, being called before the bar, would in no wise plead, but rather barked like a dog. Whereat Wrangham J. declined to proceed to sentence, saying that it were a superfluity upon the manifest judgment of Almighty God.'"

"Broadmoor is the proper home for cases of that kind," pronounced Aunt Eva. "Are you ready?"

Uncle Roger sighed as he prepared to entrench himself behind his row of pawns. Suddenly he looked down at Olive sitting idle on the sofa. He saw that she was smiling and the evidence of her appreciation appeared to encourage him very much. He patted her hand and smiled back, rapidly blinking his shortsighted hazel eyes. Then the rigor of the game encompassed him.

The starry crystals multiplied on the windowpanes. The ormolu clock ticked pompously on the mantelpiece. Intermittently the house resounded with a groaning, rattling noise, like the play of a high wind about cornices and rooftops. But the air outside was still, with the absolute immobility of petrifaction. The noise came from the venerable system of piping as it wearily strove to maintain a supply of hot water for Aunt Eva's bedtime bath.

3

Now it was on English fenland that the battle raged. The enemy had exchanged his weapon but it was still the same battle, the one that had begun long ago when James Marshall, being then young and strong in his early prime, had sailed up the gray Orinoco to Ciudad Bolivar, where the dead people lay piled in adobe huts and the living stood all day in the churches, waiting their turn to kiss the Virgin's feet and supplicate her for their own and their children's safety. Young James Marshall had soon put a stop to their devotions. He had gone to the alcalde and browbeaten that pious man into accepting the view that holy feet could spread infection as easily as any other article of common use.

And again, the elephants swayed under the Burmese sun, most majestic of beasts, and the little fleas hopped in the dust, and on men the dark boils came up in groin and armpit. There in Burma, in the walled city looking over the ricefields, had perished Charles Ducane, M.D., whose strenuous advocacy had done more than anything else to establish the reputation of James Marshall. But James had never liked him much, because of his fiddling propriety and his objections to alcohol, and had happened to be away when the plague struck him and he most needed expert attention.

Saint-Hippolyte, the lofty tomb of the lepers in Martinique, had seen the contest joined a third time. That was the scene of James's most resounding triumph. The Marshall plan of graduated injectional treatment produced results which were then revolutionary; and even now formed the basis of lepral therapy. When he left, the local paper had misquoted, with perhaps more enthusiasm than good taste: *"Fuit homo missus a Deo cui nomen erat Jacobus."* The most pleasurable memory which James retained of Martinique was that he had succeeded in seducing two French nuns.

Vile, magnificent, terrible, courageous, he had stamped through the pest spots of the earth. Under his ironshod boots died immemorial plague and scarcely less time-honored aspiration. He was quite fearless and quite without reverence. On the threshold of a sick rajah he had kicked aside the many-armed image, the tutelary god of his patient's house. The rajah recovered, James was paid, the palace doors shut tight. He was an evil ambassador leaving everywhere the mark of his own great genius and the doubt whether even its successful employment was worth the cost.

James Marshall was by training an expert in tropical medicine. Chance had made him an itinerant scourge of epidemics. In the bad old days before the Boer War the authorities were not inclined to draw any finicking distinctions between the various complaints of those who built the Empire. If they were dying in Ashanti, send the fellow who put them right in Trinidad! Consequently, a reputation, once gained, tended to increase like a snowball. Ere the days of a more specialized outlook, James had become encyclopedic, indispensable. Greatly endowed by nature, his brain was equally capable of sucking up theory from a textbook or practice from a corpse. There were inevitable gaps in a knowledge so diffuse. Many young scientists who had seen cholera only inside a culture tank could have told him things about it which he had never suspected. But though the age outgrew him as a theoretician, medicine dared not neglect his vast auxiliary power. He had learned the art of coercion in a hard school—where black-tongued men fought for water about padlocked wells—where mothers hammered on the barred huts, seeking in vain the daughters who would pass away in sanitary seclusion, bereft of the peculiar and unhygienic death rites of their race. James Marshall could organize illness. Frequently his methods created a riot: but even before they began, the rioters seemed to realize that they were fighting a lost battle; he drew strength from others' hostility, as did the giant Antaeus from his maternal earth.

The Great War had marked the last phase of his active career. The French made him a member of the Legion of Honor for his services among their colored troops. Thereafter he had retired to Gorchow, the ugly little village that lay level with the horizon on every side. A few papers to medical journals and his autobiography, hastily recalled by the publishers who found themselves confronted with fourteen separate writs for libel, had been the only public reminders that he was still alive. But the ancient daemon did but sleep, and now, in his seventy-sixth year, had awakened under a familiar stimulus.

In May the readers of newspapers had learned, without a tremor, of a severe pestilence raging throughout China. Although millions died, it was noticed only in brief paragraphs. It was a long way off and the West automatically attributed it to defective sanitation. In July, however, a large body of British troops had, contrary to any preconceived plan, to be drafted out to India. They were used to fill up gaps in the army, caused by a mysterious epidemic. People in England became anxious about their empire-building sons. Thereafter the consumption upon the world's vitality galloped.

The miserable undernourished populations of Central Europe fell in swaths: too late they discovered that a pound of butter and a few ounces of decent meat were more protection against the invader than rows of ironclad tanks and squadrons of bombing planes. In Germany the number of deaths disturbed even her rulers. It was at this stage that the doctors of the world entered into tacit conspiracy to call the destroying agent influenza—a safe, familiar name, sounding of aspirin and hot-water bottles, neither of which was any more use than an umbrella against a thunderbolt. They remembered 1918, to which the conditions, though not identical, bore a close resemblance. On the October winds the first infection sailed into England, pursuing its westerly migration. By the end of November twenty thousand people had died in East Anglia and the death roll round Bristol and the towns of South Wales was rapidly drawing level. Only America remained so far untouched, a fact which many of her citizens attributed to keeping out of European affairs.

The sufferings of Ely and its surrounding district were rather worse than the average. The villagers drew a fanciful analogy from the floodwaters which had so long oppressed their bare countryside. "Stands to reason," they said. "Anything that comes in, comes in these parts bad. There ain't nothing natural to keep it out." The disease had its own strategy: in many cases it made an early and determined assault on the keystone of a village's defense. The doctor died, and since his neighboring colleagues, even if themselves in health, were inevitably overworked by their own cases, an undefended breach was left through which the tide of sickness poured with increasing volume. Gorchow was lucky. When, a month since, prim little Dr. Milsom had dropped off, tut-tutting miserably over his own symptoms, the locality had actually derived advantage from the substitution of a far stronger, more resolute hand. Old though he was, James Marshall, as a qualified medical man, could scarcely have refused to come out of his retirement and meet the crisis. He showed no reluctance. He hurled himself into the fray with all his former abandon. He ramped round the village, cursing like a bargee, forcibly tearing its victims out of the half-closed jaws of death. The power to dictate was like a tonic to him: all his forces seemed renewed in a kind of Indian summer.

His clinical knowledge of the disease he was treating was negligible. This did not much matter, since no one else in the world was in a substantially better position. A doctor was chiefly valuable for his prestige, whose weight could allay panic and force people into obeying simple precautionary rules. James had not been on his rounds for forty-eight hours before he had earned more respect and hatred than Dr. Milsom in twenty years. Fenlanders are easily moved to both these emotions: neither renders them very articulate, but neither is lightly forgotten.

4

James walked ahead with great loose strides. Ted Fremlin's legs were short for his fifteen years, and despite the utmost efforts an irrecoverable yard separated him from his leader. Seen together, the pair looked like a rather brutal parody of Good King Wenceslas and his page: James, medievally-bearded, silver-haired, yet distorting all these traditional symbols of sanctity into the likeness of Pan; Ted, whom the village barber had been unable to attend owing to his decease, sporting a long flaxen fringe all round his bullet head, beneath which his forehead sloped back and his nose and lips slid forward into the mask of a kindly, contented little pig.

They passed the vicarage. The shrubs behind the low railing were frozen into geometrical lines. There were no softly subtended curves between the little boughs and trunks, but everywhere hard, perfectly defined angles, whose joints shone fiery-white beneath the glittering moon.

Ted blew on his cupped hands.

"Reverend Faulkner's coming over to Ma," he ventured.

"Not while I'm in the house," said James grimly.

"Ah!" said Ted. "Ah!" Young as he was, he had a great manner of saying "Ah!" The syllable seemed to proceed slowly from a reservoir of immemorial rustic cogitation.

"How the hell can I keep your mother in this world if there's a parson running round giving her a garbled prospectus for the next and destroying her resistance?" James inquired irritably.

"Ah!" said Ted. "Parson and doctor work together, like two crows in stormy weather."

"Don't be so damned sagacious," said James. "What do you think that means anyway?"

"I don't rightly know, mister. It's just a saying, like."

The double rank of cottages began to close in. Gorchow was a slender elongated village, strung out along the road, with a bulge in the middle where the church and the Lord Harvey stood back from the general building line, one on either side of a weedy duckpond. The cottages were low and whitewashed, and normally their slated roofs remained the same lusterless gray in rain or sunshine. Now the frost had pointed them with diamond. Diamond, too, was the thin film which overspread the roadway, binding it to an icy lake, making foothold precarious at the crown, and on the cambered edges almost impossible.

"I can't make it out," said James. "Put the two together and you'd have thought one would cut the other's throat."

Ted made no answer, chiefly because he had not the least idea what his companion was talking about. James was mystified by the harmony existing between the epidemic and the exceptional climatic conditions. His experience had lain in countries where the advent of cold weather was a powerful ally in the fight against disease. He felt that the enemy had disobeyed the rules. He stamped viciously with his iron-rimmed heel: tiny, seedlike sparks flashed from a projecting flint, warm and comforting against the blanched landscape.

"'Ere we are, mister," Ted observed. None of the villagers were used to addressing James as "doctor." They knew that he was entitled to the degree, but they understood that he had practiced chiefly on foreigners—blacks and suchlike. They did not call the vet "doctor," either.

James pushed open the door and entered, bending almost double to avoid the low lintel. Inside, the acetylene lamp smoked, and the kitchen range dried up the air, and Mr. Fremlin further adulterated it with a powerful shag. Ted's father sat on the sofa with one boot on and the other off. Some of his children, four or five, sprawled about the floor. On James's entry he rose and hospitably cleared a path among them with prods of his bootless toe.

"Ah!" he said, with an intonation exactly like Ted's. "Glad you come this cold night, mister."

"Where's your wife?" said James. "Upstairs?"

Mr. Fremlin nodded. James made for the doorless aperture beyond which the last tread of a staircase was visible. As he passed, a child sitting by the wall scrambled to its feet and dislodged a hanging saucepan from its nail. The child ducked but the saucepan bounced accurately off its skull.

"Ah!" said Mr. Fremlin. "See? Wants a mother's 'and, eh? Good thing you come."

James looked down at the little girl who was the sufferer from the accident. She was about twelve, very dirty, yet possessing a premature air of responsibility. Gray and white flock floated out of the baglike object which she clasped nervously against her stomach. It was not James's sympathy that she woke, it was his curiosity and his instinct for an opportunity to assert himself.

"What are you doing there?" he asked.

A second saucepan rocked uncertainly beneath the impact of his voice, more suited to hog-calling on the prairies than to interior domestic life. The girl hung her head and did not answer.

"I reckon she's been set to cut on her ma's pillow," volunteered Mr. Fremlin at last.

A pair of scissor-points peeped out between one hand and the molting sack.

"Keep the child quiet, eh?" said James. "I suppose the boys saw up the mantelpiece on long winter evenings?"

If Mr. Fremlin knew that he was being mocked, he gave no sign.

"You 'aven't rightly got it, mister," he said. "This ain't just 'er play. I'd knock 'er 'ead off, else, mucking things about. She's doing this 'ere 'cos 'er ma's got scruples, see?"

"Scruples about what?" inquired James.

Mr. Fremlin did not reply directly.

"People are going off very sudden," he said. "O' course, we reckon you'll put 'er well, mister, but if she were to die she wouldn't go comfortable unless she were rightly sped."

"Ah," said James in tones of deceptive mildness, "this sounds like one of those bits of traditional rustic wisdom. I collect them. Pray go on."

Since his father seemed disinclined for further explanation, Ted confidingly took it upon himself to supply the rest of the story.

"It's this way, mister. When some folk feels the death grip, they like the pillow pulled from under their 'eads an' shook out, so all the feathers go free. Reverend Faulkner preached one Sunday 'ow it was to do with the 'Oly Ghost, what come down like a dove. Well, there might be a dove's feather in yer pillow, though I reckon they're mostly 'ens', and shaking it out is as much as to say yer spirit can go back to Our Father in 'Eaven. It's just a custom, like. I don't reckon much to it."

"You don't?" said James. "Wise boy! Come here."

He pulled a coin out of his pocket and gave it to Ted.

"Here's a shilling," he said, "for your triumph over superstition. Hang on to it, Ted; don't let your father get hold of it or he'll take it away and wear it round his neck as a talisman against voodoo and werewolves."

Mr. Fremlin's brick-colored face took on an undertint of red. He realized that somewhere beneath the cloud of educated verbiage lurked an insult—uttered before his son, diminishing his prestige, subtly bringing nearer the day when he would have to yield over the leadership of the Fremlin herd and become poor old granddad by the fireplace.

Not even now had he plumbed the depths of humiliation, for James, who was beginning to enjoy himself, turned from covert to open condemnation.

"As for you, Fremlin," he said, "you're a bloody goddam fool! Your wife's lying upstairs, her throat passage probably half-blocked with catarrhal mucus, and you take away her pillow to chop it up! Haven't you the sense to see that you might easily choke her? And sew the damned thing up before you put it back or she'll be swallowing feathers all night."

A slow subcutaneous tremor went through Mr. Fremlin's body, like the tightening of the muscles in a plow horse as it takes the strain. He would have dearly liked to hit James in the face, and then he would dearly have liked to kick him in the stomach. But a sense of the inviolability of the gentry, strongly ingrained in his generation, and the knowledge of his dependence on the tormentor's services fell like a damp blanket across his justifiable rage.

"I reckon you came to set my wife to rights, not me," he said with some dignity, and jerked his thumb toward the stairway.

The old sprung boards wailed and groaned beneath their mounting feet. Anne Fremlin was lying alone in the upper room under a framed certificate from the Ely Agricultural Show. Her bed looked like a badly arranged stall for white elephants at a church bazaar. In their efforts to overcome the bout of shivering and preternatural cold which had ushered in her fever, the family had heaped on her every article which might conceivably serve as a covering. The two topmost of the pile were her corsets and the disreputable old mat from the bedside. Her face was violently flushed and she breathed in irregular snorts, like an engine newly started on a cold day. Their entry disturbed her, and she raised herself with the curious defensive abruptness of the semidelirious.

"Edgar," she said shrilly, "'ave you given the doctor a cup of tea? 'Ow many times 'ave I got to tell you no one comes into my 'ouse but what they get something to warm 'em!"

"I've had it," said James with an unhesitating brevity that carried conviction.

"That's good," said Mrs. Fremlin. "Pore we may be, but we got our pride in doing things proper—leastways if I'm about."

James's ear was still quick enough to identify and place the nasal, rather whining intonation of her voice.

"You come from somewhere round Cambridge, don't you?" he said, picking up one of her wrists and feeling for the pulse.

"I was a girl in Sawston and, mind you, I don't say but what I'd've done better to've stayed in those parts. Not but what . . ." Her muddled brain tripped over the complications of the sentence and its remaining part went out of her head: to be replaced by a thought which is never far absent from the minds of the sick, unless they be very sick indeed.

"You don't reckon I'm going to die, doctor?"

"I'll tell you in a minute," said James.

The cold, unvarnished answer seemed to allay her anxiety.

He took her temperature. The thermometer registered between 103° and 104°. This was a malady which played curious tricks with the bodily fire. First it kindled a great furnace in the blood so that the mercury soared and seemed on the point of breaking through its sheath of glass: but in the penultimate, the antelethal hour, came a precipitous fall, as if the coals had been suddenly raked out, and the patient died clammily subnormal. Sometimes, on the other hand, the temperature went on rising after death. If that was so, the body usually turned black in a few hours. Those were the toxemic cases.

James bent down and unfastening his old black bag pulled out a stethoscope. He had never got into the home practitioner's habit of carrying it neatly coiled above his waistcoat.

"Pull up your nightdress," he said.

Mrs. Fremlin peeked up at him, first with a kind of superannuated coyness, then with hazy but genuine distrust.

"You ain't our doctor," she said. "You ain't Dr. Milsom. You can't play yer games with me—not like that feller in the papers at Downham, what did wrong by young girls, pretending 'e was a doctor!"

The natural shrillness of her voice was strangely perverted by catarrhal obstruction. On some syllables it broke through like a steam whistle; on others the sense had to be deduced from a dull gulp.

James turned to Mr. Fremlin, who still stood in the doorway, fidgeting from foot to foot.

"I want to get at her chest," he said.

The husband advanced a couple of paces toward his wife's bed.

"Now, Annie," he said, "you got no call to take on like this. The gentleman's a doctor right enough."

Mrs. Fremlin sighed and passed a hand across her forehead.

"My mind's like a sieve since I been queer," she said. "O' course, Dr. Milsom was took last month."

She slipped up her rough poplin garment and revealed her breasts, sagging and shapeless from repeated motherhood.

"Not taking any risks, eh?" said James. "Well, well, I can see you had something there that needed looking after when you were a girl!"

Mr. Fremlin scraped his boot disapprovingly on the floor. His wife, however, took the remark in very good part. She gave a little touch-me-not giggle, as though the fever had indeed transported her back to the days of girlhood and slaps and pinches by the stile.

James stood over her, listening to the ebb and flow of the salt, sullen tide within her body. Her lungs, however, appeared to be free from the agglomeration of liquid which characterized fatal pneumonic cases. Her heart, too, was undiscouraged.

When he had finished and unhooked the stethoscope from his ears, he said:

"You don't look like dying at present."

Such frankness, even over good tidings, was a further offense to Mr. Fremlin. He felt that it was casual and indecent. Like most countrymen, he had a great respect for traditional mysteries. A little skill decently wrapped up impressed him far more than twice the amount flung nakedly at his feet. Old Dr. Milsom had satisfied his sense of propriety. Never, never would he have told a patient whether or not she was going to live or die: the temperature was his secret, even the name of the complaint transpired only in dark hints. Standing by the bedside he would shake his head and purse his lips and consult his gold turnip-watch, so that you felt you were getting the benefit of a rare and esoteric wisdom.

In fact, Mr. Fremlin contrasted James unfavorably with Dr. Milsom in all respects except one. Dr. Milsom had not possessed a beard, and Mr. Fremlin thought well of beards in the learned professions.

"I'll come again about ten tomorrow," said James. "Get somebody to take this into Ely and have it made up, first thing in the morning."

He scribbled a few symbols in his notebook, pulled out the sheet and thrust it into Mr. Fremlin's hand.

"And put that damned pillow back!" he added with gratuitous violence.

Mrs. Fremlin tittered happily. Seen through the fog which hazed her judgment, James Marshall appeared as a very quaint and amusing old gentleman. Such a one, say anything, and rare good-looking at his age! Even when they were in full possession of their faculties, women fell easy victims to James's power of fascination. It did not matter whether they were bankers' wives or kitchenmaids, they were usually willing to grant him the most outrageous latitude. The majority stubbornly persisted in the view that he concealed a heart of gold under his rough manner. They contrived to see him as one of those rugged old bears, so popular in the theater and on the films, who for two acts scandalize everybody by their unconventional speech and behavior, but in the last are invariably revealed as full of an uncommon sympathy and desire to assist their fellow men.

James was not a dear old Teddy bear. He was an aging tiger, and though, like others of his kind, he did good work in destroying minor pests, he could only properly be regarded as dangerous and antisocial.

Without further farewell he turned to the doorway and prepared to depart. But on the threshold, blocking his path, stood the Reverend Richard Faulkner, small, square, indefinably reminiscent of a good-natured terrier. James threw up his hands in mock dismay.

"Hast thou found me, O mine enemy?" he said.

"Well," said Faulkner, "I don't know about that. Neither the meeting nor the enmity is my design."

While he spoke he thought to himself that he had made the soft answer quite neatly: it was a pity, a very great pity, he felt, that he could not achieve a diction to match his phraseology. But there it was—education, won by toil and pertinacity, could teach you to say apposite things, but only birth and early environment, which were fortuitous and irremediable, could inculcate the easy and acceptable utterance. The Reverend Mr. Faulkner was not at all vain, but he regretted the fact that he had not been born a gentleman because it hindered him in his office. The Marshall household was a great problem to him, on account of the varied and inconsistent emotions which its members inspired. There was only one of them that he could meet on a basis of Christian goodwill, and that was Roger, with whom he had established a friendly community of tastes. The rest of the family provoked him to extremes, either of dislike or of affection.

"Don't dazzle her with the Kingdom of God," said James, jerking his thumb toward Mrs. Fremlin. "She might take you at your word."

"I've brought her some eggs," said the Reverend Mr. Faulkner dryly.

"She can't eat them," said James. "They'll do for the kids downstairs, though."

"Thanks," said Faulkner. "You ought to do more of this charitable organization, Dr. Marshall."

James stared at him for a moment, then burst into his great laugh.

"Not bad," he said, "not bad! It won't be long at this rate before your tongue's sharp enough for Christian controversy. I'll come and watch you spear your first heresy. Olive and I, we take a great interest in your career."

James only waited long enough to see the flush which the mention of Olive brought to the other's face. It was a gambit he had begun to employ with increasing frequency, introducing the name in tones which were a subtly offensive parody of paternal pride. Faulkner heard his heavy tread in the room below and the bang of the cottage door as it closed behind him. What a brute that old man is! he thought. Or, no—he is not a brute, because brutes have no comprehension of the things on which they trample. They charge round the world, and one must pity them because sooner or later their folly will drive them over a steep place. But Marshall knows only too well what he is doing, calculation shows in his every move. He is the only human being I have met who gave me the impression of knowing the better and finer path, and using his knowledge simply to ensure that he avoids it. He is perverse. If he were merely a militant old atheist with a taste for gibes at the church and personal rudeness, one could laugh at him. Often the things he says would sound crude, almost schoolboyish, in another man's mouth. But when they are allied with his personality, they take on a real and malignant force. He seems to be able to breathe life into the dry bones of wickedness.

Mr. Faulkner stayed with Mrs. Fremlin for a quarter of an hour. He talked to her a little in the most soothing tones he could command. Twice she interrupted to tell him that the doctor had assured her that she would be "spared." "And Jane 'Icks that was so 'igh-and-mighty with 'er inoculations a week cold in 'er grave!" She seemed to value her survival chiefly as a triumph over the late Mrs. Hicks. Once, too, she remarked: "There's a power about that old gentleman what come in place of Dr. Milsom." Finally she requested Faulkner to pray with her. In spite of habituation it still made him a little uncomfortable to address God aloud before such a limited audience. His embarrassment was not decreased by the fact that, halfway through the prayer, Mrs. Fremlin was seized with another fit of wandering in her head and stuck on one phrase, repeating it over and over again, like a broken gramophone record. The stifling atmosphere and the heavy narcotic scent of sickness made his head ache. He was relieved when he stepped out once more into the darkness. In the vicarage drive a pair of taut, trembling little forms shot up under his feet and vanished into the further bushes. They were rabbits: their white scuts shone whiter with frosty moisture. Obeying the primitive impulse which comes to men in lonely, lightless places, Faulkner spoke aloud. And like his remote ancestors, who protected themselves with runes and spells, he instinctively chose a rhythmic form of words. He recited:

> The owl for all his feathers was a-cold;
> The hare limp'd limping through the frozen grass.

5

Olive lay in her bed. When she turned on to her right side she could see through a gap in the curtains three stars, sisterly and uniform, proceeding in due order across the cold, empurpled sky.

Presently she knew that Uncle James had come in. She neither heard nor saw anything which betrayed his return. She simply knew. For as long as she could remember she had always been aware whether or not he was in the house. She regarded this power of extrasensory perception as quite natural. If it had failed her she would have felt as concerned as if she had suddenly gone deaf.

CHAPTER TWO

IN the early light the lawn glittered like a salt pan. The double row of footprints, engraved in the crisp rime, stretched mysteriously out of sight beyond the big cedars. Like the mark which appalled Crusoe, they seemed to be divorced from human presence. But soon the sun came up, small and yellow, through the spiky branches and Uncle Roger popped round the cedar, puffing and stamping his bare feet. He was wearing his woolly vest and pants, three waistcoats, a tweed jacket and plus-fours of the same material. When he came in he would put on his undersocks and overlay them with a pair of golf stockings. At present he was paying homage to the principles of Nannie Tiggerdine. Long ago she had prescribed a morning run with bare legs for Master Roger's chilblains. He was very disposed toward chilblains, and though he still got them, he always insisted that they would have been more and worse if he had not thus ruthlessly disciplined his feet. Uncle Roger was very careful with his health. He would believe almost anything about it. Every two or three months there would be a great smashing of bottles at the Manor and the basin of the downstairs lavatory would become jagged with bergs of broken glass. For James periodically found the monstrous regiment of patent medicines on the sideboard more than he could tolerate and took his own short way with them. Roger never complained. He merely retired to his room and wrote an order to the manufacturers of the same or similar elixirs.

Olive was in the kitchen. In these days she rose early, casting off the warm bedclothes before her courage failed, and went downstairs to help Dora with the breakfast. The panes in the windows were starry with a delicate crystalline deposit, the range alternately smoked and flashed into fits of sullen renascence. Being useful about the house at early hours was not Olive's idea of pleasure. But she knew that there was—in Aunt Eva's view, at least—a certain obligation on her to render uncomplaining service. Olive was aware of being, so to speak, constitutionally an orphan, just as a Christianized Hindu of the lowest caste might remember his former untouchability. A liberty which threw one so deeply into debt was sometimes scarcely distinguishable from the original bondage.

"Dora," called Olive. "Dora, have you filled the chafing dish?"

The scullery taps continued to splash. Olive called again. Dora's head peeped round the doorjamb. A faint crackle, accompanying her movements, betrayed the presence of the morning paper behind her back. Every day before the family came down she glanced through the column of Social Gossip. It was written by a man who called himself "Edward Elite." He was the younger son of a peer and he was drunk most of the time.

"Just coming, miss," said Dora.

She reappeared carrying a potbellied silver platter, from which the steam came off in slow spiral curves. Olive turned the bacon in the frying pan with particular attention to one pallid rasher which seemed to resist all attempts at cooking.

Dora said: "Lady Rosewater got a baby this morning, miss. A boy an' eight pounds. She was only five 'erself."

"How nice," replied Olive mechanically.

"Yes," said Dora. "They're one of the most devoted couples in s'ciety. Pore lady, I reckon it must 'ave been 'ard this cold weather, though."

"Well, I expect she had an electric fire," said Olive.

Dora looked greatly relieved. In spite of her lofty reading she was inclined to translate all problems into terms of her native cottage, imputing difficulties of heating and drainage to even her most glamorous heroines.

"Funny, isn't it, miss, the number of 'appy events there've been among personages this last week? First Elsie Mayne what flew the Atlantic, an' then Alma Witchell the film star, not to speak of that woman murdering 'er 'usband and 'aving it in jail. . . ."

Olive dished up the bacon and broke one of the fried eggs. The delicate blue shade was slowly creeping up her hands toward the wrists.

"Oh, I expect they were all out on the same charabanc party," she said.

It was not facetiousness, it was a mistake. The words emerged, unpremeditated, from the depths of her memory. They belonged to Nina Hassett who had come to tea a month ago and left them behind as the tailpiece of one of those mildly dirty stories she was so fond of telling.

Dora was seized with a violent fit of giggling. Much as she disapproved of iconoclasm where the aristocracy was concerned, she could not withhold her appreciation of a really proletarian sally.

"Coo!" she said. "You do say things, Miss Olive! You and Mr. James, you're a pair."

It certainly had not occurred to Olive before, but upon consideration she was forced to agree that, allowing for differences of tone and intention, her remark might reasonably have been attributed to Uncle James. She blushed because she had set a bad example of loose conversation, which Dora was probably only too ready to follow. She gave a slight twitch of her head that set aquiver the bell-shaped mass of her dark, straight hair. It was a trick which she employed whenever she wanted to shake off a fit of abstraction or the remnants of some vague daydream. Olive was very given to what Aunt Eva, more appropriately than she knew, called "mooning." Her fantasies were not the common ones of wish fulfillment. She never married a matinee idol or flew to Australia at record speed. In the subjective world of her imagining there was no place for such brisk achievement. It was a pale lunar world, almost static, and nothing there demanded effort, nothing bit to the bone. Before her, the solitary inhabitant, its beauties passed in nebulous succession, like the incidents of some splendid pageant seen through a veil of fine gauze.

Olive was quite free from whimsy, which is an elaborate creation of the chronically dissatisfied. She never saw pixies at the bottom of the garden, and she would not have been particularly interested in them if she had.

Uncle Roger came diffidently into the kitchen. He had put on his stockings and shoes.

"Can I be of any assistance, my dear?" he asked.

"I don't think so, thank you, uncle," said Olive. "Dora and I have just finished."

He wandered along the kitchen dresser staring up at the tins and crockery, just like a small child to whom the ordinary articles of domestic use are still full of mysterious possibilities. Olive knew that he would like to talk, but was too shy, even with her, to risk intruding his conversation.

"Is it as cold outside this morning?" she said helpfully.

"Yes," said Uncle Roger. "Colder if anything. It's extraordinary how the spell continues." He paused, then continued with increasing confidence: "Some people are really most illogical. Any old fallacy satisfies them so long as it is sufficiently time-honored. Now Mr. Lewis, our schoolmaster—he should be a well-informed man, but the other day when I met him he asked me if I didn't think this weather was seasonable. Seasonable! As though he hadn't noticed that in the first days of any normal December we get nothing but muggy winds and deluges of rain! Do you know what I said to him?"

"No, what?" said Olive, nursing Uncle Roger's dialectic triumph.

"I said that I thought he'd been reading too much Pickwick and looking at too many Christmas cards. I told him that I doubted if there'd been another early winter like this since 1578."

Olive's memory for historical facts was hopelessly eclectic. It chose one or two out of each century and allowed them to bestride the whole period. Any date in the later fifteen hundreds suggested only the Great Armada. Vaguely she wondered whether the Spaniards might not have been frozen up in 1578. But she was wise enough not to place any reliance on the guess.

"What happened then?" she asked.

"The ice was so thick that they burned two witches on the Ouse at Ely," Uncle Roger replied somberly. "Poor women! A most interesting record of their trial survives."

Olive did not pursue the subject. But a chord had been struck in her imagination, and as she carried through the coffee pot into the dining room she saw the pitiless ironbound sky and the splintered ice round the sockets of the twin stakes, against each of which huddled an old crone with long gray hair. She felt for a moment the weight of age-long, accumulated human suffering. She forced herself to accept the comforting—and, as she knew in her heart, cowardly—thought that death by fire might lose some of its agony for those who met it shivering.

Aunt Eva was already at the table. She did not help with meals, because, as she said, it was a valuable experience for Olive to undertake the responsibilities of housekeeping. So she remained quite passive, except for her tongue, which was always at anybody's service.

Only James's chair stood empty. He observed his own hours of eating. Nevertheless, breakfast was not a meal for which he was usually late, for by nature he needed little sleep, and of late years seemed almost to have dispensed with it. He often went to bed long after midnight and was up again before six.

Roger politely filled the ladies' plates, and they began to eat in silence.

Presently Aunt Eva looked up from the letter she was reading.

"Cousin Laura writes to say that the second girl—that's Frances—has just got engaged," she announced.

"Dear, dear!" said Uncle Roger mechanically.

"You seem to share my doubts whether Laura is to be congratulated. Apparently the man has been married before and has a child of ten."

"Ah?" said Uncle Roger. "Really? Well, well, there's something to be said for catching an old hand instead of an inexperienced bachelor."

"There's a great deal to be said against it."

"My dear," said Uncle Roger, "if it weren't for second marriages, neither you nor I would be sitting here today."

"I am quite aware of that, Roger. My own life has given me some claim to know what I'm talking about. The children of one or the other union always suffer."

She sighed. Eighty per cent of her pathos could be written off as self-pity, but there still remained a core of truth. Orsett Marshall, well known as an engineer in the early days of railroads, had married twice. On the first occasion, while still a very young man, he had run away with the Honorable Bernice Kendal. She was a very beautiful woman and she possessed a determination of spirit, rare in early Victorian days. The mésalliance, which her aristocratic relations had striven so hard to prevent, flourished for five years and was made fruitful by the birth of a son called James. Then Bernice met her death in an accident. She fell through a lofty bridge as she was crossing it in her carriage. The bridge was very old and the money for its upkeep had been regularly misappropriated for several generations. Its piers crumpled suddenly, precipitating Orsett's wife, an old farmer, and half a company of dragoons who happened to be marching over at the same time, into a deep gully full of hard boulders.

After overcoming the first distraction of grief, Orsett instituted a dignified crusade for safer bridges. He received a wide response. When Parliament deferred to the popular clamor and sanctioned a scheme for renewing scores of rotten structures, it was only natural that the young engineer who had championed the measure should be commissioned to carry it out. It was no cynicism to say that Orsett never looked back after his first wife's death. By its peculiar and almost ludicrous form, she did more for his career than she could have achieved in a long and busy life; and, no doubt, being greatly attached to him, she would not have grudged the sacrifice. He for his part remained faithful to her memory for twenty-two years, during which he built an ever-increasing number of bridges, railways, and roads. In the fabric of every bridge he caused to be buried a small silver plaque bearing the initial B.

His remarriage greatly surprised his circle of acquaintances. His second wife was the daughter of a tea broker. Nobody knew why he had chosen her, except presumably himself; and even he, in later years, sometimes behaved as though he had forgotten. She was a virtuous, small-minded woman whose natural industry made her prone to interference in other people's affairs. She became a leading light in a women's reformative society which was a menace to the prostitutes of the later nineteenth century. A very sincere mutual hatred soon sprang up between her and the now adult James. The latter had already qualified as a doctor and was on the threshold of a career which must inevitably have caused him to spend most of his time abroad. Orsett, however, with the dogged wrongheadedness of an aging man, conceived and persisted in the notion that a stepmother's animosity had driven his first-born son away from home. As soon as James appreciated the position, he thoroughly enjoyed it and exploited it with deadly ingenuity. The result was not altogether what might have been expected. No open breach occurred between husband and wife, though their relations were further cooled. Orsett retaliated indirectly upon the second generation. Eva and Roger were the unhappy channels by which his displeasure reached their mother. He genuinely, and with a certain justification, considered them far inferior products to Bernice's handsome, brilliant, ruthless son. He missed no opportunity of expressing his disappointment, either in his lifetime or posthumously, by the division of his property. His treatment reacted unfavorably on their natures, exaggerating the defects of which they had been made overconscious. Roger's lack of self-assertion became spinelessness, his love of "old far-off forgotten things" a bolthole into which he would scurry at the least sign of approaching responsibility. Eva, who inherited the less attractive features of her mother's person and character, had been born with a deep conviction of her own merits, some of which might, with a little encouragement, have actually materialized. But being continually made to feel of no account she was beset by a festering sense of injustice: until in the end there was little left in her but sourness and a determination—masquerading as duty—to see that nobody over whom she was able to exercise any control should fare better than herself. James had once said to her: "Eva, you've spent most of your life in passing on the kick."

So now, when Olive heard the verjuice and resignation mingling in her aunt's voice, her eyes wandered to the wall above the mantelpiece where the cause of all these things hung, shrined in his bossy, gilded frame. The old gentleman whom she had been taught to call Grandpa Orsett sat in a chair of dark wood; he was leaning forward and his hands rested on his knees; the pose gave him a disquieting air of watchfulness. Long iron-gray whiskers traversed his face from temple to chin, like twin girders clamped into one of his own bridges, reinforcing it against the remotest contingency of weakness. Both the superficial resemblance and the essential difference between him and James were easy to detect. The father had been a hard, courageous, somewhat insensitive man; in the son hardness and courage were alloyed with imagination, and perverted—as when three harmless chemicals combine to make a poison—into cynical cruelty.

James had been the apple of his father's eye. In Orsett's florid Victorian will he was referred to as "my dear son James, from whose birth I have reaped nothing but legitimate pride." The old man could at times show a grim and idiosyncratic humor, but this was probably not a specimen of his irony.

"Well," pursued Aunt Eva, "I'm as delighted as anybody that Frances is getting married at last. But I must say, I hope that her wedding won't be quite like poor Dorothy's."

"Eh?" said Uncle Roger with unwonted decision. "I enjoyed myself there immensely. I hadn't attended a ceremony for years. Besides, I met that librarian fellow at the reception."

"My dear Roger," said Aunt Eva, "your social experiences may have left nothing to be desired. Not everybody was so fortunate. I am not particular, but I did resent those dreadful relatives of the bridegroom. One of them, I believe, actually *was* a publican."

Olive also had attended.

"Yes," she said in her soft, remote voice, "I remember him. He had an inn in Berkshire. He said that serving people with decent beer was the first thing that had made him happy since he left the army. Uncle James talked to him for a long time."

"Your uncle was not quite himself that day," replied Aunt Eva with acid amusement, nibbling her prim lips.

And suddenly Uncle James was standing at the head of the table, beside the poker-worked leather chair.

"Aha, Eva," he said, "the Demon Rum, eh? So I was bloody drunk at the auction of dear little Dorothy's virginity, eh? You're right. It was the only way I could stand it. I haven't got your head for alcohol or your stomach for slop."

James had a curious duplicity of movement. Usually—and in particular when it was most annoying—he tramped about as though his boots were shod with leaden plates. When he wished, however, he could compass a stealthy tread which would have done credit to an Indian scout.

Aunt Eva did not reply. If similes are to be taken from the beasts, she looked like a small jackal caught crunching an illicit bone.

James sat down to table.

"Let me get you something to eat?" said Roger.

"No-o," said James, affecting to consider, "no. I think not. But if I may prevail upon you to play Ganymede, I should be grateful for half a tumbler of whisky."

Roger rose doubtfully and went toward the old Dutch chest,

chased with mermaids and boisterous dolphins.

"You must be tired after your exertions of last night," he said. "There's still a tired look about you, James."

It was an understatement. For the first time within Olive's memory the years had cast their shadow across Uncle James. The many lines on his handsome face seemed to have drawn in their net. The golden post-tropical tan of his skin was undertinted with gray. If it had not been as unnatural a disturbance as a major earthquake in England, one would have said that his hands shook a little.

Roger half-filled the glass and bore it to the table.

"A little hot milk," he suggested.

"Spoil it," said James, quite pacifically.

Aunt Eva often quoted the saying "Everything in its place" meaning "everything in the place to which convention has assigned it." She would rather have seen a man grossly overindulge in whisky at night than touch a sip of it before noon. Certain axioms of propriety had seeped into her brain at her mother's knee, and she had never thereafter bothered to examine their logical implications. She felt the final straw insinuating itself across her back. On no previous occasion had the breakfast table been openly defiled with alcohol.

"You are unwell, James," she said sharply. "Anybody can see that. Does a man of your age and medical experience really imagine that he can put himself right by abusing stimulants at this hour? Quite apart from the example which you set to Olive and the servant who has to clear away glasses reeking of drink."

James put down the whisky. The whites of his eyes, already darkened by an unfamiliar suffusion, took on an almost crimson hue: the little veins played cat's cradle across his forehead.

"Eva," he said, "come here."

Aunt Eva stiffened in her seat behind the coffee pot and her knuckles grew white against the drooping edge of the tablecloth.

"Eva," said James, "come here."

You could feel the coercive influence of a strong personality directed primarily against one object, but overflowing in its surplus force throughout the whole room.

Eva rose to her feet. She passed behind Olive's chair. Olive did not look round. She was as much embarrassed as if her aunt were being compelled to strip physically naked.

James pushed forward his tumbler.

"Eva," he said, "I'm going to stand you a drink. And I take no refusal from my boon companions."

The back part of Aunt Eva's decorous crepe dress shivered with the hidden nervous agitation of her thighs and haunches. Still she stood, unable or not daring to find words to express her disobedience.

"Eva," said James in a low, terrible voice, "drink that whisky."

Then again, much louder, but preserving in some subtle way the original dulcet menace:

"Eva, DRINK THAT WHISKY!"

His eyes shone with a cold blue fire like icebergs which the sun has leveled to the water in their last decay.

"Eva . . ." he began again, and dropped his voice to a rasping purr.

Eva Marshall was fifty-four years old. At her mother's instance she had signed the pledge to abstain from all alcoholic liquors. She had been only eleven then, but she had never since departed from her unconscionable oath. Now she picked up the tumbler—double-handed lest she splash the carpet—and swallowed from it a fair mouthful. She did not cough, as is the way of people unused to spirits, but the tears welled up in her eyes, first engendered by the caustic fluid, then by bitter humiliation. She ran out of the room weeping, as lately Olive remembered to have wept on account of her shrewish correction. Yet it was impossible to exult over such chastisement, however deserved, because the brutality of method seemed disproportionate and, indeed, a portentous abuse of natural powers.

Uncle Roger said: "You can help yourself, James, next time you wish to drink."

"Ah," said James, "Pilate washes his hands! Never mind, my dear boy, it wasn't your fault. Which, I take it, is the only assurance you require to make you happy."

Uncle Roger departed also, neither flouncing out nor slinking away, but simply leaving a scene which had become intolerable to his sensibilities. Only Olive and James sat on in the dark-papered room where the firelight climbed between the old-fashioned ramblers on the wallpaper and reflected itself against the pattern of disordered breakfast cups. The antique Swiss clock, the one good timepiece in the house, whirred and sounded a single quarter.

At last Uncle James said:

"And what is Olive thinking about? If she lets her mind go wandering so long abroad, somebody will pop in one day and pinch the vacant premises."

There was no more venom in his jocularity. He sounded, for once, like quite an ordinary old man who enjoyed a little mildly facetious backchat with the younger generation.

"I was wondering whether I could get a job," replied Olive candidly.

"What sort of job?"

"I don't really know. Other girls seem to find them. Of course, there's the training . . ."

"Do you want to become a great actress like your little friend Miss Hassett?"

"Oh, Nina!" said Olive with a kind of affectionate contempt.

Eighteen months since, Nina Hassett had departed to London, bent on conquering the stage. She had attended a school of dramatic art for a whole year, in company with two or three hundred other aspirants. At the end of that period they were all told that they were among the most promising pupils which the school had turned out, and should obtain immediate employment in the West End. And no doubt a few of them did—if not in the limelight, then under the street lamps. The majority spent several months queueing up outside the dingy offices of theatrical agents, receiving no more encouragement than an occasional improper suggestion from some elderly entrepreneur who hinted at boundless powers of furthering pretty girls who showed him favor. In the end they drifted home to Kensington and Cheltenham and Malvern where their semiprofessional status made them greatly in demand at Christmas theatricals.

"I see," said James, "that your taste runs to something sterner. Typing and shorthand are excellent things, but, for myself, I shouldn't have said that it was much fun taking down some solicitor's letters from nine to six every day."

"It would be new," said Olive doubtfully. "And it seems almost the only businesslike thing a woman can do unless she's got degrees and diplomas. Not that I think I should be very good even at typing."

"For a young woman about to take up a vocation, you seem rather uncertain which direction your call is coming from," said James.

"I don't think you need a call for ordinary kinds of work."

"I see," said James. "The direct summons is only for people like Mr. Faulkner."

"Now you're laughing at me," said Olive. Her small, serene face betrayed neither resentment nor readiness to participate in the joke.

"I merely suggest," said James—and it was a great compliment, for to nobody else did he do anything but roar out edicts—"I merely suggest that you have not the slightest desire to take up work of any kind. All you wish to do is to get out of this place, which you find alternately dull and nerve-racking."

"Oh, uncle," said Olive, "why do you make me sound so ungrateful?"

"God damn my soul," began James; a fit of heavy coughing delayed the conclusion of his sentence, "what have you got to feel grateful for?"

Olive was embarrassed.

"Well . . . the fact that I've got a home at all, I suppose."

James looked at her fixedly. His expression was neither kind nor unkind. He might have been looking at a table and deciding where it would be most useful.

"As the poet says: 'You're here because you're here, because you're here.' There's no occasion for transports of thankfulness."

"But I don't see why you should have to keep me forever."

"You pay your way. Everybody in this house pays their way."

When Uncle James said something that she did not understand —which was quite often—Olive was usually content to let it pass above her head. But the mystery of his last remark intrigued her, and his mood seemed exceptionally favorable for questioning.

"Do Aunt Eva and Uncle Roger pay?"

"Yes," said James. "By installments. Your aunt has just been settling her account up to date."

Olive could no longer mistake his meaning. But there was one implication—the most important to her—which she still did not follow.

"But you said everybody. You never . . . I mean, I don't—" She broke off in confusion.

It scarcely occurred to her to be angry or disgusted by the picture of a brother and sister kept as whipping boys to satisfy a master's sadism. She was curious and a little apprehensive. This is the last vice of tyranny, that the subjects see nothing wrong in their condition.

"You?" said James, idly spinning a knife. "You, my dear Olive, are granted long-term credit. I regard you as an investment."

There was no telling what Uncle James would say this morning! Unpractical as she was, Olive knew just enough about business to answer him in the same vein.

"I'm afraid I'm a bad speculation, never likely to show much return for your money."

"Not in cash, perhaps," said James. "In fact I very much doubt whether you could support even yourself. But my little Olive has one valuable export. That is her sympathy."

Olive might be morally apathetic but she was not a sycophant.

"Oh, but, uncle," she protested indignantly, "just because I so often say nothing, that doesn't mean I always agree with you."

"Agree?" said James. "Why the hell should you? I said sympathy, which is something altogether deeper than mere concurrence in another's opinions. It is involuntary, inborn, inescapable. If your wireless is set at a certain wave length, then, whether you like it or not, you cannot help receiving messages sent out by the station to which it is attuned. The vital force in us sometimes makes such connections—very odd ones, perhaps, but more durable than any other human bonds."

Another violent fit of coughing seized him and his eyes were clouded with water.

Olive was repelled and bewildered by Uncle James's sudden, untypical venture into mysticism. His obscure and esoteric views on a quality which he called sympathy only interested her because they were clearly intended to have some reference to herself. She felt as if the skeins of a hidden plot were tightening about her.

There was a nervous vehemence in her voice as she asked:

"What do you want from me, Uncle James?"

"I don't know," he answered slowly. "I don't know. For the first time in my life I'm backing a mere irrational hunch. You're my dark horse, Olive."

As though a spring had suddenly been touched in her brain, Olive awoke to the solution of an old problem, one that had troubled her intermittently ever since she could remember. Why was talking to Uncle James quite unlike talking to anybody else? The difference was too radical to be explained by even his extraordinary personality. Now she had it. When other people spoke, her ear followed them, picking up the thoughts as they were clothed in sound. But in conversation with Uncle James her mind sometimes seemed to get ahead of his tongue so that she positively *knew*—not merely guessed—what was coming next: even when the subject matter was incomprehensible to her. The process did not always work, and it was hard to detect, because the actual utterance followed so closely on its telepathic forerunner that the two things almost merged. The effect had been to make James's words sound like a disquieting echo of something already formulated in her own brain.

She was shocked by the support which her discovery lent to Uncle James's theory. What if her mind were in truth linked to his? It was an uncanny idea. She would rather have been physically a Siamese twin.

Olive did not possess a strong, independent personality, but, as appears in money matters, people do not value a thing the less because they happen to have little of it.

When he spoke again it was in a changed key.

"Ah, Olive," he said, "this philosophic maundering is a bad sign. I seem to hear the first shambling footfall of dotage."

He rose from his chair. Halfway to an upright position he suddenly pressed both hands into the small of his back.

"What is it?" said Olive.

"Just a touch of lumbago, I think."

She looked at him uneasily. If he were right, the lumbago had chosen an equivocal moment for its onset. Its symptoms so exactly counterfeited the heralds of another illness. All over England people were getting up in the mornings and anxiously pressing the flesh above their kidneys to detect the slightest twinge.

"Oughtn't you to keep warm?" she suggested.

She meant "go to bed" but she dared not use a phrase so directly suggestive of weakness. James did not take kindly to advice about his health. He would have bitten Eva's head off for the merest hint. Olive, however, was to some extent privileged. His answer to her was not abuse but a gesture of defiance, in which he challenged the elements to shake his constitution.

Striding through the hall, he went to the front door and threw up its latch. A great wave of cold swept in, biting against their faces. He beckoned Olive to join him on the doorstep. He exhaled deeply and the cloud of his breath went up, straight, column-shaped under the impetus of his lungs; then it trailed motionless against the atmosphere.

"Look!" he said. "The second law of thermodynamics anticipates its triumph. Absolute inertia! 'Some say the world will end in fire, some say ice . . .'"

And indeed to one looking out into the still, steel-blue air, it seemed as though the cosmic energy had finally distributed itself. The cold crystalline glow of frost might have been that starlight which, it is said, will be the last resolution, not only of kings and princes, but also of the dust which they have become.

Olive was chilled to the bone. She was too polite merely to disappear into the house, leaving James to his contemplation. But she cast about for an excuse.

"Is there anything I can do for you?" she asked.

"You might take the Rover into Ely and call at the chemist's for a parcel."

Olive said doubtfully: "Aunt Eva did tell me I wasn't to use the car while the roads were frozen."

"Well, well," said James, "so that's an end of it. Wise woman, your aunt! I only wanted you to collect a few drugs for some of my moribund patients."

"I'll be ready in five minutes," said Olive.

2

Mick, the gardener, tickled the carburetor with a skill learned from the management of secondhand lawn mowers. Olive strained on the choke. The whir of the self-starter gave place to a series of staccato coughs as the engine shook off its numbed sleep. Presently the revolutions became steadier, and Olive signed to Mick to unstrap the muff from the radiator. Gingerly she let in the clutch. The old Rover crawled jerkily over the cobbled patch which had formerly been the Manor's stableyard. Behind her, Mick shouted a few words of incoherent advice.

She went out by the back drive into Possett Lane which debouched, after a quarter of a mile of bumps and potholes, on to the main Ely road. The village showed scarcely a sign of habitation. The street was empty except for a couple of elderly women exchanging a few words at the door of the post office. Even they seemed to be constrained and uneasy in their attitudes. They did not look into each other's faces as they spoke, but glanced continually at the ground or over their shoulders. They had an air of covert apprehension, like children playing marbles in a cemetery.

Even at 20 m.p.h. the wheels behaved erratically, taking on an independent life whenever two of them simultaneously found frozen puddles. Olive drove with care and concentration, but she completely lacked that effortless harmony with the petrol engine which characterized most of her contemporaries. She behaved on the road as though she were a promising beginner of fifty. She did not like acting chauffeur to any of the neighboring girls because she knew that her methods were a long-standing joke.

Gorchow lay behind her and the road began its monotonous journey between a parallel of frozen dikes, on whose farther banks the pollarded willows marched in undeviating line. The feathery tentacles, which at other times drooped so softly, stood out now like spiky coronets, seemingly diaphanous with accumulated ice. Field upon field, the fenland stretched back against the horizon— pasture and sugar-beet and plowland in successive swaths. In the slight mist the chimney of the factory, where the beet was cut and boiled, took on an airy, unreal dignity, which rivaled the more distant spire of Ely cathedral.

By the junction of a side road a man was standing, staring up at the ancient and battered finger post. Olive recognized him immediately and halted the car.

"Hallo!" she said.

"Hallo, Olive," said the Reverend Faulkner.

"Would you like a lift anywhere?"

"Well, I did mean to take a little healthy exercise. Where are you going?"

"Oh, I just have some things to do in Ely."

"As a matter of fact," said Faulkner, "I've got a friend there that I haven't seen for a long time. Should I be in the way?"

He did not sound very convinced about his motives.

"Of course not, Dick," said Olive.

Her tone, and the use of his Christian name, drew from him a smile of pure pleasure. He had an attractive smile, of the kind that wins its possessor a reputation for frankness and honesty, but is more often attributable to good teeth.

Olive, as usually happened when she interrupted the car's movement, had allowed the engine to die. While she was restarting it, he remarked:

"That signpost's rather quaint. Have you ever looked at it?"

Olive began to laugh.

"Have I not! 'Ely 9 miles, 3 furlongs, 17 poles.' I was with Uncle James when he knocked it down."

"Whatever for?"

"He said it was a revolting example of pseudo-scientific precision. When the constable came round about it—terrified, poor man—Uncle said that he would go along and replace it personally, when and if he was satisfied that the measurements were absolutely accurate and not misleading to the public. Nothing happened. I suppose the County Council stuck it up again."

"I'm afraid I rather like it," said Faulkner. "It seems to me one of the few signposts that is genuinely anxious to give information. However, your uncle and I don't often see eye to eye."

"I know," said Olive, trying valiantly to change up into second. "I think," she added, "that he'd be more annoyed to find that you agreed with him."

"And yet," said Faulkner, "whenever I meet him I have the feeling that there's no need for us to fight all along the line. In fact, I should definitely say that we had certain things in common, if it didn't sound as though I were one of those awful clerics who breeze about determined not to recognize hostility, even when it's shoved in their faces."

"Uncle can't stand anything or anyone connected with religion," said Olive.

"That's just my point. If he's made up his mind that Christianity is repugnant to him . . . well, he's entitled to his own view just as I am to mine. But why let it poison his whole attitude toward me and destroy every vestige of civility?"

"Uncle is like that," said Olive fatalistically.

"But why?"

"Well, I don't know," Olive admitted. "Sometimes I honestly think he's got a devil or something."

Faulkner laughed.

"I don't suppose he'd be flattered to hear himself explained by such an anachronism. He'd bite your head off."

"Not mine," said Olive, with rather naïve pride. "Besides, he sometimes gets quite . . . well . . . fanciful himself. He talked to me for a long time this morning and said some very strange things: then he laughed at what he'd said and pretended it was all nonsense. Perhaps it was. I don't know."

"Don't you let him bully you—or poison your mind."

"Dick!" said Olive, jerking up her head.

"Sorry. That wasn't up to the standard of charity expected of my cloth."

"Well, you shouldn't have said it to me. I owe a lot to Uncle."

"Do you know, you reminded me of him just now. When you threw up your chin I could almost see a beard on it. I often think that family likenesses come out much more commonly in gesture than in physical resemblance."

"I dare say," said Olive in a small, deliberate voice. "But you see, I'm not really one of Uncle's family. Or perhaps you knew?"

A lorry approached on the opposite side of the road. It was traveling much too fast and its wheels, wavering across the frozen crust, churned up a spray of broken needles. Olive gripped the Rover's steering wheel with strained attention. As the lorry flashed past they both saw into its hold, where the canvas covering had slipped back and revealed the high-piled cargo. It was carrying a large number of plain wooden coffins.

"No," said Faulkner levelly, "I certainly didn't know. I realize, of course, that James was not born of the same marriage as your other uncle and aunt. D'you mean that you're only his niece by the half blood?"

"I'm not his niece at all," said Olive firmly. "I'm nobody's niece."

There was very little for Olive to read at the Manor. Aunt Eva still favored *East Lynne* and similar works. Olive had been driven to them faute de mieux and had consequently become familiar with the tableau in which the heroine tests her lover by proclaiming that she is "nobody's baby." All the same she could not help wishing, either that it was untrue or else that there was a moral certainty of her turning out to be the lost scion of a ducal house. The Reverend Faulkner did not assist her at all. But she had burned her boats and could not now retreat.

"Yes," she said firmly, "I'm an orphan, I expect. I was picked out of the gutter."

"What, by James?" said Faulkner.

"I don't really know," said Olive, "but I think some kind of institution probably did the actual picking, and Uncle James came along afterwards. Anyhow, he adopted me. I've been here ever since I can remember."

"Good Lord," said Faulkner mildly. "The locals are usually pretty well au fait, but they all think you're the child of a deceased sister of your aunt."

"Well," said Olive, "Auntie tries to give a wrong, respectable impression about me. One can understand it."

She had expected her disclosure to make more of a sensation. Little given though she was to histrionics or the enjoyment of a scene for its own sake, she had already drawn up her forces to counterattack at the least sign of patronizing sympathy or shocked dismay. She was disconcerted when he entirely failed to pursue the subject.

Eventually her anxiety to know how he had really been affected forced her once more to assume the initiative.

"I don't know if I shall be here much longer. I'm thinking of getting some work."

"I shall be sorry if you go away, Olive. Though, of course, I think it's quite natural. Gorchow . . ." His voice tailed away regretfully, leaving his opinion of Gorchow to be inferred.

Olive was rather pleased. She had wanted to know that he would miss her.

"I don't mind the village," she said. "But I feel I must live my own life."

The Reverend Faulkner winced slightly. Olive at times reproduced echoes of the most unfortunate type of fiction. It was, as he recognized, a failing due rather to lack of individual emotional experience than any innate love of cheap clichés. He felt ashamed of even this tolerant diagnosis, because she, on her side, might have inwardly criticized his own faint ineradicable plebeian accent; and he was certain that she never did.

"Olive," he said. "I should never try to persuade you to tie yourself to a tiny place and a limited society in which you felt that you were wasting your days. But you have told me that you don't dislike Gorchow. Would it prevent you from leading your own life, as you put it, if you were to marry me? That is, if you would consider the idea at all," he added hastily.

Olive tardily recognized that this was the goal which had all the while been before her subconscious mind. Now that she had achieved it she was thrown into a flurry of disconcertion. She was probably the only girl left in England who could have sincerely received a proposal in the spirit of a Jane Austen heroine. She did not go so far as to swoon, but she nearly put the Rover into a telegraph pole.

"It's very kind of you, Dick," she said at last.

"Good heavens, this isn't a charitable offer! Or are you just trying to refuse politely?"

"No," said Olive. "At least I don't think so. I don't really know. You see . . ."

"Well, suppose you think it over and we talk about it again in a week or two's time? Provided, of course, that the flu hasn't nipped us both in the bud by then!"

He clasped his square, short-fingered hand for a moment over her gloved one where it gripped the wheel.

"Dick," she said, "you are silly to go out in this weather without a hat or gloves. Your fingers are blue."

"See how I need somebody to look after me!"

"Yes," agreed Olive. "But it ought to be somebody capable and efficient. And, anyhow, I don't think that's all men expect from their wives."

Faulkner smiled. In the clear space, the semivacuum created by the expense of emotion, he saw himself in accurate proportion against the enormous background of contemporary life: the unimportant representative of a creed which seemed to be ceasing to affect the world except as a social institution; a clergyman and therefore, in the eyes of many of his fellows, a paid hypocrite. The vision scarcely depressed him at all. He had that more creditable kind of self-sufficiency which comes from complete absence of ambition. He had no great wish to convert unbelievers or to reform the morals of other people; not because he doubted that these things were desirable and capable of being achieved, but because he knew that he was not built for such work. He accepted his own limitations as laws. He was not thereby prevented from fulfilling his duties conscientiously, but his performance of them tended to aim at preserving the status quo, or, more concretely, at leaving Gorchow no worse than he found it. His private religious belief, which he kept distinct from his profession, was rather a fixed state of mind than a thing capable of motive force and development.

Often it seemed to him that in Olive he detected a spirit similar to his own, though less conscious of itself; and that by associating his life with hers he might secure, beyond the possibility of destruction, that inward peace which he prized above all things. Other moments came, too—but more rarely—when she raised doubts in him and he wondered whether he was not reading something into her character which had never been there, mistaking the results of repression and an incurious mind for a philosophic tranquillity. He knew that it was possible for some men to hypnotize themselves into seeing the most marvelous and admirable patterns simply by prolonged staring at a perfectly blank surface.

He was very fond of Olive but little in love with her, and for even that little her physical attraction did most to account. No woman was likely to get more from him.

In Ely the streets were all light brown, carpeted with loose gravel to counteract slipping. Olive stopped at the chemist's shop.

The man inside explained that by chance Uncle James's consignment of drugs had already been sent.

"A young fellow I know was taking his van your way, and I asked him to drop the parcel. I hope I've not done wrong. I wouldn't like to make Dr. Marshall wild."

The last words he said with great feeling, and Olive had to reassure him at some length.

When she came out, Faulkner told her that she could not make the journey for nothing. He asked her to have lunch and go to the cinema. She accepted a little doubtfully, wondering whether it could be held to prejudice her free decision on the question of marriage.

Olive enjoyed films. The hackneyed stories often failed to thrill her, but the motion picture as a device never lost its appeal. She liked the disembodied way in which the actors flicked on to the screen out of nothingness, and at the end were swallowed up again without a trace. The theater was extraordinarily empty. The program had begun but hardly more than a dozen people were watching it. As they took their seats Faulkner gave an exclamation of dismay.

"I am a fool," he muttered. "We never ought to have come here."

"What do you mean?" said Olive.

"Didn't you hear that announcement they gave out over the wireless last week—about the advisability of keeping away from all crowded public places which it wasn't absolutely necessary to visit? They mentioned cinemas particularly."

"Oh, yes," said Olive, "I remember. Because of the epidemic."

"A room like this, full of warm, stale air, is probably a deathtrap."

"I don't believe we're any more likely to catch flu here than elsewhere," said Olive with surprising decision. "Nobody knows how you get it. The BBC warning was bunk. Uncle James said so."

"Well," said Faulkner, "I'd rather it was he than I who had the responsibility of putting it to the test."

"Sit down in front, there!" shouted somebody behind them.

They both flopped into seats.

"Of course," said Olive, "if it really makes you uncomfortable to stay, I'll come out, too."

Faulkner did not reply, but settled himself in his seat. He had recently attended too many highly infectious deathbeds to be very alarmed about his own safety.

As she picked up the threads of the story now on the screen, Olive began to feel rather embarrassed by her insistence on staying. The film was a comedy and it depicted the preposterous adventures of a poor family who won an enormous prize in a sweepstake. The father tried to shoot grouse with a machine gun, and the mother's attempts to break into Society were crowded with solecisms. It was all extremely crude, but it would have been at any rate mildly amusing if it had not been so unfortunately apropos.

"I think, after all," whispered Olive, "that perhaps it isn't really safe and we ought to go."

Faulkner was amused.

"Your tact alone would make you a marvelous wife," he said. Then: "As a matter of fact, I wish they'd called me in for expert consultation when they made this film. I could have given them a few hints on the more subtle psychological aspects."

Olive was not quite sure whether he was being rather helpful or rather callous.

Faulkner had a good superficial knowledge of his parishioners' domestic affairs. But for accuracy and detail it was nothing to Gorchow's investigations into his own family history. Every English village is a kind of co-operative private inquiry agency: antlike, the inhabitants collect each his crumb of information, then they pool results, and ultimately a formidable likeness of the truth emerges. The completed story percolates slowly to the houses of the gentry, but it gets there in the end, passing from gardener to cook, and thence abovestairs. Olive knew the saga of the Faulkners from many repetitions, for it was, in substance, the perennially popular tale of the man who found a crock of gold. Alf Faulkner had kept a small garage on the outskirts of Northampton. One day he filled in a football-pool coupon for the first time. He won fourteen thousand pounds. During the inevitable celebration he met a charming stranger in a West End bar. This man persuaded him that it was foolish to be content with such a comparatively paltry sum. There was, he said, in London an institution called the Stock Exchange which paid higher dividends than any pool and did not demand nearly so much troublesome brainwork. Folly has no right to escape its conventional reward. Alf Faulkner should have returned to his tires and pumps, enriched by nothing except bitter experience. Indeed, the stage was fairly set for a horrible warning. Mr. Faulkner's new friend had just finished a sentence of eighteen months for stock promotion. He was an ingenious and unprincipled fellow with a great talent for finance. As it happened, however, he had now decided to turn over a new leaf, at any rate in so far as to test whether it was not possible under modern conditions to make money without either contravening the law or doing any hard work. Accordingly he did not merely put Mr. Faulkner's winnings in his pocket and disappear, but proceeded to lay them out in series of dizzy speculations. Partly because he had a run of phenomenal luck, and partly because he was very expert, he succeeded in multiplying the eleven talents by four or five times, even allowing for his own commission, which fluctuated between twenty-five and forty per cent of the profits on any deal. While it lasted, the arrangement benefited two people and had the additional moral advantage of keeping one of them out of almost all temptation. But Mr. Faulkner was probably fortunate that his mentor was struck down by a taxicab on the second anniversary of their meeting and died before the tide of chance could turn. The old man did, however, deserve credit for his decision, taken immediately on learning the news, that he now had quite enough money and should consult more sober authorities on how to keep it.

Before the arrival of the check from the pool promoters, Dick, the eldest child, had been looked on as the family's crowning achievement. His father and mother often said they did not know where the boy got his brains from. Privately, of course, both meant that they acquitted the other of any share in his heredity. Dick won a scholarship to the local grammar school and from there he won another, sufficient when supplemented by certain charitable funds to send him to Cambridge. During the years of his education he grew far away from the tousled urchin with the attractive smile who had once played with spanners and empty oil drums on the asphalt patch outside Faulkner's De Luxe Garage. But the more impossible it became for him to conform to their standards, the greater his parents' pride in a son whose manners so clearly marked his higher status. His mother would exasperate him by fondly calling attention at table to the difference between his and her husband's methods of eating food. At first, when he visited his home, Dick conscientiously tried to revert to type and to put temporarily out of his head all those turns of speech which belonged to a different society: he was a kindly and modest youth, and if he could not honor his parents, he believed that he should at least humor them. Soon, however, he realized that his efforts were misdirected. They honestly preferred that he should be out of place in their circle; if he had been at home there, they would have felt that he had nothing to show for his education. Unfortunately, as he came to see, their motives were not altogether disinterested. Mixed up with a genuine altruistic pleasure in watching their child surpass them there was an unworthy and snobbish joy in being able to patronize their neighbors on the strength of a superior possession. Alf Faulkner soon became a nuisance in his favorite pub, with his references to "my son at Cambridge." And Alf had not yet won that fortune.

Dick's success continued at the university. He had gone up as a sound but uninspired classical scholar. He was not really very interested in the ancients of the pre-Christian era: he found, or fancied, in all of them some common element, antipathetic to his taste. As soon, however, as he was introduced to the earlier medievalists, in particular the ecclesiastical writers, he found his proper milieu. He developed a personal sympathy for the early Fathers, unworldly men who wandered in bewildering fashion between bathos and the sublime, trivial anecdote and apocalyptic fervor. He so distinguished himself by certain researches into their works that he was given the unofficial offer of a college fellowship. He turned it down for two reasons: he did not relish the prospect of a life spent among dons whose only outside interests lay in gossip and mildly homosexual attachments; in the second place, he had allowed himself to be so far seduced by his studies as to believe that they offered a practical guide to conduct in this world. Origen and Jerome and Porphyry so obsessed him that he seriously wished to imitate them. And since the contemporary world offered no facilities for retirement to the desert—not at any rate without great expense and probable publicity of the worst kind—he decided, faute de mieux, to enter the Church. In those days the vicarage at Gorchow was not before his eyes; rather he saw the tawny sands and the tunneled habitation and the fabulous lions gathering round to hear his preaching.

He had barely entered the Training College when he received a copy of the Northampton paper which headlined the announcement "Local Man's Epic Gamble." Underneath was a picture of Alf being presented with his check on the stage of the local cinema. Dick had not the least objection to cash gained by lottery and he could not help feeling relieved that he was now backed by something besides his own brain. During the next two years, sudden prosperity made little change in his home, except that his father congratulated himself more frequently and paid less attention to the garage, while his mother had a new electric vacuum cleaner. Dick remained quite unaware of the operations which were even then being conducted in the stock markets.

The letter beginning "Dear Son, I think I can now say as I am rich" and ending "Hoping this finds you as it leaves me" arrived at a time when his ordination was already in sight. It came as a great shock. Sandwiched between those two phrases was the news that his father had bought a small house outside Market Harborough in which he hoped to spend the rest of his days as country gentleman. He naïvely explained that he thought Dick was admirably qualified to assist his plans. The suggestion was that he should abandon the Church—which no longer offered any social advancement that money could not more quickly procure—and settle down as a kind of major-domo to guide his family through the intricacies of high life in Leicestershire. If he needed any further occupation, there would be funds available for the purchase of, say, a partnership in some old-established local business.

Dick would have been less enraged if he had believed that these proposals were framed in a spirit of conscious and blatant cynicism. He knew what had happened: his mother, who had always been a snob, ever since she lady's-maided in a castle, had got hold of his father and superimposed on his simple, rather "Paycock-ish" mind the picture of himself sitting in a paneled hall telling the butler to fetch his guest, Lord X, another glass of sherry. He replied in biting terms, of which Alf understood just enough to be gravely offended. Thereafter Dick's relations with his family were strained. He would have been willing enough to make it up, but, in point of fact, he had outlived his usefulness. "My son who was at Cambridge" no longer constituted a paying gambit in a society where the statement was merely taken to indicate that he had not been at Oxford. "My son who is a clergyman" was definitely bad medicine and provoked such remarks as "How too earnest of him, my dear!" Alf certainly carried out his design. He went to live in a district loud with the baying of hounds and the manners of huntingfolk. The Faulkners rapidly became a county joke. They employed a first cousin as their chauffeur and several times, after meets, Mrs. Faulkner had been seen sitting with him on the running board, her fashionable shoes eased halfway off her feet, while she blew on a nice cup of tea from the thermos. To do them justice, the Faulkners had too much sense to push themselves in the crude manner of stage nouveaux riches: for which they were ultimately rewarded with the kind of affectionate contempt anciently accorded to court fools.

There were two other children. The utmost exercise of Christian charity could not reconcile Dick to his brother Roddy who, by some obscure personal magic, invariably converted his surroundings to the likeness of a street corner. A derisive whistle after passing housemaids seemed to hang perpetually on his lips, and when he hunted in a topper he gave the impression that he had mislaid his cloth cap. Josephine, the sister, was a far more sympathetic character. She was a thin, pretty girl with ash-blond hair and waxen cheeks, hectically splashed with a color which was, alas, natural. She was riddled with tuberculosis of the stealthy, lingering type. She had been to a sanatorium in Switzerland for six months, but her mother had brought her back, saying that what she needed was not this foreign air, but "building up." Now all day long she lay on the sofa, surrounded by rejected offerings of cream and meat essence, mourning her youth and strength, reading novels and judging them with an acumen beyond her education. On the rare occasions when Dick visited his home, he always found pleasure in talking with Josephine. But she depressed him terribly. She was so thin, her voice was so faint that she might have been released on parole from among the strengthless, twittering ghosts of the Homeric underworld.

3

When they came out of the cinema the air had turned smoky-blue with the approach of night. A few snowflakes drifted through the dusk, thin and crisp, as though they were shavings sliced off by a lathe from the frozen sky.

"I wish it would snow properly," said Faulkner. "That would break the spell. But the temperature stays too low."

Olive thought: When the frost dissolves, and water begins to run again, and the boughs of the trees move and drip, everything will be different. I shall be stronger and clearer and more certain of myself, because to my mind also the thaw will come. In this weather I feel like Lot's wife.

They drove back to Gorchow in silence. Once by the wide junction of two dikes they heard above their heads the whistling sound of pinions. In these days the wildfowl had deserted their accustomed pathways of the air, finding that northward the broads and shallow inlets of the sea were locked with ice: they descended, some to Cambridgeshire, others to Suffolk, seeking in vain a haven of open water where the reeds grew lush from banks of mud. They were pathetic in their flights of fruitless reconnaissance, creatures of instinct defeated by a mood of nature which rendered useless their inherited experience.

Olive dropped Dick at the vicarage gate.

"Thank you," he said. "Think about me a little, Olive, and of what I said this morning."

"Yes," said Olive, "I will. Perhaps, when the frost breaks, I shall know the answer."

Olive did not possess a latchkey of the Manor. She rang. Her hand was scarcely off the bell before the door popped open, revealing Aunt Eva standing on the threshold, obviously "in a state."

"Olive," she said, her voice squeaking and grating with emotion, "where have you been? Of all the heartless, ungrateful girls . . ."

"The road was perfectly safe, aunt," interrupted Olive wearily. "And anyhow Uncle James told me to take the car."

"Your Uncle James! It will be a long time before you have another chance to use him as an excuse. I don't suppose that even he ordered you to remain out all day and half the night!"

"I went to a film with Mr. Faulkner," muttered Olive.

"And of course you couldn't telephone in case we needed you or the car!"

"I'm afraid it never occurred to me."

Aunt Eva licked her lips, anticipating the pleasure of reporting disaster and simultaneously laying the blame for it on another's shoulders.

"Apart," she said, "from allowing us all to wonder whether you had driven into a dike and were lying drowned at the bottom, you may well be responsible for your Uncle James's failure to recover from the attack he developed at midday. A few hours in these cases often make all the difference, but we could not get hold of a doctor until after four o'clock. Of course, if there had been anybody here who could have been sent to catch him on his rounds, no doubt your poor uncle would have received earlier attention."

While she was still speaking Olive pushed past her and, with moistening eyes, began to run upstairs. At the far end of the top landing were two opposite doors. One gave entry to Uncle James's bedroom, the other to his laboratory. The latter was ajar and beyond it, glimmering palely in the semidarkness, Olive could see the double row of glass-stoppered bottles. She had always been fascinated by the laboratory, though her visits to it had been comparatively few and seemed to have become even rarer since she had grown up. Once, however, on her twelfth birthday, Uncle James had called her inside and allowed her to watch while he performed mysterious rites with something called a "culture." Afterwards he cleaned his hands with cyanide of potassium, discoursing ghoulishly on the fate of others who had done so and overlooked some crack or abrasion of their skins. Olive had fidgeted and held her breath throughout the operation, filled with the same fearful curiosity with which she had watched a man crossing a tightrope on a bicycle. Nothing happened, and she had not really believed anything would. Not to Uncle James.

She hesitated for a moment, then tapped firmly on the left hand door.

"Is that you, Eva?" It was Uncle James's voice, but strangely distorted. To her mind rose the image of a railway track, its iron level cluttered with the debris of a landslide.

"It's me—Olive," she said.

"Come in," said Uncle James. "Just in time to witness my dissolution!"

He lay propped up on three pillows. He was greatly changed within a few hours. Superficially he seemed to have been treated with a youthful elixir, so many of the lines and wrinkles had disappeared from his face. Only when one looked closer did one see the baneful cause of his rejuvenation—the feverish tightening of loose tissue and the rosy unnatural flush superimposed on tired flesh. Olive realized with a shock that Uncle James had lost his immortal quality.

"I'm sorry to hear you're not feeling well," she said decorously.

"I've got something which society has agreed to call flu. I shall be dead within twelve hours. My bloody lungs are going."

"Uncle!" said Olive.

"Uncle!" he tried to mimic in a ghastly falsetto, but the vocal effort swamped the back of his throat in liquid and he began to choke. She stood helpless and frightened while the paroxysm ran its course.

"Physician, heal thyself," he croaked.

Aunt Eva came in without knocking. She went to the somber, old-fashioned dressing table and opened one of the top-layer drawers.

"James," she said in a bright, antiseptic tone which dissociated her from all personal sympathy, "you've been coughing. I left my own favorite tincture up here and now I'm going to give you some."

In her own eyes Aunt Eva was heaping coals of fire. A she-Lazarus, she proffered the curative draught to him who had lately spurned her underfoot. No suspicion of doubt assailed her as she calmly and authoritatively prescribed for one of the greatest medical figures of the era.

While the syrupy nostrum flowed into the spoon James lay quite still, save for the throb of the veins in his forehead and the light twitching of his long, supple fingers.

"Perhaps you'd prefer me to give it you," said Aunt Eva. "Then we shan't spill any."

She pushed forward the brimming spoon. James docilely opened his lips. This was her triumph. Men were only big babies. Their harsh phrases withered under the shadow of illness, and were replaced by a lamblike obedience to the dispassionately ministering female.

Suddenly, on the point of taking the draught, James threw up one hand, barring the way to his mouth.

"Now, now!" said Aunt Eva, soothing the refractory child.

"Eva," said James, "how do I know this stuff is wholesome?"

"Don't be absurd. You can look at the bottle if you wish. The recipe or analysis or whatever you call it is printed on the label."

"Ah," said James. "I don't suspect the original ingredients."

"Then what do you mean?" Aunt Eva's voice rose to shrillness.

"My dear Eva, I have great confidence in the devoted nursing of relatives. In my experience it usually achieves its object. Sometimes the patient recovers, sometimes he dies."

Aunt Eva stood, still holding the spoon with commendable steadiness, while the last traces of color drained out of her wan cheeks.

"Auntie," began Olive, "he doesn't mean . . ." She stopped, realizing that she had only called attention to the innuendo.

"And after all, Eva," pursued James, "why shouldn't you take your chance to poison me? The toxicology may be weak, but the spirit is willing. A few drops of rat bane, and you'd be seated on the family throne. I don't suppose Roger would even put in a claim. Why, damn me, if I held your views, I should feel a moral obligation at any rate to try powdered glass!"

Olive looked at Aunt Eva's face. It was neither angry nor disgusted: it had an aghast expression, as though she had suddenly seen her own suppressed likeness in a particularly repellent and vicious ape. James had this magnetism, whereby he could draw out and vivify evil thoughts, of whose embryonic existence their begetters had scarcely been aware.

Trembling, she said: "Your uncle's in a fever, Olive. He doesn't know what he's saying."

"Don't worry, aunt," said Olive. "He knows perfectly well you'd never really poison him."

"A very apt summary!" muttered James. " 'The poor cat i' the adage,' eh?"

"You go and rest," whispered Olive. "I'll stay with him and ring if I should need you."

She felt a faint glow of pride as Aunt Eva obeyed, murmuring about nerves and lack of appreciation. She could never before remember having taken even partial command of a situation. Only when she was alone with James did her confidence ebb a little. Suppose that in delirium he forgot her established immunity, suppose he turned and rent her?

The fire hummed in the grate and awoke dull glints in the dark mahogany furniture. Blue-bulbed, the reading lamp suffused pillow and bedhead with a dim glow which seemed to melt into the sick man's features so that it no longer resembled superimposed light but a sinister phosphorescence of the flesh.

"Well, well," said Uncle James, chuckling harshly. "It's always the theoretician who makes the fuss. The practitioner takes things in his stride. I can distinctly remember poisoning three people —outside the ordinary medical routine, of course—and I can honestly say I never felt any ill effects."

Olive pulled up a chair to the bedside.

"Did you really?" she asked.

"Yes," said Uncle James with a simplicity which carried the force of truth.

"Aren't you afraid, then, if you believe you're going to die?"

"My God, Olive," said Uncle James, "that damned lascivious cleric has been corrupting your mind. I don't suppose he's got the guts to go for you physically. Lose your honor, my girl, embrace a fate worse than death, but don't put up with mental fumbling."

Olive's pacific temperament gave her one advantage over most of the people who crossed swords with James Marshall. She never tried to play him at his own game.

"I'm sorry," she said gently, "that we should talk about this when you aren't yourself, but I think I'm going to marry Dick Faulkner."

"Indeed?" said James. "I congratulate you on your sense of strategic timing. Up go the banns on one side of the church wall and down goes the old man's coffin on the other! No doubt you'll find Roger very amenable in the matter of consent."

Olive might have considered this a reasonable interpretation of her conduct if she had believed that Uncle James advanced it with any genuine conviction.

"Will you tell me something?" she asked in her soft, sweet voice.

"I don't know," said James. "What?"

"Do you like making people hate you?"

As he lay, the bedclothes molded themselves to every contour of his still magnificent body. Supine, he resembled a petrified image of the Count Baldwin or some other crusading paladin, long-bearded, enshrined in the panoply of disinterested valor. For the first time Olive realized how handsome he had been, and indeed still was.

"My dear child," said James, "I don't recollect that I ever concerned myself with other people's animosity. And if you personally are under the impression that you hate me, let me advise you to consult yourself again!"

Olive sighed. As usual, he managed to usurp three-quarters of the right in an argument. She did not hate him. Even her disapproval became acute only in spasms. By some sleight of will he had jockeyed her into the position of a confederate, who had no right to be scandalized by his misdoings.

"Come closer, my dear," he said.

She pulled up the wicker bedside chair. James stretched out his hand. She took it automatically. She could feel the blood beating, harsh, rhythmic, indomitable, through the knotted veins. Presently she had the curious fancy that the pulsations of her own body had begun to keep time, marching in step with an alien heart.

From downstairs came a series of soft, ringing notes, almost unrecognizable as the music of the gong which Dora normally took pride in rousing to an ear-splitting clangor. More than anything else those tentative beats brought home to Olive a sense of disorganization and impending calamity. She looked into Uncle James's face with a new anxiety. He had turned his head, and his eyes fixed her in the full beam of their cold, unwinking stare.

"Do you want anything?" she asked uncomfortably.

"Yes," said James, "I do. But could you give it me?"

"Of course," said Olive. "Just tell me."

"I want life," said James. "Any brand will do."

Olive did not know how to treat this demand. Perhaps it was a joke, or again perhaps it was a feverish delusion which ought to be shelved by tactful humoring.

At last she said: "I'm sure you'll keep the life you've got. But even if you shouldn't, there's always the hope that you'll exchange it for something better."

"Pah!" said James. "I know what's in your mind. You're trying to push the goods your paramour travels in. My requirements are less pretentious. I've always found that this material plane offered me plenty of scope. All I want is a body that will stick to it."

Olive thought that this must be Uncle James's peculiar way of showing remorse. She was not surprised, since she had been brought up to believe that remorse was inseparable from sinful deathbeds. Moreover, in view of his character, she did not think that he had begun to show it a moment too soon. But it was not her part to exaggerate its pangs, so she answered in soothing and rather priggish tones.

"You may be sure that we shall all do everything possible to keep you with us."

"Ah," said James, "how I distrust these damned collective promises!"

"I promise," said Olive. "I, personally, won't let you die if it can be helped."

She felt rather noble when she said this. She could only wish that Uncle James might appear more frightened and less purely resentful at the prospect of death. He retained his unique faculty for debasing other people's gestures. The new "Florence Nightingale" Olive looked very like the old Olive subserviently anxious to remove annoyances.

"You've set your name to a hard bond, my little Alcestis," said James.

"What did you call me?" Olive asked.

Still clasping her hand, as though to complete an electric circuit, he began the story of Admetus, whose virtuous wife was ready to take his place among the ghosts of Hades. Although his cough and his breathing grew progressively worse, he related the fable with taste and felicity of expression. She was reminded of something she had once heard Roger say: "James has been a great doctor. He could have been great in any sphere which he chose, even poetry."

Dora came in, bearing a little tray on which stood a solitary glass of milk-and-soda.

"Dora," said James, "I can't take that stuff unless it's diluted. First go to the washstand. Now tip it into the water jug. Thank you. That's right. Now I'm sure I shall get the goodness out of it, as we say in medical circles."

"Uncle!" began Olive. But Dora interrupted:

"Please, miss, your aunt says for you to come down and have your dinner, because she or Mr. Roger will be up to keep the watch."

"Magnificent!" coughed James. "The Celtic touch. Roger and Eva taking turns to keen about my bier!"

Poor Dora was completely baffled. She knew that this must be one of Mr. James's jokes and she would have liked to show her appreciation, if only she could have combined it with the respectful sympathy proper to extreme illness.

"Tell them that I shall be staying here for a little longer," said Olive. "You can leave something cold for me on the table. I shan't want much."

She basked for a moment in a glow of new-found importance. There was nobody else whose presence in the sickroom would be even tolerated. Aunt Eva had already once been put to rout: and since she was the only alternative choice as ministering angel, Olive was justified in considering herself as indispensable.

Uncle James's breathing grew progressively harsher and more labored. The tiny malignant organisms, multiplying at incredible speed inside his lungs, were steadily bringing nearer the moment when he would, almost literally, drown in his own secretions. Now his eyes had lost their insolent, unwavering stare and opened and shut intermittently with a fluttering movement of the lids. His hand, too, still clamped on Olive's, grew alternately damp with sweat and dry like an evaporated stalk. He remained silent for long periods, and when he spoke it was in snatches, apropos of some private, uncommunicated train of thought. Gradually, however, the disconnected utterances lit up the general trend of his mind.

Uncle James was still unreconciled to the prospect of death. Automatically, from force of long habit, he continued to cast about in his mind for means of repelling the invader. Perhaps, too, in the feverish recesses of his brain he invoked powers which his scientific conscience would have scorned to recognize.

About half past nine Roger put his head round the door. He did not come completely inside because he held some very peculiar ideas about infection. His attitude toward germs was roughly that of a soldier in the trenches toward bullets: the greater the area of the body which was exposed, the greater the chance that one of the hostile agents would find its mark.

"Sst!" he whispered. "I thought I'd let you know that Dr. Mailey rang up. He's trying to find a nurse. Anyhow he says he'll be round soon."

Olive nodded.

"Grave risk you're running, my dear!"

The strain of subdued hissing irritated his throat and he strove desperately to suppress a cough.

"Roger!" James's voice was a croak, but an imperative one. "Come in here."

Roger obeyed most reluctantly. James rolled over to face him.

"I don't like that cough of yours," he pronounced. "Get Mailey to look at you before he comes up here. I've no wish to be alarming, but it sounds to me as if you may soon be needing his attentions more than I do."

The habitual diffidence of Roger's expression became alloyed with fear. His round cheeks seemed to deflate. Courteous, as always, he muttered his thanks to James for sparing him a thought in such circumstances, then he hurried from the room. Outside, they could hear the power of suggestion acting on his larynx in a violent succession of coughs.

James was noticeably revived by working off his surplus malice. He seemed to benefit in much the same way as certain people do by bloodletting. He said:

"And now I suppose he'll run round saying his prayers and swilling pints of patent-medicine muck."

Olive backed away from the bed.

"I think it was a very cruel trick. You know how he worries

about his health. You can't do anything but hurt and annoy others, even when you say you're nearly dying. You're—you're like one of those creatures that hang about houses, plaguing people and—and throwing coal."

"This is most refreshing," said James. "I thought at first you meant a sadist. But coal-throwing is a new departure in perversion."

"You may be a sadist too," said Olive, exasperated by inability to complete her indictment. "But that's not the word I want. Pol—pol—"

"Poltergeist," supplied James. For a moment the obstructions in his windpipe cleared and his voice resumed its normal volume. The effect was intensely startling, as if he had suddenly broken into a triumphant shout of "Eureka!"

He seemed infuriatingly pleased by a remark whose intention had been anything but complimentary. He repeated the word "poltergeist" several times, and a shrewd speculative look came over his face, momentarily chasing away the blurred shadows of illness.

"Coal-throwing, eh? Not very subtle, but no doubt the spiritual world has its roughnecks. Ah, Olive, almost you persuade me that I've been wrong all this time in classing psychic research with the investigation of lampposts by Pekinese. Acquaintance with a really unscrupulous poltergeist might well have lightened my last minutes."

The improvement of his powers was transient, a valedictory flash from the graying clinker of a once-mighty furnace. At quarter past ten he began to cough up semipurulent mucus. The white, glossy beard which had always sprung so immaculate from his chin became a mass of soiled and matted hair. A little later he complained in choking tones that he was losing all sensation in his extremities. And indeed the bluish tint of numbness was clearly perceptible on his fingers. Olive took his hand again, and by chafing vainly tried to restore its circulation. Unless the doctor comes soon, she thought, he can spare himself the visit.

Olive was not sorry for Uncle James. But now that she was faced with the certainty of his disappearance from her world she felt an acute sense of loss. It was, as she knew, a selfish emotion, compounded of regret for the destruction of a landmark and something deeper, more elusive. It was as though she were watching perish a part of herself—a part which she, perhaps, detested, but one from whose fortunes she could never be entirely dissociated, because her will to break free was itself chained to an invisible warder. As the strength left James's limbs, she imagined that she could feel a proportionate ebb in her own vitality. Depression and lassitude and a curious stupefaction, a blankness almost of the mind, assailed her. When at length Dr. Mailey arrived, he found her doubled forward in her chair by the bedside, her face touching the edge of the blanket, her arms hanging loose and puppet-like below her knees. She might have been sleeping an exhausted sleep; she might have been drugged or hypnotized; she might have been in a paroxysm of hopeless mourning.

But Dr. Mailey's own condition did not encourage him in superfluous analysis of other people's. He wore the dazed look of a man who has been subjected to continuous overwork. His eyes had a tranced stare and he moved stiffly through the nightmare of an unending mortuary. He was quite young and very keen, but he no longer looked either of these things.

Aunt Eva accompanied him. Olive dimly perceived their entry and forced herself back into an apologetic show of life. The doctor bent over Uncle James and lifted his hand to feel for the pulse. James opened his eyes and tried to say something. At the second attempt he barely managed to articulate the words:

"Wasting your time."

"Nonsense," said Dr. Mailey, and the hollow tonelessness of his voice travestied the sentiment. "If you were in as bad a way as some of the patients I've pulled through . . ."

"Bloody impudence," came the hoarse reply. "Brains of a second-year student."

The perfunctory examination continued. It might have been a specimen case. All the symptoms were present in their most uncompromising form. A young Olympics athlete would have stood little chance of survival. Seeing that James had relapsed into apparent coma, Dr. Mailey turned away, shrugging his shoulders.

"Well," he said, "I'm afraid I must accept the patient's own diagnosis. We can do nothing but wait."

"Can you give us any hope, doctor?" asked Aunt Eva in a bated, pharisaical voice.

Exhaustion had stripped Mailey of conventional pretenses. He realized that for every tear shed over James's death there would be two for his survival.

"I think I can set your mind at rest," he said. "There's virtually no chance that he'll recover. He'd be dead by now if he hadn't a constitution in a thousand."

Without warning the respiration from the bed changed its note and the sufferer's limbs were constricted by a fierce cramp, so that they stood out like corrugations against their covering. Dr. Mailey feverishly rummaged in his bag and began to assemble the parts of a hypodermic syringe.

"This only has a very temporary effect," he said. "But I always administer it in these cases"—he spoke in jerks, exposing the right arm, inserting the needle, preparing to depress the pump—"because it gives them a chance to recognize people and say any last thing that they have on their minds."

He drove home the injection. For perhaps half a minute Uncle James continued in his coma. Then the strychnine showed its violent tonic effect, comparable to the necromantic raising of corpses. James Marshall's eyes opened, he raised himself up on his pillows, his spirit resumed its semideserted habitation.

"Ah!" he said, looking round him. "The vultures—and my little Olive! Au revoir, Olive! Remember you promised me . . ."

He fell back, and the impact of his body sounded dully against its support of down and linen.

"Disappointing," said Dr. Mailey. "It often lasts much longer. Of course, he's old . . ."

Nevertheless, James did not die then, in that final dramatic collapse. He died ten minutes later, in an inconspicuous manner, far otherwise than he would doubtless have wished. Only Dr. Mailey was capable of distinguishing between the semblance of death and its reality.

"He's gone now," said the doctor.

Olive laughed harshly, derisively.

"Poor kid!" said Dr. Mailey. "Tired out. Get her to bed, Miss Marshall. Hysterics won't help any of us."

Unresisting, Olive allowed Aunt Eva to take her arm and escort her from the room. Aunt Eva was sniffling a bit, but Olive's face was dry as sandstone. Dr. Mailey watched them go. Then he turned to the bed and perfunctorily tested the reflexes to assure himself of death. He stopped and glanced down into the corpse's face.

"You damned old sod," he said. "You look as if you might pop up like a daisy any minute."

CHAPTER THREE

EVEN in the most favorable conditions, Roger would have been unhappy and embarrassed by the nature of the business. To be forced to conduct it while looking at his own distorted image was almost more than he could bear. Yet Mr. Simcox meant to be helpful. One might perhaps deplore his occasional lapses into salesman's patter and the knowing, confidential inflection which crept into his voice, when he spoke of hinges and beveled finishing and other mysteries of his craft. But his face and figure—nobody could fairly blame him for those. There was no copyright in such things. He was perfectly entitled to walk the world looking like a caricature of Roger Marshall. One could do nothing about it except to regret the malicious exaggeration of the modeling.

Two rather bowlegged little men regarded each other from opposite sides of the fireplace. Both had round bald patches in the middle of their skulls, and plump well-fed faces. But whereas Roger's zone of surviving hair was a decorous iron-gray and clung neatly to his scalp, that of Mr. Simcox fluffed itself out like a half-grown halo, flaunting its bilious carrot-colored strands. The cheeks were another offense. Roger knew perfectly well that his own inclined to fullness, but surely they did not sag into those ridiculous overblown pouches, surely they did not threaten his collar with engulfment? On pretense of straightening his tie, he cast a hasty glance into the mirror. To his disturbed eye he appeared to be very like Mr. Simcox indeed.

"There's one other little item, sir," resumed the undertaker, "that I'd like to call to your attention. Would you be needing extra labor at the grave?"

"Well—I hardly know," said Roger. "Why? I always—er—understood that the parish employed a sexton."

"Ah," said Mr. Simcox in a faintly superior voice, "but think of the ground, Mr. Marshall, think of the state it's in!"

"I suppose it's rather hard."

"Hard, sir! You wouldn't believe! My men were half a day soaking it with hot water before we could lay poor Mrs. Cotter, over at Haines, to her rest."

"Well," said Roger helplessly, "perhaps you'd better send a man to assist the church authorities. I really don't know what's usual in these cases."

"You may be sure I shouldn't impose any unnecessary expense, Mr. Marshall. Not like some of these firms calling themselves Funeral Experts. Why, I could tell you . . ."

Roger held up his hand despairingly.

"I have every confidence in you," he protested.

Mr. Simcox picked up his black hat. He was, however, appallingly difficult to divert from any train of thought, once embarked on it.

"Of course, it all mounts up," he admitted reflectively. "Some people have been keeping them a few days, what with the weather and the shortage of accommodation in the yards."

"Keeping whom?" asked Roger vaguely.

"The defunct," said Mr. Simcox. Then, seeing the look of disgust on Roger's face, he made speed to add: "Not that I was for a moment suggesting it to a family of your class. Just a little curiosity I've come across in my profession!"

"Good-bye, Mr. Simcox," said Roger firmly, thinking that he would rather the vultures had his remains than this frightful little cad.

"At your service, sir. I think I have a note of all requirements, but if there should be anything else I can do before Friday, don't hesitate to call me. As I always say, my time is my clients'."

Mr. Simcox often told his wife what an asset it was in his line to be able to chat with the gentry in a manner which made them feel that they were entrusting their dead to somebody of culture and refinement.

As the door closed behind him Roger shuddered with relief. Then he returned to the mirror.

"Detestable little bounder!" he muttered. "Thank God, James isn't here. I should never have heard the last of my twin-double."

Olive strayed in aimlessly, as though she had no more reason for choosing this room than any other.

"Hallo, uncle," she said, her listless manner warming to a faint show of surprise. "I thought I saw you going down the drive."

"No," said Roger.

"It looked just like you."

"It was the undertaker."

"How funny! Even the walk was the same."

"For God's sake, Olive!" exclaimed Roger with unwonted petulance. "Anyone would think you were keeping on about it deliberately."

Olive sat down with a daily paper and opened it at random. She chanced on an article headed "Be Yourself." It sounded as though it might contain exactly the kind of advice which she needed. She did not feel at all like herself today. She felt—to use an equivocal phrase—as though she were only half there. Unfortunately, the same paralysis seemed to have attacked her power of concentration, and she could not take in more than a couple of consecutive sentences. Presently she gave up and allowed the page to swim before her as a mass of blurry, disconnected symbols.

Meanwhile Roger had settled at his desk and taken out his notes and the tied bundle of his manuscript. For five years now he had been engaged upon a work provisionally entitled "The English Judiciary in the XVI and XVII Centuries." Embalmed in his tiny, meticulous handwriting lay all that remained of the old ermine-clad sages who, under Elizabeth and the Stuarts, had sat in Westminster Hall or traveled England, exercising the commissions of Oyer et Terminer and Jail Delivery. The scheme of the book was biographical, for Roger was too diffident to embark on any avowed history of the law itself. He contented himself with collecting anecdotes from obscure sources and reporting the dicta of his subjects which best illuminated their personalities. Already he had reached on the latter part of Charles II's reign, a period which gave him great satisfaction, partly because it marked the approaching end of his labors and partly because it contained his favorite character, Sir Joshua Wrangham, who had then sat precariously on the judicial bench. Apart from the historic interest of his career, Wrangham J. had another claim on the Marshall family's attention, for he was an ancestor in the direct paternal line. He was a very fine judge, and also one of the few for whose removal a petition has been laid before Parliament. Roger's faded eyes gleamed with a new life as he turned over his transcript of the authorities. Dug out from the libraries of Lincoln's Inn and the British Museum, the old intrigue revived in all its dignified absurdity. The list of Sir Joshua's improprieties, as set before the House, made curious reading. It flashed with the tinsel of hearsay and jewels of slanderous invention.

> Item. He, the said Joshua Wrangham, did irreverently and contrary to the course of nature, hick-hock before meat during the saying of the Lord's Grace, and in this habit continues to the scandal of all true Christians.
>
> Item. He, the said Joshua Wrangham, not having the dignity of his office before his eyes, did familiarly and lewdly conduct himself with a serving-maid, one Betsy Rinkler, in his own house, saying that she was his little trollop and that he had a mind to tup her, and one time (as his housekeeper Mrs. Nott doth testify) most lustfully lifting her undercoats. . . .

The paragraphs dealing with his alleged partiality on the bench were less amusing, probably because they had less substratum of truth. Sir Joshua had collected enemies from all quarters: in an age when every public man was suspect either to Catholic or to Protestant sympathizers, he had the unique distinction of being equally loathed by both. But, at any rate in the matter of the petition, the old fox tricked the chase. For he caused it to be put into the heads of certain roistering young relatives of his persecutors that it would serve their cause if they appeared in court at his next sitting and created a disturbance. When they proceeded to do so, he committed them all to jail for gross contempt. And as he was the only person who, in his capacity as judge, could order their release, there was naturally a lull in the efforts to remove him. Indeed, he continued in office to the day of his death, declaiming torrential and highly flavored judgments in a style which alternated curiously between shrewd modernism and archaic dignity.

Roger sometimes reflected that there were certain points in which the old Caroline judge must have resembled James. But this was a comparison which he always refrained from pressing, out of reverence for Sir Joshua, who, whatever his defects, had many times shown himself to be on the side of order and goodwill. He went to work with a sense of guilt. It seemed callous to be taking up his private concerns again under the roof which still covered a dead man. If he could not honestly mourn his half brother, then perhaps he ought to spend a while lamenting his inability to do so. But unless he busied his mind, it was filled with recurrent visions of Mr. Simcox and Mr. Simcox's handiwork, which he had been called upon to approve. Who could have believed that it was James who lay upstairs washed and prinked and bland like an old beau taking a nap before he set out for some party? Not Roger, for one. Death had extracted the essence of the man; that the shell was better void than inhabited in no way reconciled him to the great horror of emptiness. He forced himself to complete a footnote and a couple of uneasy pages.

Upstairs the telephone rang and was silenced in the middle of a peal. Eva came in, wearing a black crepe dress.

"I've unhooked the receiver," she announced. "These wretched vulgar papers have got no respect for privacy or sorrow."

"What did that one want?" said Roger.

"Oh, details for the obituary, of course. I don't mind telling them where poor James was educated, but I do object to being asked whether I can throw any new light on what the man chose to call the Hollister scandal."

"Quite," said Roger. "No good purpose in digging up that business."

During the Boer War James had conducted certain researches on behalf of the government into parasitic complaints affecting the troops. The results, though achieved too late to affect the war in hand, had been brilliantly successful. Just before publishing them, James had got rid of his chief assistant, Charles Hollister, on the grounds of obstructionism and incompetence—charges which did not accord with the dismissed man's honorable scientific reputation. Eventually Hollister brought an action in the courts, claiming that he had been sacrificed to his superior's desire to enjoy the sole credit. After a long struggle James received the verdict on mainly technical grounds. The judge, however, intimated severely and distinctly that there were more kinds of disgraceful conduct than the law could touch. Hollister shortly afterwards had a nervous breakdown and committed suicide. He left a long and dignified letter of protest. The many people who had from the first sympathized with his case redoubled their outcry. The matter was widely canvassed in the press and private conversation, and though ultimately it blew over without positive damage to his career, James did not, for once, go scot free of his iniquity. Years later, when his services in the Great War were being publicly acclaimed, people still whispered connecting him with "that dirty business." It was said to have cost him a knighthood. Even now, in these first post-mortem hours, when, if ever, a man may expect to enjoy the charity of disproportionate praise, it sprang up, evergreen, from the obituary pigeonholes.

In a deep, dreamy voice Olive suddenly observed: "Hollister had himself to thank. He was the type who'd be done down in a kids' nursery."

"Well!" said Aunt Eva. "And what do you know about it?"

"What?" said Olive, starting.

"Never mind, my dear. It's very natural, after all, that you should want to stand up for your poor uncle."

Surely the speed with which she had transfigured James's memory was a record. The simple maxim *de mortuis* was put to shame by the wistful "poor" with which she now prefaced his name. One would have suspected insincerity even in an early Christian martyr who referred thus to her tormentors. But Eva was not deliberately playing hypocrite nor giving a self-conscious exhibition of charity. She was simply irradiated by a profound joy which disposed her toward extreme forgiveness. The cause, though hidden from herself, was apparent to all her intimates. James was dead: the bond of her oppression was broken; she was free, and who could tell if she might not now be rich? The old evil days had vanished, the chronic sores had healed up, as if by magic, and like the ordinary victim of public-school bullying, she found herself able to look back with kindly tolerance, and almost to swear that suffering had done her good.

Roger left his desk and began to prowl round the room. He stopped beside Olive's chair and glanced down at her relaxed figure. His expression was puzzled and vaguely apprehensive.

Eva followed his eyes.

"She needs a tonic," she said briskly. "Do you hear, Olive? We shall none of us do any good by allowing our natural sorrow to get the better of us."

Olive answered with a curt monosyllable which Roger was certain that he had misheard.

"My dear child," said Aunt Eva, "balls or dances are out of the question while we are in mourning. Besides, you've always said you don't care for them." She began busily to take the pins out of an antimacassar and smooth away a crease. "I want to have everything in order for Mr. Marten's visit," she said.

"Eh?" said Roger. "The solicitor?"

"Yes." Her voice became elaborately casual. "I forgot to tell you, I thought it proper to ring him up and let him know of our loss. He immediately offered to come over this afternoon with—with the documents relating to the estate."

"I suppose you mean James's will," said Roger.

Something in his tone put Aunt Eva on her dignity.

"Nobody could be less mercenary than myself, but, in my opinion, the sooner we know the true position the better. There is the question whether we continue to live in this house, for one thing."

"Oh, quite," said Roger hurriedly. Then he chuckled.

"Really, Roger!"

"I'm sorry, my dear. I wasn't laughing at anything you said. I was just thinking of an old play I saw years ago—must have been in the school holidays. I remember one scene where a family was gathered round to hear a will read—each expecting the lion's share, of course. It turned out that the testator had given them all something, but he'd arranged his gifts with a view of causing the maximum embarrassment—an old lady got a keg of whisky, and that kind of thing. It was most amusingly acted."

"No doubt," said Eva, "but it seems to have been in rather questionable taste."

A cold little serpent of doubt slid into her mind, chilling its warm security. Was there any ulterior purpose behind Roger's ambling reminiscence? Could it perhaps have been intended as a warning, or even as a cynical estimate of her own prospects? Suspicion and anxiety grew in her so that she was soon unable to contain them in silence.

"Olive," she said, "I don't think those shoes you have on are at all suited to mourning. Just run upstairs and change them for a pair that are rather quieter."

Olive obeyed indifferently. She crossed the room with a heavy dragging tread. Nobody listening to her footfalls would have said that they belonged to a young, slim girl. Roger thought that she was utterly dispirited and emotionally worn out by her first contact with death. Eva thought that she was giving a display of petulance, and making a clodhopper exit to show that there was nothing frivolous about her footwear.

Eva waited for a few seconds after the door had closed, then she said:

"Roger, did James ever mention his will to you?"

Roger shook his head.

"He was hardly likely to."

"Why not? You're a lawyer. He might very well have consulted you on some technical point."

"My dear, in the first place, James had all the professional advice he needed. In the second, he never held a very flattering view of my abilities. Anyhow, I should not say that he was the type of man to tie his property up or indulge in any complicated dispositions. No, James's will is probably of the terse and forthright kind."

"Do you—do you think he's likely to have done anything eccentric?"

"Quite likely," said Roger dryly. "Of course, one can always apply to have opprobrious and insulting words struck out so that they obtain no publicity. But the actual distribution of his property is irrevocable."

There was a pause.

"I suppose we're the only two people close enough to be called real relatives," Eva said musingly. "I expect, though, some of the money will go to scientific institutions."

"Aren't you forgetting Olive?" said Roger. "For all practical and legal purposes, she's his only daughter."

"But, surely, nobody could leave a child like that in control of money? It isn't as if you and I would fail to provide for her in every possible way. Besides, I always thought that people under twenty-one couldn't own property."

"My dear Eva," said Roger in a gentle but decided tone, "none of these things is quite as you suppose. Without going into details, I should advise you not to build too high on any hopes of benefiting by James's will. Personally I expect nothing—nothing, at any rate, to my advantage. Knowing his peculiar character, I think we ought to be proof against disappointment."

"You're just being absurdly cautious," said Eva, with a kind of despairing pettishness. "You won't admit it, but you know perfectly well that it's natural to have expectations from an unmarried brother—even if he was only a half brother and didn't always show a proper family affection."

Roger was so staggered by this last understatement that he had nothing more to say. He picked up the *Times* and began to read the correspondence column. A well-known health faddist wrote about the epidemic. He inveighed against the habit of frowsting—his "King Charles's head"—which he alleged to be the influenza's greatest ally. Like rabbits petrified by the nearness of a stoat, people were huddling round their firesides, growing wan and debilitated in an atmosphere supercharged with infection. Rather let them seek the highways and byways and the keen fresh air, which he described in his peroration as "Nature's prophylactic, the supreme antitoxin which God has put within the reach of all men, rich and poor, alike."

All this eloquence only made Roger uncomfortable. He remembered that he had not been out of the house for two days. No wonder he had coughed again this morning. Already he saw himself laid out, awaiting the attentions of Mr. Simcox. But perhaps there was time to make amends. He left the room hastily and put on his coat, his mittens, and his lined snowboots.

It was not unpleasant in the garden. The round sun shone yellow as butter: its disk was very remote, very small, like a gold piece clipped by coiners. It gave out no warmth, the icicles in its direct beam did not drip. He walked round the naked herbaceous border toward the rough patch irregularly planted with small conifers. One of those unobtrusive cats which, like comets, only appear at intervals and thereby acquire a preternatural significance, was trying to stare a dwarf fir out of countenance. The cat was couchant and its tail, ringed with tortoise shell and white, switched idly to and fro. The dwarf fir remained perfectly still. It was a most dignified vegetable. Too big to suffer from the inroads of mice about its roots, too small to tempt man to cut it for a Christmas tree, it led a tranquil existence of guaranteed neutrality. No birds perched in its branches. The cause of its attraction for the cat was beyond conjecture. Roger was very fond of cats and he liked to see them confidently doing unaccountable things with an air of inward purpose.

When he strolled on, the soothing influence of the cat waned and he drifted once more into vague, lowering apprehensions. He tried to pretend that he was mourning the loss of a brother: to which his conscience, more honest than Eva's, immediately gave the lie. Or he was upset by Simcox and his gruesome niggling over graves; quite true, the man's appearance was sufficient to upset anybody, but it did not go far enough. Intuition told him that his frame of mind did not relate to anything that had already happened: this was a shadow of approach, cast by things not yet come.

The intense cold from the ground began to nip at his well-covered toes. He turned onto the graveled drive, in the direction of the house. He had not walked far before he was roused from his reverie by the crunch of overtaking footsteps. He saw behind him a sturdy youth, carrying an irregular bundle wrapped in brown paper. He waited, and soon Ted Fremlin greeted him with a tilt of his cloth cap.

"Well, Ted," he ventured uneasily, for he knew himself to have no technique with the villagers, "what brings you along this way?"

"I was carrying this 'ere up to the Manor," replied Ted, indicating the package.

"What is it?"

"'Olly," said Ted. "Ma couldn't get nothing else in this weather."

"Er—very nice," said Roger, floundering after some connection of thought. "But why exactly are we getting this present?"

"It's for Mr. Marshall that's dead. Ma done it a treat, all wove round in a circle."

"Oh," said Roger, "a wreath! Well, that's extraordinarily kind and sympathetic of your mother."

"Ah," said Ted, "Ma thought a lot o' Mr. Marshall. She reckons she wouldn't be 'ere now but for 'im."

"Of course, he went to see her only the other night. So she's better now?"

"She sat up in bed and done this."

"I'll take it back with me. You must give our warmest thanks to your mother and father for their very kind thought."

"Ah!" said Ted, drawing up the syllable from his secret store of profundity. "This is from Ma. It ain't from Dad."

"Your mother may have made it, but I'm sure your father joins in the gift."

Ted shook his head.

"Nur. Nothin' disrespectful, sir, but Dad don't feel like Ma about Mr. Marshall."

Roger was not accustomed to this honest differentiation between those who wished to pay tribute to the dead and those who did not.

"Perhaps," he suggested, "your father thought that, since Mrs. Fremlin was the patient, the wreath would come better from her alone?"

"Mebbe," said Ted with obvious disbelief.

Roger was suddenly nettled by the boy's stubborn, callous refusal to make any concession to civilized pretenses.

"Possibly," he said, descending to retort, "your father and others in the village will feel rather differently about Dr. Marshall's death if they themselves fall ill and can't get attention!"

"Ah!" said Ted. "I shouldn't wonder."

Ted was invincible. He had the strongest natural armor in the world, for he never exposed himself by venturing a definite opinion on anything outside his immediate experience. He touched his cap again and began to plod homeward down the drive. Watching his square, assured little figure and the firmness of his gait, Roger forgot his irritation and allowed his thoughts to slide toward the pastoral fallacy, which at intervals besets so many educated men —"How much happier I might have been if fate had made me a plowboy!" He was still toying with the idea when he discovered that his woolly muffler had slipped and was no longer completely protecting his throat. He sighed as he readjusted it, and shifted the mass of brown paper to avoid the holly barbs which here and there pricked through his mittens.

2

Eva was defying her own precept. The square of embroidery had rested so long untouched on her lap that she could not plead that she was merely snatching a moment's rest for her eyes. She was mooning. Her spirit was away on the Grand Tour and, having just reached Florence, would not be recalled. An apartment, perhaps: but was there any reason why she should not be able to afford a small villa? The Fascists? It was only people ignorant of a country's language and customs who had difficulty in adjusting themselves to an unfamiliar political regime. The contessa was calling. Today she had brought a very handsome young man with beautiful black hair and a black shirt. "Miss Marshall, may I present my son Vittorio. He is a good boy but so wrapped up in politics." (Carelessly.) "He tells me that they have made him president of the Fascist Council in our district." The young man bent and kissed her hand. "Donna Marshall," he said, "I am honored to make the acquaintance of a lady for whom my mother has so much respect. If ever I can use my small influence to smooth any little annoyance, only command me." The contessa smiled approval. "We do not think of Donna Marshall as a stranger in Florence. Vittorio will see that nobody makes the mistake of treating her as one." The whole conversation was, of course, conducted in Italian, and in neither fluency nor accent was Eva appreciably inferior to the other two. Later, at tea, she had to switch from Italian to French and from French to English, for the party had been increased by the arrival of a British diplomat, his titled wife, and an elderly actress, retired from the Comédie-Française. The actress had played only classical roles, she had been a household word in the more creditable sense, and if the spice of some old scandal still clung about her, it was very faint, almost deodorized by the sanctity of her present life. When they left, the guests said: "Ah, Donna Marshall, nobody entertains like you. You are a true cosmopolitan." And one of them—Vittorio probably—complimented her on her gift of tongues. "You refute the general reputation of your countrywomen."

This emphasis on linguistic skill might seem mundane and unromantic in an imaginary world where difficulties of intercourse are usually solved by ignoring them: but actually it was at the very core of the daydream. Most people surpass the average in one capacity. Eva had a genuine talent for languages. She spoke French well, though she minced and exaggerated the accent. She had been at a school in Tours, and she had always kept up her knowledge; chiefly, of late, on the pretext of improving Olive's education. In both German and Italian she could manage something better than the usual tourist's jargon. She set an inordinate value on her proficiency, because she had so few other legitimate outlets for pride. She knew from bitter experience that she was not and never had been physically attractive: yet she still pathetically believed that the ability to repeat the same prim commonplaces in a sufficient number of foreign tongues might earn her the reputation of cleverness. She kept a large pile of grammars and conversation guides in her bedroom. She believed that they were the distilled essence of a mysterious admirable quality called "cosmopolitanism." She could say "Good morning," "What time does the train go?" "I want the cloakroom" in Greek and Russian.

She had shut up the villa for a season. She was traveling back to England to make an important decision connected with her "affairs"—say, to sell or not to sell the rocketing shares of that gold mine for which the diplomat's wife had given her a whispered tip. She was breaking the journey in Paris, staying a night at the Meurice: outside there was a tinkle of dishes as the garçon de chambre brought up dinner to her room. . . .

He dropped the dishes. Dora dropped the dishes. The crash resounded through the Meurice, through the Manor. Fantasy and the household crocks disintegrated in the same catastrophe.

In the hall Dora stood rubbing her bottom and looking down on a chaos of pottery, roast potatoes, and Brussels sprouts. The leg of mutton was lying under the gong.

"You wicked girl!" said Eva.

"Ooh, miss, I'm sorry. I caught me 'eel."

"And haven't I told you before about wearing those ridiculous high shoes?"

Smarting above and below Dora was stung into rebellion.

"Well, miss, we don't all want to look like bits of God-knows-what!"

"Don't be impertinent! You've ruined our meal and destroyed two expensive pieces of china. I shall deduct it from your wages."

"Oh, you wouldn't, miss, you wouldn't do that, not if you knew what it was to want the money," protested Dora in anguished tones, thinking, no doubt, of some long-coveted piece of finery.

She must have believed that the pathos of her appeal had gone home, for Eva did not pursue her threat.

"Pick everything up," she said shortly. "See if you can manage to make the food eatable. And for heaven's sake try to do your work properly in future!"

Eva was more than a little given to the cruder forms of superstition. Without being a confirmed omen hunter, she often drew an imaginary parallel between the course of her own fortunes and the outcome of some exterior, unconnected event. In the present instance, she was also subconsciously swayed by a higher principle —that of doing unto others as she would herself be done by. She felt that it was hazardous to mete out a short measure of wages to Dora, while her own financial prospects still trembled in the balance. "If you knew what it was to want the money . . ." The girl might have been inspired, were it not obvious that she had never considered her mistress as sharing the same need. Breakages were expensive, but she had been right not to take the risk. O God, O Florence, O contessa, remember my forbearance!

3

Mr. Marten arrived about half past two. He was a first-class family solicitor of the old school. As soon as he came into a house, anybody who belonged to the same tradition automatically offered him a glass of sherry and a biscuit.

When he had taken his refreshment, Roger led him back to the lounge. Olive and Eva were already occupying two of the four chairs collected round the center table. Eva was knitting furiously, Olive was doing nothing and looking as if she enjoyed it. After the conventional greetings, Mr. Marten sat down, unlatched his brief case and snapped elastic bands.

"As a matter of form," he said, "I always begin by reminding my clients that no will has any binding force until it has obtained probate."

Roger nodded. Eva and Olive both followed suit, the one because she liked to appear knowledgeable, the other because she felt that she ought to show an intelligent interest.

Mr. Marten began to read:

"This is the last will of me James Orsett Marshall of the Manor House, Gorchow, in the County of Cambridge, M.D., F.R.C.S., Chevalier de la Légion d'Honneur. I have made no previous wills, testaments or codicils, but in deference to the customary legal flummery I hereby revoke them all—"

"You will appreciate," said Mr. Marten, looking over his spectacles, "that this was the testator's own choice of words."

"Yes, yes," said Eva impatiently. "Nobody would hold you responsible."

". . . I appoint my half brother Roger Marshall of the address aforesaid and Ernest Snow Marten of 3 Dean Close, Ely, to be the executors and trustees of this my will.

"I give the following legacies and annuities:

"(a) To Delia Frances Pond the sum of £4,000 as a perpetual souvenir of a very pleasing and fruitful friendship—"

"Who is this woman?" interjected Eva shrilly. In the same breath she supplied her own theory. "Is the whole fortune eaten up with gifts to loose, designing hussies?"

Mr. Marten put down the will deliberately.

"The estate is quite a large one and this happens to be the only bequest outside the family. I'm afraid I have no information about Mrs. or Miss Pond or her whereabouts. I had hoped you might be able to assist me."

He looked at Roger, who shook his head. Eva subsided, realizing that she had gratuitously exposed a skeleton.

"—An annuity of £250 to my half sister Eva Janet Marshall during her life so long as she shall continuously reside within the British Isles not absenting herself therefrom for any day or part of a day."

Eva sat bolt upright, the handkerchief between her fingers screwed to a pellet. She took in the words quite clearly, though the voice which uttered them seemed unreal, a mere projection of her own forebodings. How did he guess? She had never babbled of her dreams. Then she remembered with a dull despair his inhuman instinct for the weak joint, the spot where the blow would cut most deeply.

Mr. Marten's voice flowed levelly on.

"—An annuity of £400 to the said Roger Marshall for his life or until he shall marry any person who has professionally appeared upon the theatrical stage or in any cinematograph picture."

Olive could not control a giggle. Roger smiled, too, but wryly, appreciating that, if the press got hold of such a proviso, it would prove more than a harmless joke.

"—I have regretfully seen fit to impose the above conditions for the protection of the annuitants' morals. Upon breach by either of them the said Eva Marshall or Roger Marshall of the condition attaching to his or her respective annuity, such annuity shall forthwith cease and the capital moneys and investments for the time being representing the same shall become payable to the said Delia Frances Pond for her absolute use and benefit."

Eva was exasperated by the mere repetition of the unknown Jezebel's name. When she thought of that woman, sitting waiting to grasp her own modest legacy, if she should so much as venture on a day-trip to Boulogne, her heart churned and a little of the mud, which lies at the bottom of repressed minds, spurted out.

"All old men ought to be made to have operations. Then they wouldn't sacrifice their own families for harlots."

"My dear Miss Marshall!" said the solicitor.

"Eva," said Roger. "I think you'd prefer not to hear any more. I'll listen to the rest of this document and let you know later of anything that affects your interests."

"I'm not going out of this room before I've heard every syllable. And not then, till I've asked Mr. Marten a few questions."

Her face was quite mottled, like a thrush's egg.

Marten shrugged his shoulders. He did not fancy the office of executor.

"—All the rest and residue of my property of whatsoever kind, whether real or personal, I give, devise, and bequeath to my adopted daughter Olive Marshall absolutely."

He paused.

"There follow certain clauses in common form, relating to the appropriation of funds to meet the annuities, and to the right of a trustee who is also a solicitor to charge for his services. I don't know whether you'd like them read."

"No, no," said Roger.

"The will is duly signed and attested."

Roger turned to Olive.

"My dear," he said, "I could have wished that James had used rather different language in certain parts of his will, but I think his provision for you, as the person whom he has chosen to carry on his name, is entirely proper. I congratulate you."

His sincerity was beyond question.

Olive inclined her head a little, continuing to look straight in front of her. A faint, enigmatic smile gathered at the corners of her mouth.

Marten addressed himself to her.

"Of course, Miss Olive, your uncle, when he made his will, did not contemplate that he would die before you had attained twenty-one. As you probably know, you will not have personal control of the property until that age. In the meanwhile your uncle and I, as trustees, must administer it in accordance with certain rules laid down by law."

"That will hardly affect her," said Roger. "She's twenty now, and by the time we've got the estate together—"

"Stop!" said Eva in a voice which belonged to the last act of an old-fashioned melodrama. "Are we to sit here discussing this disgraceful will as though we were content to abide by it?"

"Madam," said Marten, "I really don't know on what other basis we can discuss it."

"Is there no flaw in it? I've noticed that lawyers can generally find an objection to nice, honorable, proper wills!"

"I drafted this will myself," said Marten wearily. "In my opinion it is perfectly valid. If you are thinking of your own annuity, I can only say that conditions as to residence have sometimes been held void, and I therefore took particular care to render this one binding."

"Then I think you acted in a very unfair and unkind manner. You had nothing against me, and yet you deliberately helped to coop me up in this country, where I can starve for all you care!"

"Eva, you should apologize to Mr. Marten," said Roger. "He was bound to exercise his skill to carry out a client's wishes. It was no concern of his what form those wishes took, so long as they weren't illegal."

"Thank you, Mr. Marshall," said Marten.

"All the same, I refuse—"

Olive spoke.

"Oh, chuck it!" she said. Her tone was rough, not so much in its actual timbre as in its inflection.

Eva drew in her breath with a slight whistling sound.

"We haven't had to wait long for the first results. It's wonderful what a little money can do in so short a time. We don't count now, Roger. We mustn't expect even common civility from an heiress, though we may have slaved to bring her up and supplied her with everything, from the manners she once had to the clothes she wears on her back. I always said that we'd get nothing but ingratitude from a poor-class foundling chit."

Olive rested her chin on her hand and listened. Then she jeered: "Would you like to see my strawberry mark?"

"Roger, are you going to listen to me being insulted in this way?"

"Eva," said Olive, "do you know what you are? You're a damned silly, sterile old cow!"

She did not shout. Her tone was flat, almost impersonal, as if she were reciting a lesson. The incongruity between her manner and her matter seemed to point the insults.

Eva did the only thing that was left for her to do. She burst into tears. More overwhelming than her anger was the shock of surprise. For years she had cherished this creature to her bosom, under the impression that it was a docile and rather insipid little dove: now, without warning, she felt the unmistakable stab of a viper's fang.

She was oppressed by a curious notion that time had maliciously run backwards, returning her on its current and forcing her to resuffer old evils of which, by all canons of justice, she should not have been put a second time in peril.

Roger rose and opened the door for her. Except that he had no table napkin in his hand, they might both have been re-enacting the climax of the scene in which Eva first made the acquaintance of alcohol.

"My God, my God, my God!" Roger was muttering to himself, as he came slowly back to the table. At last he said quite distinctly, "My God, Olive!"

"What, uncle? I beg your pardon," said Olive, giving the familiar little toss of her head with which she recalled her wandering thoughts.

"I don't want to rebuke you in front of Mr. Marten, but I can only say that you've behaved with a rudeness of which I should never have believed you capable."

"I'm awfully sorry," said Olive. "I ought to have been attending. I really did listen to the first part of the will, but then I got sort of drowsy. Was there anything I should have heard?"

"I don't claim to understand your attitude," said Roger after a pause. "But this frivolous pretense of innocence seems to me like another piece of misplaced cynicism."

He was forced, however, to admit in his own mind that, if he was right, Olive had suddenly developed, among other things, a very pretty talent as an actress.

Her face and Roger's face wore almost identical expressions of puzzled bewilderment, as though both were straining to catch at something beyond the normal range of their senses. They continued so long in their quest that Mr. Marten, although he was not given to gratuitous interference, decided that he must take a hand.

"Well, young lady," he said, striving to infuse a paternal note into his voice, "suppose you go and think things over. And before long I'm certain you'll come back in a different frame of mind, perfectly ready to offer apologies where they're due. One must never let good fortune go to one's head, you know."

Under Eva's rule Olive had become as used to periodic ejections as any family cat. In itself Mr. Marten's proposal did not strike her as at all odd or unreasonable. She was only disconcerted by the serious view he seemed to take of her behavior. She must have hurt him very deeply. She could quite see that any man would be annoyed at having motored twelve miles to read a paper to a drowsing audience. On the other hand, she had mooned on many other important occasions without causing nearly so much offense.

"All right," she agreed. "I'll go upstairs."

Marten held up his hand.

"It would be better if you could see your way to take a short walk in the garden."

"Oh?" said Olive. "Why?"

"I don't think it would be advisable for you to incur the chance of meeting your aunt at present. Eh, Mr. Marshall?"

Roger nodded.

Olive began: "I'm sorry, I really don't quite see . . ." Then she looked again into the two men's faces, and detected the urgency behind their persuasion. "Oh, well, if you say so . . . then, of course . . . but it's so cold."

"If your own coat isn't in the hall," said Roger, "then by all means take mine."

Olive trailed desolately out of the room.

Roger nervously shifted photographs on the mantelpiece into exact, geometrical alignment.

"I suppose I ought to apologize to you, Marten," he said.

"You needn't bother, Marshall. This isn't the first difficult scene my practice has brought me into contact with."

"Difficult? It was so damned queer. You probably won't believe me when I tell you that this is the very first time I've heard Olive say an unkind word to anybody!"

"Judging from her general manner I should have thought she was quite incapable of the language she used."

"Well, there you are!" said Roger helplessly. "She is—but she used it!"

Mr. Marten did not say anything for some seconds. Then he suddenly inquired:

"Did you know that I lost my eldest boy a couple of years ago?"

"Why . . . I'm afraid I didn't. Otherwise I or my sister would certainly have written to express our sympathy."

"He was thirteen and a half," continued Marten in a deliberate, unemotional voice, "when he was killed by a fall from a hayloft. He was what my wife and I naturally called a healthy boy full of animal spirits. At the same time I could understand strangers thinking that he was rather a young hooligan. He loved fights with other children, piercing whistles, practical jokes, and hard balls which always went through windows. Jeremy, my second child, was quite different. Ever since he could hold a pencil his sole enthusiasm had been for drawing animals. I should say that he was definitely a sensitive, retiring, artistic type—if that doesn't sound too much like the fond parent! Anyhow, Jeremy was about ten when Michael died. You couldn't expect a child of that age to mourn very deeply, particularly since he had never appeared to be much in sympathy with his brother. In fact, I had at times been called in to put a stop to bullying by Michael. However, no sooner was the funeral over than Jeremy ran completely amuck. He seemed to go out of his way to smash things, he acquired one of those terrible pistols that discharge blanks in your ear, and the climax came when we found him and a little local ragamuffin ducking each other's heads in a sewer. The change was so astounding and deplorable that we took him to a psychologist. He diagnosed the trouble straight off. The child had been deeply subconsciously impressed by his brother's superior strength and daring, and he felt lost in a world which no longer seemed to contain those qualities. So he set about supplying them for himself. Technically, I believe, the process is called 'compensation.' We had the devil's own time with him for a few weeks. But the psychologist was right. He told us not to show that we noticed anything and the phase would wear itself out."

Roger listened attentively.

"Thank you," he said. "So you really think . . . ?"

"I only met your deceased brother on three or four occasions," interrupted Marten, "but I noticed that he had—er—certain well-marked characteristics."

Roger agreed: "Of course, the resemblance struck me at once. It was almost uncanny. I only hope to God poor Olive won't keep this compensation business up for long. Frankly, James was not a man whom one would wish to have commemorated by a living copyist."

"Today's performance may easily be the first and the last. Now, if you'll excuse me, I must be going."

As he was about to climb into his car, he remembered a point that had hitherto slipped his memory.

"By the way, I suppose we shall have to insert the usual advertisements for this lady called Pond."

"Oh, naturally," agreed Roger.

"You can't give me any clue which might save the expense?"

"No. Our ignorance was quite genuine. My sister and I knew very little about James's private affairs. I can only suggest that she is to be looked for among friends of his earlier life. He rarely left the neighborhood in later years and I think we should inevitably have heard of any local . . . acquaintance."

Marten thought: All the same, she is probably a barmaid in Haines or Ely.

As he drove off into the gathering dusk, under the cold pale sky, flecked like curdled milk, he was filled with an emotion that came rarely to his well-ordered mind. Hatred. He hated the flat, sinister eastern countryside! He hated its vacant, cunning face and the vacant, cunning faces of the inbred cottagers and the big houses of the gentry, those fine white elephants whose bland façades so often concealed a deep-seated internal canker.

Next year perhaps he would retire and go to live in Bournemouth.

CHAPTER FOUR

STANDING there, one on either side of the half-open door, they looked like a pair of little figures annexed by some medieval craftsman to an enormous and daedal clock. Soon, one felt, machinery would whir and they come stiffly forward, he to bow and she to curtsy; each keeping step with the chimes. They were both too worried to notice the comic, rigid symmetry of their attitudes.

"Are you sure?" repeated Roger.

"Of course I am. I've looked all through the house—even in the room where *he* is."

"Perhaps she felt better and went out."

"Then she'd no right to. I distinctly told her that she was to stop in bed all day."

"Did she seem more herself when you went up after lunch?"

"Not really," said Eva, hesitating. "She . . . well, she was like a person with mild concussion—quite all right, so far as one could see, in her body, but only half aware of what was going on around her. Of course, she's so dreamy at the best of times . . . !"

"And therefore," said Roger, "there must have been something very distinctly wrong or it wouldn't have made any impression on you."

"Well, you saw her for yourself at breakfast."

"I thought then, and I still think, that she is suffering from shock," Roger declared so vehemently that he might have been shouting down an internal skepticism.

"You mean—grief?" suggested Eva doubtfully.

"No, I don't. I mean that she was allowed to sit for hours in that room—where she never ought to have been—while her adoptive father died visibly in front of her eyes. There's a limit to what the human mind can stand. After a certain point it goes dull in its own defense."

"Roger, do you think her memory can have been affected?"

"Well, my dear Eva, anybody could see that it wasn't working normally this morning."

"Oh, that!" said Eva. "I believe she was very much ashamed and thought that the best way of passing off her yesterday's conduct was to behave as though nothing had happened."

Roger felt as if a series of ton-weights were descending on his shoulders—a dead brother, an unstable niece, a sister who explained everything by reference to her own frequently petty standards.

"You can't believe that," he said. "The toughest of these modern girls couldn't have carried through such a pretense. She'd inevitably have given the game away by being too sulky or too anxious to make amends. Olive had no idea this morning that she had behaved at all unusually toward you."

"Unusually!" said Eva. "Language like—" she stopped, rejecting the personal comparison which naturally suggested itself—"like a fishwife!" she concluded lamely.

Roger shrugged his shoulders.

"I'm afraid that anybody suffering from amnesia isn't particularly likely to remember where she owes apologies."

Eva took him up: "Amnesia! I've read about it in the papers. Don't you remember that society girl who disappeared and was found a week later wandering round the Cardiff Docks? It was all over the placards. Roger, we've got to find Olive before the same thing happens to her."

"Don't be absurd, Eva. How the devil could Olive get to Cardiff from here?"

"Isn't it almost as bad wherever she gets to? Do you want the place infested with reporters asking questions, then going away and insinuating that she's probably run off with a man?"

Roger was tolerant. He had suffered too much from human impatience to be otherwise. Even so, he could scarcely restrain himself from pointing out that Eva's concern appeared to be purely selfish, that she showed no signs of minding if a deranged Olive fell into a pond and was drowned so long as the occurrence did not provoke unfavorable publicity. He let her off with a slightly acid warning, uttered in her own interests.

"I'm afraid that in any case we shall come in for quite a lot of attention from the newspapers, once probate of James's will is granted. I am not well versed in journalese, but I think you should be prepared for a few headlines such as 'Scientist's Will Ban: Kin Forbidden Actresses, Gay Paree.'"

"I thought you told me that insulting language could be suppressed."

"James unfortunately took the trouble to disguise his insults in the form of sincere solicitude for our moral welfare."

With an effort Eva restricted her mind to its quota of present evils.

"Somebody," she said, "must find poor little Olive and bring her home."

"In all probability she has done nothing more sensational than taking a long walk. However, if you feel anxious, perhaps I had better go out and see if I can trace her movements. There will be people in the village who have noticed her."

Roger's disparaging tone was a creditable imitation of unconcern, but it was not by any means perfect. His voice jumped on the higher notes and his mild, shortsighted eyes wandered into the corners of the room, like those of a child who fears, but does not really expect, that something very nasty will pop out from the shadows.

2

The hanks of rope, tied to the crossbar of the lamp-post, were pulled taut by small circling forms. The children swung beneath the unlighted glass and sang in thin treble unison:

> Sally go round the moon,
> Sally go round the stars,
> Sally go round the chimney pot
> On a Sunday afternoon.

Olive stood in the middle of the street and watched them, burying her hands in the pockets of her raincoat, hunching her shoulders to raise the collar round her throat. The lilt of the little catch took hold on her and she began to sing it in her own brain. When the children swung, she swung: the moon and the stars and the quiet Sunday chimney pots tumbled beneath her in acrobatic confusion. She was that Sally whom they celebrated, the meteoric wanderer, buoyed by a great wind which swept through the empty chambers of her mind. Like a box kite, she floated at the mercy of alien and ungovernable blasts.

She had walked a long way since the compulsion had seized on her and driven her out from her warm bed. She knew roughly the ways which she had taken, and she had in her mind a clear general recollection, stored up from many previous visits, of the scenery through which she must have passed. But her brain had made no individual record of things seen and felt, it had noted none of the tiny variable details which distinguish one journey over familiar countryside from another. She knew that she had crossed the frozen brook at Pike's Spinney, but she could not remember how the tall reeds had looked in their prison of black ice—whether it closed tight round them in a strangle hold or stood back a little, breached by their emerging stems. Always before she had noticed such things. So faint were her reactions, she might not have covered the distance in person, but merely have sat drowsing in a chair while a film of certain landscapes was run through very fast, in blurred monochrome.

She understood that this insensitiveness was due to a kind of preoccupation. At the back of her mind something ticked with dull insistence: every little beat was trying ineffectually to break through into her conscious mind and warn her of a task neglected. There was a duty . . . a grave, important duty . . . your duty . . . to be done. That was all the little alarum could articulate: patiently it returned to the beginning and repeated the same incomplete formula.

She was harassed by her inability either to disregard it or to interpret the practical significance of its message. It had convinced her, but it would give no clue how she should act on her conviction. It had become painful to lie there in bed while her mind raced endlessly in pursuit of a will-o'-the-wisp. Presently the very walls of her bedroom seemed to hum with the same small, reproachful notes. Perhaps, she thought, as she pulled on her clothes, it will die out in the fresh air, or else it will guide me where it wishes, by the rules of hunt-the-slipper, beating fast for "hot" and slow for "cold."

And, indeed, as she walked, the ticking, though it did not vary its rate, took on a lower, less plangent note. From which she judged that it had partially accomplished its object by inducing her to leave the house; but would not be silenced until, by trial and error, she should discover the place where her work was waiting. Several times she experienced moments of quasi revelation, in which she felt herself to be well versed and competent in the still-undefined thing that she must do. The less she consciously exercised her brain the stronger the reassurance. Let her mind be as nearly as possible blank, and there would be space for powerful allies to enter and stand beside her.

The children round the lamp-post saw her watching them and began to show off. They swung higher and with more abandon, each throwing his whole weight on to the strands of rope. Presently there was a disaster. A boy of seven or eight, and a pretty, dirty, dark-haired little girl, perhaps a year his junior, were both clinging to the same trailer. Up they went and down they went, and the iron stanchion creaked under their onslaught. But it was the rope that broke. The boy dropped neatly on his toes, but the little girl was taken off her guard. She toppled over backwards, her head striking the pavement with an audible bump. The rest—no more notable for loyalty than the general run of children—glanced briefly at her inert form and dissolved into the dusk. Some of them had lately become quite accustomed to bodies in the house, but they knew that such things ought not to lie about the streets.

Olive went unenthusiastically to the rescue. Like many other very young women, she had a qualified love of children. She adored them lying asleep in cots or otherwise quiescent, but their needs and activities embarrassed her. She sat down on the curb and put the child's head against her lap, preparing to examine its injuries. Almost immediately, however, it revived and tried to struggle to its feet.

"You've hurt yourself," she said, restraining it. "You must wait till I've looked at the damage."

It took her some time to satisfy herself that there was no open wound. The little girl's hair was so matted from lack of combing that the thicker tangles might have been caused by clots of blood. Eventually she found the point of impact, a round, unbroken swelling at the back of the skull.

Olive was not normally tolerant of dirt. She defined the term widely, with what she had several times been told was a ridiculous fastidiousness. This was a remarkably unkempt, not to say filthy, little girl. Paddling about in her hair was an occupation which carried no insurance against parasites. Nevertheless, after the first moments, Olive felt grateful to her protégée. The trivial responsibility seemed to restore her self-possession and bring her back into relationship with simple, commonplace things. The ticking, also, dwindled in volume until it was no more than a muted echo. But it crossed her mind that this could scarcely have been its true purpose—to lure her here to nurse a child with a sore head.

"Where do you live?" she asked.

"Dahn road," said the child noncommittally.

"Well, when you feel strong enough, you and I will take a little walk. We'll go down the road and you shall show me your mummy and daddy's house."

"Nah," said the little girl, "you come abaht the rent!"

She had evidently (and in all probability forcibly) been warned against blandishing strangers.

"Of course, I haven't," said Olive. "I just want to make sure that you get home all right. You had a horrid fall."

"I can taike it, miss," said the little girl.

Olive wondered how she got the cash to enable her to pick up cinema lingo.

"I know you're very brave," she said. "Now, listen, I'll give you a penny to tell me your name."

Groping in the raincoat pocket she discovered, by pure luck, three coppers to support her promise.

"Mavis," the child muttered, eyeing the coin.

"Mavis what? What's your daddy called?"

"Thrupp."

Olive paid. She knew the parents, though only by sight. Throughout the village, people were fonder of talking about the Thrupps than of talking to them. She lifted Mavis gently into an upright position and scrambled to her own feet.

"Now I'm going to take you home," she announced.

"Nah," protested Mavis, hanging back against her skirt.

"But why not? Don't you like your home? Don't you want to see your nice pussy again?"

The last was a fairly safe venture. The inhabitants of Gorchow were extraordinarily addicted to cats. They seemed to live by taking in each other's kittens.

The child did not reply. Getting her home would obviously mean dragging her dead weight the whole way. Olive yielded unwillingly to what seemed to her to be pure blackmail. She held up a second penny between finger and thumb.

"I might give this to a good, obedient girl," she suggested.

"Nah," repeated Mavis.

"But why 'nah'—I mean, no?"

"Dad said 'e'd warm me be'ind if I come 'ome before supper."

"Surely he doesn't want to keep you out at night in this weather?"

Mavis nodded vigorously, beginning for the first time to appreciate the pathos of her position.

"'E's wild. The new baiby's took sick an' don't stop crying. Dad says we got enough bloody trouble without me."

A great wave of feeling mounted in Olive, lapping at the borders of her mind, preparing the engulfment. Not indignation, not sympathy with either the child or her harassed parent, not anything but pure urgency.

"What's wrong with the baby?" she asked, almost snapping.

"'E got the flu, and 'e chokes, and there ain't no doctor any more."

Olive set off with fast, heavy-footed strides, dragging the surprised child after her.

"Come on, you little bastard," she said.

Mavis understood that kind of talk. She was used to it. All the same, she felt that in some obscure way she had been cheated of her lady—the pretty, helpless one with the pennies.

3

Punctually, as though they had been waiting in the wings to

obey a stage direction, Roger and Faulkner came into sight round a bend of the street, barely missing their quarry by a couple of seconds. They had met by chance on the outskirts of the village, as Faulkner was on his way back from a funeral. Roger was very glad to have recruited him for the search, though it involved the difficult task of explaining why there was a search at all. Unwilling to go into distasteful details, he had to fall upon hints and generalities which, to his own ears, sounded either ridiculous or unduly sinister.

"Yes, but what do you mean when you say she hasn't been herself?" repeated Faulkner for the third time.

"I'm sorry, I can't put it any other way. Her manner and her behavior have changed. When we find her, you will no doubt see for yourself and form your own opinion."

"Has she actually *done* anything abnormal?"

"Not yet," said Roger rather grimly. He found Faulkner's gently implied skepticism a little trying, and did not mind if he succeeded in frightening him.

"But," said Faulkner, "I saw Olive only two days ago and she seemed to be in ordinary health."

Roger replied: "You forget that James was still alive then."

"Of course, the death would be a blow to her. You think it has affected her . . . nerves?"

"I don't know," said Roger.

"Well," said Faulkner in a much less comfortable tone, "if you say that she ought not to be out alone I'm sure you're right. We must get hold of somebody who has seen her."

Privately, however, he was still half inclined to attribute the fuss to Roger's old-maidishness.

They walked on as far as the duckpond. Now that the pipes were all frozen, many people had taken to cutting blocks out of its almost solid ice and melting them down for household purposes. The edge presented a weird, jagged aspect, as though some powerful monster, balked of its wonted drink, had gnashed furiously on the hard casing.

"Where are we going?" said Roger.

"I don't think we can do better than visit Mrs. Hole. She's an old friend of mine and without exception the most inquisitive woman

I ever met. She sits all day long in her parlor, peeping through a gap an inch wide in the lace curtains. But she sees more than most of us would from a French window. She can give you a list of everybody who has passed up or down the street within the past twenty-four hours."

Roger was pleased that his companion now seemed to be taking the quest seriously. And so he should if the general view of his intentions toward Olive were correct! Roger liked Faulkner very much. Occasionally, however, it crossed his mind that it would be a pity if Olive's children inherited the Northampton voice. Afterwards he was always deeply ashamed of himself. He knew that he had been brought up in an era when snobbery was part of a gentleman's equipment. He and Faulkner suffered from different forms of the same disease—inability to escape entirely from their earliest influences.

4

Mrs. Thrupp was a gypsy by birth. Mr. Thrupp was one by habit. Between them they kept as nasty a cottage as one could find in East Anglia. It was full of dishcloths and underclothes. Apart from these things, it contained few of the ordinary necessities of life and many tawdry luxuries, some procured by coupons, others by stealing. (Mrs. Thrupp went to Woolworth's every Saturday afternoon.) She was very fat and greasy looking, yet beneath the jowls and mounds one could still detect the remains of that prettiness which had formerly been her chief source of income. Even now she managed to come by more gin than anybody in the village could account for. Her husband was physically a perfect foil. Lean, meager, dry-skinned, with long drooping mustaches, he looked like an old-fashioned solicitor's clerk, who, having had an accident with the petty cash, had lost his wardrobe and his self-respect. In fact, he was an expert nocturnal poacher, whose days were spent in whittling away at what were ostensibly clothespins, but always looked better designed for anchoring a rabbit snare.

Olive knocked briskly and pushed open the door. The child Mavis dodged to and fro behind her back, uncertain, now that it came to the point, how far and how long the presence of gentry would protect her.

"Whatcher want?" said Mrs. Thrupp, regarding Olive without pleasure.

"Haven't you got a kid ill?"

"An' what if we 'ave?"

Olive's shoulders squared and her jaw stuck out and her mouth became long and thin. It was difficult to say who had the advantage in truculence.

"Have you let a doctor see it?"

"Gor' love us!" said Mrs. Thrupp, affecting amusement. "She asks me that! Where'm I goin' ter get a doctor these days? 'Ad two, we 'ave, in these parts lately, and they muck off theirselves. I don't suppose you'd be aware o' that, though, miss," she added slyly.

Olive kicked her heel on the uncarpeted stone floor.

"You know damned well," she said, "—or if you don't it's no excuse—that there's been a recent regulation to deal with this kind of emergency. If you ring up the local medical officer, he'll see that you get attention within twenty-four hours. Failure to do so may make you responsible for any resulting death."

Mr. Thrupp rose with slow dignity from his seat on an old sugar box, covered with a piece of disused bedspread.

"See 'ere, young woman," he observed, "nobody asked you in 'ere. S'pose you buzz off an' let us mind our own business."

He eyed the shrinking Mavis in a way which threatened a "warming" of unprecedented severity.

"Well, well," said Olive in a throaty purr, "the magistrates were rather skeptical about the other little chap who met with an accident in your house, two years ago. Tipped up a kettle, didn't he, though he could hardly crawl, and scalded himself to death, eh? I shouldn't be surprised if you had to go to a higher court to get rid of this one!"

Both the Thrupps were manifestly frightened by this accurate and brutal summary of their last appearance before the magistrates. They were used to threats from persons in authority—old enemies such as the sanitary inspector—for whom familiarity had bred contempt. But they did not know what to make of a young girl who dropped in at their house and seemed not only anxious to pick a quarrel but more than a match for them in the art of browbeating.

Mr. Thrupp contradicted appearances by showing himself the tougher of the pair.

"You might get yerself 'ad up fer slander, my girl."

"And I might get your dirty neck stretched," replied Olive.

Mrs. Thrupp signed to him to come off the aggressive tack. She put on a whining gypsy intonation which would have sickened anybody but a Romany novelist or a drunk at a country fair.

"See 'ere, missy, you don't think we treat our little bebby right, bless 'is eyes. D'you reckon you could do better by 'im nor us as 'ave 'ad five and reared three?"

"How the hell should I know till I've seen the child? It may or may not be a hopeless case."

"What does a kid like yerself know about physic?" burst out Mr. Thrupp.

"'Ush, Fred!" muttered his wife. "You dunno what 'er uncle teached 'er. Mebbe she'd better taike a look at young George if she feels that way. We don't want no more trouble in this 'ouse."

"Okay, yer ladyship," Fred agreed offensively. "This way ter view the heir apparent."

He moved over toward a corner of the room.

"You're not going to come very pleasantly out of this unless you mend your manners," said Olive. "I don't know if you realize the weight attached to the report of a qualified practitioner."

"Good Christ, Fred, don't make no trouble. We didn't know you was a doctor, too, miss. My 'usband don't mean nothing."

A faint sibilance pervaded the room as though a kettle were gently boiling on the hob. It was an ordinary sound in Gorchow, for the cottagers lived largely on a poisonous concoction of stewed tea.

Mr. Thrupp produced his son with the bored air of a conjuror producing a rabbit. He pulled the cover off what had appeared to be merely another small case, pressed into service as an occasional seat. But the box lay hollow side uppermost and was padded internally to form a rude cradle, from which the whistling sound unmistakably proceeded. Even a healthy infant would have had trouble in breathing freely packed away under a layer of thick material: it was a wonder that little George, who had the influenza to contend with as well as his canopy, had not suffocated long ago.

"There y'are," said Mr. Thrupp. Mavis tried to slip upstairs behind his back. "As fer you, you little bitch, I'll teach you to play this game twice!" he added in a savage undertone.

Olive inspected the baby. It was difficult to say where the signs of neglect ended and those of illness began. George had sores at the base of both nostrils, and a red patch at either corner of his mouth. Seldom had anybody obliged him by wiping away saliva or corrosive mucus. He would have appeared a wretched infant at the best of times. Now his little cheeks were gray and sunken, fiercely contrasting with the strangulated red of his temples. The veins in that area were so puffed that they might have belonged to an old, port-soaking clubman. George could not get his breath. With every attempted intake he whistled dolefully in a minor key.

Olive lifted the child from his bed with a kind of clumsy, unfeminine certainty. She pushed one of his eyelids back with her finger. The whites of the pupils were violently suffused.

"In fifteen minutes or so," she said, "you'd have had one less mouth to feed."

"For Christ's sake, don't keep on!" muttered Mrs. Thrupp. "Let's see *you* do something fer the pore kid."

"Get me some boiling water."

Mrs. Thrupp lumbered to the wall and pulled back a length of curtain, revealing a tiny cupboardlike scullery. Dirty plates were heaped high on the drain board of the sink. Among them were a couple of saucepans. She started to fill one of them from the tap.

"Wash that thing out, you slut!" shouted Olive.

When Mrs. Thrupp turned round she fully intended to throw the saucepan. Then she found that she dared not.

Olive put the child down and began to stroll round the room, examining its objects with an air of insolent appraisement. She was obviously convinced of her own paramount importance. She would have been laughable if the brusque certainty of her manner had not made it extremely difficult to keep her real age and sex in mind. Mr. Thrupp was not notably imaginative, yet whenever he took his eyes away from her figure he caught himself next looking up in instinctive expectation of being confronted with a large and turbulent male—say, an inspector of police.

His wife came in with the scoured saucepan and set it to boil on the kitchen range. Then she slipped back to the scullery, for no obvious reason except that she did not relish the living room.

Olive finished her tour by taking something from the mantelpiece. It was a new-looking cigarette holder, of the very cheapest kind, which end in a small, tubular vulcanite mouthpiece.

"This been used?" she inquired.

Mr. Thrupp shrugged his shoulders.

"Shouldn't wonder. One of Ma's silly crazes goin' down the village with that in 'er mouth, tryin' ter look like a laidy."

He spoke with exaggerated casualness, endeavoring to avert any comment on the unusualness of such fal-lals in rustic circles, and preparing to disclaim all knowledge of where and how the article had been "won." Olive had given him a profound shock, and he would not have put any unpleasant, nosy conduct past her.

All she said was: "I shall want it. Fetch me a knife, too."

"What sorter knife?"

"Pointed and very sharp. You must have one in your line of business."

Mr. Thrupp took his orders without a murmur, though they happened to involve going out into the bitter night and hunting round the lean-to shed where he kept his nefarious tools. He did not profess to know what this girl was about, but somewhere at the back of his mind had sprung up a vague, unformulated hope that she was going to do something which might simultaneously save him a lot of trouble and involve her in as much again. Mr. Thrupp always derived a spiritual, as well as a practical, satisfaction from seeing somebody else pull his chestnuts out of the fire.

"Shut that door, you fool!" she shouted after him, and he had to retrace his steps to obey.

Olive turned her attention again to little George. He was whimpering thickly, and his small red hands were clenched as he pressed them against his jaw, trying ineffectually to push aside the slow constrictor. She carried him over to the lamp and, opening his mouth, peered down his throat. Then she laid him on the table and sounded his chest and back.

The disease showed a great range of attack, but, at the same time, a curious fidelity to particular methods in particular cases. The baby's lungs were not seriously affected. Those of children seldom were, for in the very young the germ seemed to concentrate all its venom against the upper part of the respiratory system, producing violent laryngitis with swelling and sometimes ulceration of the throat tissues. In this respect the symptoms closely resembled those of diphtheria. Despite their severity, they were not nearly so dangerous as the pneumonic type, more prevalent among adults. In proportion to its powers of resistance, an infant, which received prompt and adequate treatment, had a far better chance of surviving than a grown man. If, however, it was neglected it would almost certainly perish, either from the actual closure of its windpipe or else from heart failure brought on by the continual effort of breathing. George was rapidly going by the former way. Olive tried how far she could insert her little finger into his gorge. It was like palping a mass of close-knit sponge.

The water started to bubble. As Mrs. Thrupp was lifting it off the fire, Mr. Thrupp reappeared with the knife and laid it on the table. They avoided each other's eyes, as though they were ashamed of their obedience. In both their faces was the same mixture of curiosity and incomprehension and alarm. Olive carefully scrutinized the long sinister blade which tapered into a spike for punching holes. By luck it was clean and almost new. She threw it carelessly into the steaming pan. A few drops jumped and stung Mrs. Thrupp on her bare arm.

"You bitch, you done that a-purpose!"

Olive merely looked at her and pitched in the cigarette holder.

"My Fairy Smoker!" gasped Mrs. Thrupp. "'Ere, this can't—"

"Let 'er be," said Mr. Thrupp grimly. He now took the view that if only Olive were given enough rope he might well acquire some right to damages or compensation against her. "Watcher going to do, miss?" he asked.

"Take a long shot to save your brat. If it doesn't come off I shall have the satisfaction of knowing that the child's better out of your care."

While the ill-assorted tools were still boiling, she took George, and seating herself with him under the lamp, gently explored the baby flesh and the soft underlying muscular wall of his throat. Neither the removal from his cot nor the unfamiliar touch could pierce his exhausted torpor. He lay still in her arms with closed eyes, having almost abandoned the cruel struggle. The whistling in his throat had ceased because the air could no longer force a passage.

Olive commanded: "Put a lid over that saucepan and pour the water away without touching the things in it."

While she was waiting on Mrs. Thrupp's unhandy maneuvers she pulled out a handkerchief and wrapped it loosely round her right hand. It was a big square of linen, once the property of James, which she was in the habit of carrying in her raincoat.

She took the knife delicately in her covered fingers, she held it up to the light, then, without hesitation, at the spot which her eye had marked, she plunged it into George's throat.

5

Faulkner started so violently that his head banged against the outside of the uncurtained window, and his clerical hat was knocked ludicrously down over his face, shutting out the terrible picture.

"Stop her!" he shouted. "For God's sake, stop her!"

As he gathered himself to dash for the door, Roger gripped his sleeve with a hand whose trembling vibrated through both their bodies.

"Don't!" he said, in a kind of whisper, as though his teeth were clenched, "the only chance is to let her finish."

"Finish?" Faulkner cried. "They'll say it's murder."

"Look," said Roger, "look, you fool!"

Clearly visible against the lighted interior, Olive was proceeding with her self-appointed task.

While they watched, she took up the sterilized cigarette holder and began, now strengthening, now relaxing the pressure, to insert it between the red lips of the incision.

"Not yet, not yet," muttered Roger, restraining another of Faulkner's efforts to break loose.

Inside the room the two Thrupps were on their feet. Their faces were twisted with horror of the act and fear of its consequences to their own skins. They looked like a pair of "framed" criminals. Faulkner made a great effort to control himself.

"Do you realize," he asked, "that we're standing by while Olive commits herself to a criminal asylum? Why couldn't you have told me straight out that she'd lost her senses?"

Roger still kept his gaze fixed on the window. At the same time he fumbled with the knot of his scarf. He wrenched open his collar, regardless of the evil properties which he had always attributed to cold night air. Low down, beneath his Adam's apple, showed a reddish, linear puckering of the flesh.

"I had it done myself," he said.

"What?" said Faulkner.

"Tracheotomy. For diphtheria. It saved my life."

"An operation—without anesthetics?"

Roger nodded.

"It's a last resort. They don't often have to perform it nowadays."

"Oh, God!" said Faulkner, sighing with momentary relief. Then his fear came back on him: "She couldn't know how to—not successfully . . ."

Roger suddenly regained natural command of his voice, though his frame was still shaken by nervous tremors.

"I pray to God," he said, "that what she has done is the work of an unskilled, courageous girl, anxious to save a child's life. But knowing the little I do of surgery, I'm afraid that the only result consistent with my hope is failure. If that child lives, not by a fluke, but because the operation was properly carried out . . ."

"But—" began Faulkner.

"Come," said Roger with a kind of cold fortitude, "we should go in now."

Three times already had Mrs. Thrupp repeated the phrase "murdering little toad." But, for all the attention she received, even from the object of her abuse, she might have been murmuring some soporific commonplace. Olive did not seem to be taking any further interest in the proceedings. She sat and nursed the monstrous combination of little George and the cigarette holder. Yet, despite this outward indifference, her attitude toward the child had undergone a subtle change. The curve of her back and the angle of her crooked arms had suddenly become feminine, protective, maternal. She no longer looked to be handling little George more as a case than as a baby.

"Cut 'is pore innocent throat! I'll cut yer dirty liver out!" screamed Mrs. Thrupp, tormented by a growing certainty that she would be fixed with half the blame.

"Good evening," said Faulkner from the doorway.

He always greeted his parishioners politely, and the habit asserted itself in defiance of the situation.

"Looks like you might have to say a prayer, reverend," said Mr. Thrupp with more composure, jerking his thumb toward the baby.

Roger pushed past into the middle of the room.

"Nonsense!" he proclaimed. "Utter nonsense! Now you, madam, perhaps you'll have the decency to express gratitude for what has been done on your child's behalf!"

"Jesus Christ!" ejaculated Mrs. Thrupp.

"You can thank Providence later and no doubt Mr. Faulkner will be pleased to assist you. I was referring to my niece."

"'Ere," said Mr. Thrupp, "let's get this right. That's our kid. She cut 'is throat. We saw 'er."

"And helped her," added Faulkner.

"My niece," said Roger, "has exerted her skill to operate on your son, and in return she hears herself cursed in the filthiest terms."

He was trying to carry things off after the manner of James, but the Giant's Robe sagged and wavered about his shoulders.

"Operate?" said Thrupp. *"She cut 'is throat!"*

"Of course, she did. What is an operation but using a knife on somebody?"

Mr. Thrupp shook his head.

"She dunno 'ow, properly. Not a kid like 'er."

"Doesn't it occur to you that she may have received some training from her uncle, who was one of the most distinguished doctors in Europe?"

"Mebbe. I didn't rightly think of that," admitted Mr. Thrupp. "But I still reckon this is a funny business, what should 'ave been done in an 'orspital."

"And how do you suppose the child would have survived till it got there? Can't you understand that it has been wounded simply in order to provide it with the means of breathing?"

Unfortunately Mr. Thrupp's general ignorance was leavened with a certain psychological perception.

"Well," he said, "if it's all O.K., mister, why the hell are you in such a mucksweat?"

He pointed to Roger's forehead on which the telltale drops glistened and slid and hung against the barrier of his eyebrows.

Faulkner was much the younger man. Though he had taken the shock harder at first, he threw off its effects more quickly.

"I suggest," he said in a tone that was the quintessence of normality, "that somebody should pay a little attention to the child. After all, it is the chief subject of this discussion."

He peered over Olive's shoulder.

"It seems to be doing very well for a victim of murder," he observed.

And indeed the change in little George's appearance was unmistakable. The red congestion of his face had so far subsided that it was possible to distinguish the dirt. The drastic treatment seemed to have caused him very little pain, and though once or twice he sought to disengage a hand from his shawl and investigate his throat, the tubing was obviously a source of more curiosity than distress. He was whistling again, but now with a cheerier note as the life-giving air rushed in by its strange conduit. He had bled hardly at all.

Having seen for himself, Mr. Thrupp was obliged to change his ground.

"'E looks lighter now, but 'ow're we to know 'e won't pop off sudden in a few minutes?"

"He won't, if you do as you're told conscientiously."

Mrs. Thrupp pointed suddenly at Olive.

"You're all ready enough to talk but the one who done the job. Why don't she say nothing? She'd a saucy enough tongue in 'er 'ead awhile back. Barging into other folks' 'omes!"

"Olive!" said Faulkner gently. He repeated her name thrice, each time louder, until it sounded as if he were calling somebody back from a distance.

"Yes?" said Olive in a dull, drugged whisper, without lifting her eyes.

"My dear..."

"Poor little baby! It's hurt its throat. I've never... seen a baby like... this one."

"She's hopelessly overwrought," broke in Roger. "This has been too great a strain for her. If you'll be good enough to take your offspring, madam, my niece will come straight back to bed."

Mrs. Thrupp took the child out of Olive's limp arms and held it like a lighted firework.

"What does 'e do now?" she asked. "Go round the rest of 'is life with this in 'im, advertising the Fairy Smoker?"

"Don't be stupid," said Faulkner. "What's been done is only an emergency measure. You must get hold of a doctor as soon as possible."

As if a tide had turned, animation—her own animation—was rapidly flooding back into Olive's body, restoring to it the power of independent action. She rejected the offer of Roger's arm, and approached Mrs. Thrupp.

"I hope I haven't been a nuisance," she said diffidently.

Mrs. Thrupp gasped.

"Gor!" she said. "Butter wouldn't melt in 'er mouth!"

Her husband followed them out into the street. He still believed that he ought to be able to turn the situation to account if only he could grasp it from the right angle.

"This is a queer business, reverend," he grumbled. Getting no reply, he ventured on a more definite line: "Maybe she ain't certified, like, to do operations?"

"Of course, she's not a qualified doctor. But she or anybody else is entitled to take steps to save another human being from imminent death."

"Ah!" said Mr. Thrupp, pulling his long mustache. "She acted very funny—now, didn't she? 'Asty one moment and mild the next. I'd've said she didn't rightly know what she was at 'alf the time. I don't reckon 'er family would want this talked of?"

"I'm getting cold," said Faulkner and strode away to catch up with the other two.

The men walked one on each side of Olive. Their speculations kept them silent. When they had nearly reached the Manor gates, Olive suddenly said:

"I suppose I fainted or something."

6

In the third notebook Roger found what he had been seeking, the passage which ran through his head like a steady refrain repeating itself between the wild improvisations of his fancy. Drawing closer to the lamp he set himself to read his own handwriting:

Action for Damages for the Ensorcelment of Cattle. Winchester Assizes. Spring 1676. Before Wrangham J.

Then followed a note on the curious and, at that date, somewhat anachronistic nature of the claim, which was one of the last civil proceedings in England to be based on allegations of witchcraft. Richard Hamaker had sued Ezekiel Tite, pleading that the said Tite, a neighboring farmer, had revenged himself for a dispute over boundaries by bewitching the plaintiff's herd of cows. In this wicked conduct he had the assistance of his wife, "a reputed solicitress of hobbies [goblins], noxious spirits and all magick inquiry." The effect on the cattle was deplorable. Blotches and sores appeared on their hides: their nostrils ran, their eyes were scalded; it was said that flies had been seen to emerge from their mouths in large numbers—"a malignant sign patently averring unnatural mischief."

Even the forceful Wrangham was somewhat shaken by the cataract of improbable assertions and denials which constituted the evidence. His ultimate judgment in favor of the plaintiff-owner of the cows was a triumph of legal impartiality over private common sense. But Pilate would have envied the dignity with which he washed his hands of all supernatural questions.

Concerning the active operation, nay more, the veritable existence, of subterraneous demons I have no clear knowledge. Yet I apprehend that since our law has oftentimes condemned both men and women to suffer death on charge of devilish associations, so when I sit upon this bench I must give credence to such things, at least *quasi figmenta juris.* I find upon the testimony that the Defendant has indeed summoned pernicious spirits to damnify the herds of the Plaintiff. Though why the imps of Satan should yield to the importunity of one that can have no literacy of invocation, passeth my understanding.

Roger sighed. Then he reread the first sentence.... "Concerning the active operation..." Ah, wise Sir Joshua, he thought, could you have stood in my shoes today and still preserved that firm, agnostic calm?

Slowly he started upstairs. The second story was in darkness, and when he tried the switch no illumination followed. He clicked his tongue at the fallibility of fuses. All the rooms above the first floor would be affected. He retraced his steps and took one of the candles from the mantelpiece of the lounge. Bereft of electricity, the house became a strange, unexplored region. His shadow went before him, a monstrous herald. The flame of the candle guttered and swayed. Its light fell with a queer, eclectic distribution, seeming to pass over some objects in a flash, while on others it lingered meaningly. It picked out the body of Hope and her battered lyre, in an engraved reproduction of Watts's painting which hung on the second floor. Roger had always despised it as an example of the worst type of sentimental symbolism. Now the candlelight dignified it with a peculiar and sinister bitterness.

In the bedroom Roger removed his waistcoats one by one—the black, the cardigan, and the brown-beige which he wore surreptitiously under his mourning. A crushing depression had settled on him. It was a familiar mood, though it came less frequently nowadays than in his youth. He felt himself struggling, yet being swamped, like a swimmer in a strong sea, by the fierce, combative nature of existence. He knew that his arms were too feeble to beat the current, yet some instinct forced them to continue their weary threshing. He supposed that he had never had the guts to sink. He associated this sensation of helplessness particularly with the years in which he had striven to build up a practice as a solicitor. It automatically recalled to him the long, cheerless, resonant corridors of the Law Courts and the loitering clerks, wetting their lips in anticipation of their lunchtime drink, and the bustling counsel, who compensated themselves for second-rate practices by shoving and barging among the bystanders in the effort to create an illusion that their time was to be measured only in guineas.

He broke his custom of reading in bed, though the candle still had half its length to burn. As soon as he slept, he was representing the Reverend Faulkner in some unspecified but vital proceeding which involved the cross-examination of his half brother. James stood in the witness box, and his beard and his blue eyes sparkled with maleficent power. He kept on refusing to answer the question which Roger could never remember to have put. "This little rat," he proclaimed, "sags at the belly. No goddam guts." His lordship the judge was lost in a gray mist and either could not or would not interfere. It was awful. It was worse than any of the things which habitually occur to those that plead before the courts. The voice of James continued, multiplying on itself, like an echo between concave rocks. Presently the sound lost all characteristics of speech and became a mere series of dull percussions. Bump, bump, bump.

Roger went from sleep to wakefulness in one instantaneous bound. He was sweating and he was sitting bolt upright, though he could not remember to have raised himself on the pillows. He listened. Only the clock, and the doubtful chirrup of some small bird, deluded by a false lightening of the east. Then again he heard the steady squeak of the ceiling above his head: not the noise of old boards as they contract or expand in changing temperatures, but that other one which is evoked only by the passage of a living creature. Darkness is a terrible thing to a man who cannot account for everything that it contains. Then the smallest chink in the wall of reason opens on a chaos peopled by monstrous invaders. Roger felt for the switch. Even as his hand closed on it he remembered that the wires were dead. And once more he heard a movement, not loud, not stealthy, but horribly casual in the room above.

His heart raced. Like the wheels of a train it began to thump out a single exhortation. "You must go up and see, go up and see, you must go up and see." Roger was not of the breed to which terrors unknown are always worse than those faced. At most times, if he had learned that there was a repulsive specter behind his back, he would not have turned round to put his fear to the test: he would have hidden his head and trusted that if he left the horrid thing alone, it would do the same for him. Now, hearing sounds from a room which he knew ought not to contain anything capable of physical movement, he was strongly tempted to block his ears and pacify his mind with a few platitudes about the deceptiveness of human senses. But his conscience forbade him. He believed that it was his imperative duty to investigate. He had no definable reason for his belief, save that when a household had been disturbed by one abnormal occurrence it was good sense to watch for another and try to correlate it with the first, in the hope that the accumulated evidence would point to some explanation.

He swung his legs over the side of the bed and groped for his slippers. He donned his thick camel's-hair dressing gown. If he shivered he did not intend that it should be from cold. The candle, after a moment's deliberation, he refrained from taking. It was bad not to see, but worse to have a distorted vision. He mistrusted the flickering, bud-shaped flame, in whose light something always seemed to be lurking just beyond the corner of his eye.

He kept his hand on the banisters to prevent himself from stumbling. Much as he would have given for human companionship, he had no wish to waken Eva, who in one way or another would certainly have defeated his object. As he mounted he held out to himself little promises of reward: When the funeral is over, the house will be quiet again and I shall take a short holiday. I shall go and stay by myself in London where nobody knows me and nobody can bother me. Perhaps I shall do a little reading in the British Museum.

Something suddenly pattered and squeaked with grating sharpness. The sound came from behind the laboratory door. He jumped and nearly lost his footing on the stair tread. Then he thought of the mice, and remembered the chance remark of a workman employed some months ago: "You can't never rid old houses of 'em. Mebbe you hear 'em mucking about in the joists at night." Of course: mice had been the cause of all the disturbance upstairs. Naturally. Undoubtedly. Not very pleasant, perhaps, to picture the little rodents gamboling around one's brother's corpse. Mice. Not rats. Rats were much worse—charnel creatures of indiscriminate appetite. But surely there was no need for a middle-aged man to rise at dead of night and paddle about death chambers dispersing vermin?

He had almost succeeded in justifying retreat, when his reason struck back at him in full force. If there were only mice in James's room, why not enter and shoo them away? It might not be obligatory, but it was the natural thing to do. Refusal strongly suggested fear: and since he was not afraid of mice it would appear that he was taking cover under an insincere pretense.

Roger sighed. His conscience had a half nelson on him. There was no middle way between advance and surrender to undisguised cowardice.

The handle turned and the hinges gave in oiled silence. He resisted an impulse to hurl the door back with a shattering, heartening crash. Two little steps and he was inside, amidst the smell of cut flowers and death and another fainter perfume which he knew to be familiar but could not, in the perturbed state of his mind, identify. Cold! God, how cold it was in that place! Fires are not burnt where the dead lie, often for good reasons affecting the body, occasionally because religious belief sees in them an evil omen. There was nothing that could be called light in James's bedroom, only a gray tint in the immediate neighborhood of the half-open door. Straining his eyes into the dark, he could just distinguish the outline of the nearest bedpost. Then the door shut behind him: gently, demurely, with a quiet little click of triumph. Sometimes a draft will close doors in this deliberate fashion. Roger was seized with panic and rushed wildly to reopen his line of communication. He had hardly gone a pace before he collided with a wall bracket. A vase fell, striking first his leg, then the carpet. Clammy water began to permeate his pajamas, and he trod on a scatter of juicy stalks. All sense of direction left him, and the room became a sealed box about which he blundered like a bee on a windowpane.

James said: "God damn it, Roger, are you playing at housebreakers?"

Roger would not have believed that he could so easily endure to hear the unmistakable utterance of the dead. He did not realize that the dim, unformulated suspicions, which had already gathered in his mind, were helping him to meet the crisis with the resolution of a man forewarned. He was horrified, but at present it was a dull, narcotic horror.

Carefully he found the wall, aligning himself against it, so that his shoulders received a welcome support.

"James," he said without a quiver, "where are you?"

"Ah," replied the voice of James, "can't you guess? I am in a beautiful region of light and flowers, of course, you bloody fool! And everyone is very happy. Papa is here and so are our respective mammas. They are very happy. We get what we want by just thinking about it. That's what comes of being on a higher plane."

"I should have thought," said Roger, "that whatever your new status, it might have cured you of mocking at other people's sincerity."

"In that case, my dear Roger, the horrors of death are greatly exaggerated in your mind."

"James," said Roger, "perhaps it sounds ridiculous, but I'm not concerned to pry into your private affairs. You may be in torment or a kind of limbo or even condemned to earthly wandering, for all I know. In any event, I wouldn't insult you with my sympathy. But for the sake of Charity, let Olive be. Let her alone, d'you understand?"

"Well, well!" said James. "Oughtn't you to hang garlic round her neck and drive a stake through my heart?"

"You may be sure I should, if I believed either in physical vampires or in superstitious remedy. But I knew you alive, James. It was never the body you preyed on, it was the personality."

"I suppose," said James more mildly, "that you hold me responsible for even the most discreditable feats—such as saving a child's life."

"No doubt in that instance you justified yourself, though you chose the most revolting means and were probably actuated by nothing more than the pleasure of exercising your skill. I should be satisfied if I could believe that, having once used Olive for a legitimate purpose, you would refrain from repeating the performance maliciously, to cause damage."

Out of the dark came a familiar, rasping, deep-throated chuckle.

"Still the same Roger! Talking like a second-rate attorney's clerk! The reason you don't like my little alliance with Olive is that you foresee it causing a certain amount of social embarrassment to yourself. Still, don't worry. I think we shall concentrate on Eva.

She reacted well the other day, when my will was read."

Roger clenched and unclenched his hands over the cord of his dressing gown. The half-frozen air seemed to have an astringent quality, drying up his tongue like the kernel in an old nut.

"James," he said in slow and difficult appeal, "if I am to believe my senses, you have by some means managed to retain control of certain faculties after death. Isn't that enough for you? What further need have you to invade the mind of an unhappy and helpless child?"

Gradually he was recovering full command of his articulation. On the final plea his voice rang out with more than its normal strength.

"Haunt us if you must, James. Go on haunting us if the sport doesn't pall. But for God's sake do it honestly in your own guise, and be ashamed to hide behind a girl's skirts. I'd offer my own body for your damned experiments, if I thought it a feasible exchange."

After this there was a pause so lengthy that Roger half hoped, half feared that his words, striking home, had offended the unquiet spirit. But at last it answered:

"Nothing could give me more pleasure than to be congratulated on the preservation of my bodily vigor, even though it is the kind of compliment usually kept for decayed centenarians. All the same, my dear Roger, are you quite sure that you have an accurate view of the position?"

"Yes," maintained Roger stoutly.

"Then we must put the matter to the test. Besides, how can a poor corpse put its alleged physical powers to better use than by shaking hands with the man who has just expressed such noble and altruistic sentiments about his little niece? It's a duty and a privilege."

For an instant the words hung suspended and meaningless in Roger's brain. But with the first rustle of movement from the direction of the bed, their message burst upon him in a great flash of crude, instinctive terror. Many persons can bring themselves to hold converse with the dead, but the number who will endure to have contact with a supposed materialization is infinitely smaller. Wise commercial mediums recognize this: apart from the mechanical problems involved, the dear departed is seldom asked to lay a ghostly hand on the believer's person.

"I forbid you to touch me," he shouted. "Leave me alone, leave me—" Then, irrational with terror, he cried out: "I won't have you decently buried if you touch me."

"Ah," said James, moving, it seemed, cautiously, gradually, through the darkness, "now, if you could promise not to bury me at all, I might consider your offer. Just suppose, as you evidently do, that I am still in control of the dignified framework of James Marshall. That's not going to be very much use to me after a few months underground. No, my dear Roger, when the old house falls to pieces, it's only logical to find another."

His approach was weirdly light-footed. You would never have believed that the soft, delayed footfalls could belong to a six-foot man. It crossed Roger's mind that perhaps he was no longer amenable in the same degree to the laws of gravity.

"You could be embalmed," gasped Roger, clutching at the last ludicrous straw of propitiation. "I swear I would see to it."

"A poor second best! There's no flexibility in a mummy. I'm not attracted by an existence of perpetual paralysis."

Roger felt a touch on his wrist, light, exploratory, of an arctic coldness. It seemed to run up his arm, shriveling and numbing the flesh. He snatched his hand away, failing to notice when he struck his knuckles against the wardrobe and made them bleed.

Panic, a thousand times stronger than before, seized him. His mouth opening in dumb sobs, the cord of his dressing gown flailing about him, he beat and tore at the solid wall as if he were trying to uncover a sealed exit. He was touched again on the shoulder. A cannoning lurch threw him against something whose pointed metallic hardness reawoke his capacity to feel physical pain. The switch went up, the labors of five men who had spent the past hour repairing a broken cable on the Ely road were rewarded, the room was flooded with light.

For a moment he was dazzled. Then the golden blur cleared from his eyes. His mind, like a supersensitized film, registered every detail of the room in an instant's exposure. He saw James lying on his bed, frock-coated, surrounded by flowers, his features set in a smug, ironic mask. He saw Olive. She was standing almost at his side. One hand made a stroking movement in the region of her chin. The other was stretched out in the act of giving the victim another prod. Her eyes were pulled down, like a Mongol's, at the corners, accentuating her expression of cruel, detached amusement. You would not have been surprised if there had come a hissing from her hair. She looked like Medusa decked out as a young woman of the period.

Roger fell down in a faint. Olive remained looking at him. Gradually the diabolic glow faded from her features: as if the lights had been dimmed in a theater, not to hide the substitution of scenery, but because the actors had suddenly decamped with all the properties; or as if a god had deserted his vocal image, and, in place of the oracle, stood a dumb, insentient log.

CHAPTER FIVE

THE girl on the far side of the carriage opened her handbag and began to make up her face. The train jerked, and the paper which she had been reading ever since she had got in at Ely shot off her knees and slid halfway under the opposite seat. Delia bent down and retrieved it, instinctively smoothing its crumpled leaves. As she handed it back she could not repress a smile.

The girl thanked her brightly. Then she said: "I can see you think it funny that I should be reading this."

"In that case I'm afraid I must have appeared very impertinent," replied Delia.

"Oh, not at all," said the girl. "Most people probably wouldn't have noticed you smiling. It just happens that I rather go in for psychology and observation—you know!"

"Perhaps that is why you read the *Daily Worker?*"

The girl shook her head. She was an attractive little thing, with a round pink face and short, curly auburn hair. "Irrepressible," that was the word she suggested.

"Not exactly. You see, I'm working through communism."

Delia was sure that this girl talked with indiscriminate mateyness to everybody in trains, buses, and any other public place. Someone, she thought maternally, ought to drop a word of warning in her ear. Angela and Joyce had strict instructions about noncorridor compartments.

"Does that mean that you are a communist yourself?" she asked, looking at the girl's clothes which were expensive but curiously somber. Perhaps, thought Delia, she wears them in order to appear presentable, yet at the same time sympathetic toward the downtrodden proletariat.

"Yes," said the girl, "I am at the moment. It's only temporary, of course."

"That's very broad-minded of you. Most people imagine that their present phase will last forever."

The girl was obviously delighted with the compliment. She bubbled with pleasure.

"It's so nice to find somebody who understands one's point of view. You see, I've realized that one has simply got to experience all these things—I mean, anybody who isn't utterly dim always goes through the communist period."

"I see," said Delia, trying not to laugh. "That's most original. You're deliberately anticipating your own development. What happens when you come out at the other end of communism?"

"I haven't decided what I shall take up next. But in any case one is bound to be *enriched psychologically*, if you see what I mean. For instance, I've never regretted the six months I spent with religion."

"My younger daughter is in the religious stage. Do you think she'll get over it as quickly?"

"That depends," said the girl, wrinkling her nose judicially. "If it's just a case of vestments and the new curate, it probably won't last long. On the other hand, if it's a real sort of urge . . ."

She really is rather a sweet little imbecile, thought Delia, and there is a kind of acuteness about some of the things she says. She hit off poor Joyce with her romantic Anglo-Catholic enthusiasm and her Masses and her bedroom decorated like a second-rate Continental shrine.

"I'm afraid I've been doing nothing but talk about my own affairs," said the girl winningly. "I wonder now if you'd tell me something about yourself?"

Delia began to feel faintly alarmed. She had not reckoned on being invited to a bout of soul-sharing. However, having had her amusement, she could not decently refuse to pay for it.

"I don't think I'm very interesting," she said hypocritically, "but if there's anything you'd specially like to know . . ."

"There is," said the girl. She stared at Delia with round, intense blue eyes. "What do you use on your nails?"

The bathos was too much. This time Delia could not stifle her amusement. The girl was hurt. She did not see the joke. She had that peculiarly feminine type of mind, rather like a sieve, which reduces all questions that pass through it to a uniform bulk and weight.

Delia tried to make amends by a polite and detailed answer—but the conversation lapsed. The little local train crawled on with the painful slowness of an injured worm. Delia rubbed a clear patch on the misted windowpane and fell to watching the cold, desolate pageant of fields. The complete absence of variety or elevation gave the landscape an unreal, two-dimensional appearance. The natural law of perspective did not seem to operate on it. It repelled her, but she could understand the attraction it had for others. In that unbroken, omnipresent monotony a man was not dwarfed: his vitality took on an increased significance against the absolutely passive background. Just as there was no physical barrier to his movement in any direction, so, you felt, his will might be unlimited in its range. She smiled grimly to herself, reflecting that this was at any rate a convincing explanation why one person had chosen the district for his home.

The girl who had been studying her *Daily Worker* looked up again as the train began to brake.

"This is my station," she said. "I suppose you're going on?"

"I don't really know," Delia confessed. "I want a place called Haines."

"But here you are, my dear! They'll simply die when they see *two* of us on the platform. They haven't had such a crowd since the year dot."

They clanked to rest by a collection of shacklike station buildings whose most prominent feature was an enormous door, labeled "Gents." There was also a station master's cottage with a rockery outside on which the name "Haines," picked out in white stones, had been almost obliterated by the homogeneous whiteness of the frost.

The girl opened the door and motioned to Delia to go first. Delia's estimate of her immediately rose a point: she set a high value on good manners in the young—not from any excessive idea of the merits of age, but because a certain formality of etiquette seemed to her a pleasant and orderly thing, and order was the keynote of her whole philosophy.

A porter came toward them with a leisurely air as though he were selecting a particular client out of a choice of several dozen.

"Will you put this on my cab?" said Delia. "I have one ordered—by telephone, last night. Lady Pond's the name."

"Blast!" said the girl. "Just my luck! If you've bagged Percy's chariot, I shall have to walk it."

"My dear child, if you're going the same direction as myself, I shall be very pleased to give you a lift."

"I must get to Gorchow before half past two."

"By coincidence, I happen to be going there myself."

"Well, honestly, I wouldn't bother you, only there's about as much chance of getting another car here as picking up a date in the Sahara."

They followed the porter out past the ticket gate. An old Renault was parked in the roadway outside. By it stood the driver flapping his arms and stamping his feet and protesting to himself in a continuous running mutter. Percy, the taximan, was the result of a long series of unions between the neighborhood's best families. Inbreeding had rather affected his development. Locally he was known as "Silly Percy"—a description which connoted neither lunacy nor mental deficiency, but a kind of atrophy of the understanding beyond the sphere of basic common sense. Percy would never have allowed himself to be underpaid his fare, but he might have believed that the moon was made of cheese. Fortunately his weakness did not affect his competence as a driver.

As soon as he saw them, he favored the girl, whom he obviously knew by sight, with a rather suggestive grin.

"My dear," she said to Delia, "isn't he frightful? I always feel he'd like to get me behind a haystack!"

"I want you to take me to the Manor, Gorchow," said Delia in her clear, decided tones.

She almost always managed to get the best and most uncomplaining attention from servants. She had a knack of addressing them with a combination of civility and complete assurance of her natural right to command. But Percy was something outside her previous experience.

"Ur!" he said. "You didn't ought to come in for the port wine and cake but what you do your bit at the church, first."

Delia turned to her companion:

"I take it he is . . . safe?" she said.

The girl also was looking surprised: though not apparently for the same cause.

"I say," she said, "you do know that they'll all be out, don't you?"

"I hadn't really thought about it. But presumably they won't mind a caller waiting for their return."

"Well, if you're an old friend. . . . But I should have thought it might be a bit embarrassing . . ."

Delia was not accustomed to have the propriety of her actions thus weighed and doubted.

"I have come from London in order to see some people called Marshall on a matter of business. Evidently you and the rest of the neighborhood are intimately acquainted with their movements. Have they gone away, or is there any other particular reason why I should be unwelcome?"

The girl looked at her watch.

"In ten minutes," she said, "they'll be at a funeral. Where I ought to be."

Delia's beautiful smooth mask of upper-class efficiency showed a perceptible crack.

"Good heavens!" she said. "Is—is another of the family dead?"

"I hope not," said the girl. "Anyhow, this is the old man's funeral —Uncle James's."

"I'm sorry," said Delia. "Very stupid of me. I'd heard . . . but somehow I imagined that he died several weeks ago."

"Did you know him?"

"Yes," said Delia.

"Then," suggested the girl, with that somewhat irritating brightness, as of a troupe leader instructing her brownies in self-reliance, "I should think you ought to turn up at the service. I mean, it would make the Marshalls take a definitely better view of your business."

Delia had recovered sufficiently to say: "I hope you don't imagine I want to sell them a vacuum cleaner!"

"Of course not," agreed the girl. "I heard your name. If I wasn't off snobbery for the moment, I'd admit I was frightfully thrilled."

Silly Percy was not naturally impatient. He had a pastoral mind and he enjoyed a good browse. But he had already waited some time, and the intense cold was beginning to stiffen his limbs.

"Dilly-dally," he muttered, "dilly-dally. Like a pair o' bloody 'ens!"

"I feel we ought to be moving," said the girl tentatively. "You can decide where you're going on the way."

Delia meekly climbed into the frayed leather-smelling interior of the cab. The girl followed and, plumping down beside her, pulled up her dark-colored skirt.

"Excuse me!" she said. "But I've got a damnable man-eating garter. It bites a piece out of me each time I sit." Then, without any perceptible pause, she reverted to a former topic. "You must be Sir Joseph Pond's wife. My dear, I do envy you. He looks simply marvelous in his photographs in the newspapers. I mean, quite apart from that terrific wig. So calm and penetrating. I loved his cross-examination in the Bailey divorce. 'Were you or were you not intimate with this unfortunate woman?' And after that, of course, anybody could see what a cad Lord Ivan had been!"

"Really," said Delia in a suppressed voice, "I seldom follow my husband's cases."

Percy started his engine at the fourth attempt and gingerly let in the clutch. They began to move.

"My name is Hassett," said the girl. "Nina Hassett. Not of course that you'd know it. Daddy's just a retired colonel, and too bourgeois."

"I doubt whether you yourself are naturally adapted to communism," replied Delia, disapproving of the last remark with the unoccupied half of her mind.

"Oh, of course, it's the battle against environment that is hardest for all nonproletarian comrades. . . . I say, it strikes me that you must know an awful lot of interesting people."

"You're most flattering," said Delia. "Why?"

It was hard not to be flattered by such uncritical recognition of one's status. But the silly kid went and spoiled it in the next breath.

"Well," she said, "you seem to have been a friend of Dr. Marshall, for one thing. I believe he was definitely big in his own way. Long before my time, of course, but he'd really done things, hadn't he?"

"Yes," said Delia, "Dr. Marshall did a great many things."

"I believe I ought to go through a Flo Nightingale period," said Nina. "I'm just too ignorant about famous physicians and diseases and drugs. . . ."

Delia leaned forward and touched her on the knee—a Chelsea

gesture which is wrung from Belgravia only under stress of considerable emotion.

"You like to hear about celebrated people?" she said. "Let me tell you the only lesson that I've learned from them. Don't be a silly little snob. You'll pay for it in blood and tears."

Nina took her outburst quite calmly, not realizing that she had been treated to something altogether outside her new friend's ordinary repertoire. She herself had lived so long in a warm bath of enthusiasms and confidences that she was rendered more or less insensitive to any rise of the emotional temperature.

"The moment I saw you, I could tell that you'd *suffered*," she remarked complacently.

Delia, somewhat ashamed of herself, was thankful when it appeared that Miss Hassett, having paid tribute to her own powers of observation, was quite ready to change the subject.

"Don't you think the Marshalls are rather a peculiar family?" she said. "I don't mean that nastily because I'm terribly fond of them all—especially Olive. . . ."

"The late Dr. Marshall was the only one I've ever met," replied Delia.

"Well, he was miles the most interesting. I used to be terrified of him when I went to tea as a child. But later I found him sort of fascinating. Don't imagine I'm the type of girl with a morbid passion for old men."

Delia sighed. Her acquaintance was like a child carelessly jabbing sticks into a pond: all the old buried mud was churned over and floated up to foul the surface. She did not want to hear about the Marshalls at all; but if hear she must, let it be about any other one of them than James.

"How does your friend Olive come into the family?" she asked.

"My dear, too romantically. James found her on the doorstep or something and made her his adopted daughter. And yet a lot of people always persisted that he was heartless!"

"Did they?" said Delia faintly.

"Yes. You know what I think? I believe some woman soured him when he was young, and then he retired behind a mask of cynicism!"

Delia looked out the window. They were crossing a patch of

common. A clump of trees lifted a spidery fretwork of branches against the curdled sky. Delia was not given to looking for sermons in stones, but she managed to extract a certain comfort from their dull endurance. After all, she thought, I have only memories, ghosts of things a long time past, to contend with.

"Miss Hassett," she said rather sardonically, "I wonder whether in your search for experience you've ever considered turning novelist?"

"No. But I've been on the stage. I thought the drama was my natural art-form."

"I should doubt it. Never have I heard a more astounding and original theory of James Marshall's character. And, believe me, it was a character that gave many people cause for profound thought."

"You're being sarcastic," said Nina good-humoredly. "And it doesn't sound as if you'd much like my poor old sugar-daddy." Then, with a stiffening of moral tone: "Anyhow he's dead, and seeing that we're practically at his graveside, I think we ought to get into a more religious frame of mind."

"Isn't that sort of thing the opiate of the people?" queried Delia.

"Oh, I know!" said Nina. "But I'm not here in my private capacity. I'm representing my parents—they've both got colds—and they believe in it, and anyhow I like to do things properly."

The car turned off to the right down a side road, in the middle of which there was an unbridged water splash, now solidified into a large block of ice. The wheels skidded and whirred aimlessly on its smooth surface, but their impetus carried them across. About a quarter of a mile farther on they came in sight of a house set back behind a dense shrubbery of laurels.

Nina pointed to it. "There's the Manor."

Delia leaned forward and opened the glass panel which communicated with the driving seat.

"You can take me to the church, after all," she said.

"Ah, that's better!" replied Percy approvingly over his shoulder.

She scarcely noticed his daft impertinence. She was too occupied with her thoughts. A little while ago she had shrunk from the prospect of attending James Marshall's funeral. Indeed, she had firmly resolved that at the last minute she would invent some pretext to excuse herself, even if it involved walking up and down outside the church for an hour of frozen discomfort. Now it seemed to her that she saw more clearly. Chance had sent her this opportunity of laying an old specter, and it would be folly and ingratitude to reject it.

Gorchow sprang up in front of them. It gave Delia the impression of an excrescence which had been missed when the fenland was rolled out and flattened by the waters. It had no air of confidence in its own purpose. Yet evidently men had once thought otherwise. The church was of an entirely disproportionate splendor—a large, tall-towered piece of Norman architecture whose artistic importance was recognized by the labels "Teas" and "Cycles Repaired" on an opposite cottage wall. The eastern counties are thronged with these great ecclesiastical leviathans, stranded by a gradually receding tide of population and prosperity. They are sad places, quarter-filled, much needing a mason's repair, giving out the hollow ring of isolated coins on vast salvers, inherited from an age of bygone munificence. The churchyard had gates of chased iron. The path that ran up to the porch was lined with old mossy graves, but that part of the burial ground had long been filled and superseded by a new area on the other side of the chancel. As they drew up, several dark-clad figures vanished into the interior of the building. The air vibrated with the faint droning murmurs of an organ.

"Wait for me here," she said to Percy. "I shall want you afterwards."

"Nobody ever went in but they came out better," replied Percy apocalyptically.

"Poor thing!" said Nina without bothering to moderate her voice. "He was 'saved' when he was seventeen and religious places always have a bad effect on him. He once drove me to a wedding and then stood outside the church shouting that it was better to marry than burn!"

Inside the door they skirted an enormous font. The cold light of early afternoon, filtering through the stained windows, became charged with a misty, purplish tincture. On first entering it was hard to recognize any face more than a few yards away. Delia tried to slip into one of the backmost pews. The girl restrained her.

"Everyone is sitting farther up," she whispered.

Delia pointed to her light-colored clothes.

"You'll only be more conspicuous if you languish at the back," said Nina. "All the villagers will turn round and stare at you and then go home indulging in the most *drastic* speculations."

From the little she knew of villages Delia agreed that this was probably true. She allowed herself to be persuaded, despite a suspicion that Miss Hassett was chiefly interested in retaining the company of somebody whom she believed to be important.

The verger put them in a pew far up the aisle. They had it to themselves and Delia got the corner seat. The congregation was not large—about thirty people in all. The majority were easy to place, either as villagers or as representatives of the local gentry. There were, however, a few elderly men of professional appearance who did not fit into either category. A couple sat in front of Delia, nursing their shining top hats and exchanging an occasional remark in undertones. Delia suddenly realized that she had met one of them at a friend's house. He was an eminent surgeon. Like the others, he was probably present to pay his last respects to an eminent colleague. Knowing him to be a most religious man, a strict Baptist, she hoped, for his peace of mind, that he was merely attending on behalf of some official body and had no personal acquaintance with the deceased.

Delia knelt down and put her face between her hands. James Marshall, she said in her heart, it may be that I have been brought to this place for a good reason. I am going to forgive you, once and for all, for everything, forever, absolutely. And I am never going to remember you again. And I do not know whether my forgiveness is any help to you, but I hope so, none the less because I forgive you as much for my own sake as yours, to put a final settlement to everything that happened between us and to cancel it as though it had never been.

Nina touched her elbow. The cortege of mourners was entering. Four professional bearers carried the coffin, for Roger had cheerfully waived his claim—a decision which Mr. Simcox applauded because he loathed to see the symmetry of his funerals spoiled by some stumpy relative who insisted on butting in among his dignified six-foot mutes. "I hate to see a client go to his rest lop-sided," he used to say.

So Roger followed with his sister at the head of the double file. Delia's preconceived picture of all Marshalls was modeled on James. She was surprised and slightly disappointed when, instead of a train of swashbucklers, she saw a little pink baldish man, who reminded her of some small cony, and a sour-looking spinster with bottle-shaped shoulders.

Behind them a young girl was walking alone. She held her head bowed forward, almost touching the lapels of her coat so that her face was only visible in profile. Dark, elastic, bell-shaped, the fringe of her hair escaped from under her black felt hat. Very sweet, thought Delia, but very country-mouse: a decent dressmaker would soon make you too proud of yourself to wander along in that listless, sloppy manner. Then it struck her that perhaps the circumstances made it unfair to criticize a person for her dejected appearance.

Nina Hassett, however, seemed to have been thinking in much the same way.

"I say," she muttered, "poor Olive looks positively *filleted*, don't you think?"

Possibly Olive caught some faint echo of her friend's voice. She hesitated and glanced round. She looked quite different in full-face.

Delia saw it at once. She had not used her mirror these many years for nothing. Even so, she might have been able to pretend that she was deceiving herself but for the gasp of confirmation at her side.

"My God!" said Nina. "Now I understand why I've felt the whole time that I knew you. You might be her . . . elder sister."

That was what Miss Hassett called tact.

"I'm going out," said Delia, scarcely able to control her voice even in a whisper. The modest lipstick on her mouth glared out against the pallor of her bloodless cheeks.

She rose uncertainly to her feet. Immediately the rest of the congregation did likewise. They might have been acting in preconcerted mockery of her distress.

Then she saw that it had become impossible to leave without showing the grossest disrespect. The chief mourners had separated into their pews, a handful of cousins bringing up the rear, and the priest was already advancing toward the coffin which lay at the altar steps, its chromium handles winking saucily in the lamplight. The service began.

"I am the resurrection and the life, saith the Lord: he that believeth in me, though he were dead, yet shall he live: and whosoever liveth and believeth in me shall never die."

Olive was standing in a curious oblique attitude, half-turned toward the pews behind her. A spasm passed over her features molding them to lines of subdued derision. Oh, God, thought Delia, that was *his* look: looking at me from my own face!

The little tubby man tapped Olive on the arm, gently recalling her attention to the ceremony. When she faced about, she seemed forthwith to revert to the weary, bewildered child who had plodded her way up the aisle. It was as if the strings controlling a marionette had suddenly been allowed to sag. From near-hatred Delia veered toward a profound pity. What sort of life must this girl have had that she should command no natural graces, no mean betwixt defiance and wretched inertia?

A black cloud was gathering on the horizon of Delia's mind. Every moment it increased in size and engulfed a little more of the hitherto serene prospect. She knew its composition. It was made up of old guilt and new responsibility.

The choir had begun to sing the 39th Psalm: "I will take heed unto my ways," they sang. And Delia's heart answered in antistrophe: "Would that I had done so in my youth!"

The singers' voices sank to a honeyed supplication.

"O spare me a little that I may recover my strength before I go hence, and be no more seen."

Olive's shoulders began to vibrate, as if shaken by heavy sobbing. Delia could not believe that such hysterical surrender to grief was natural or healthy. Though she tried not to look through biased eyes, it seemed to her incredible that the man in the coffin could have inspired a heartbroken affection.

Under cover of the second psalm Nina Hassett adopted the tactics of prison life, chanting her comments to the rhythm of the verses.

"I don't think Olive is at all well—da-da-da. She looks—da-da—awful. I hope she isn't going to—da-da—'consume away in thy displeasure.' I mean, I think she may have flu."

This struck Delia as the most intelligent suggestion which her companion had yet made. It was consistent with the majority of the signs. She did not stop to consider why she should feel so relieved at being able to attribute somebody's condition to a frequently fatal illness. If she had been asked, she could only have admitted that she was glad to find a cause so concrete and objective.

Faulkner took his place at the lectern. He read admirably, spacing and timing the words to perfection, without turning them into a vehicle for dramatic exhibitionism or a casual monologue. The most captious critic could only have complained that he was reminded of a very fine performance by the prize elocutioner of a night school.

"So when this corruption shall have put on incorruption, and this mortal shall have put on immortality . . ." As when thunder peals in the distance, the sound first made itself felt, not through the ears, but as a tremor impinging on the subconscious mind. Delia was aware of it several seconds before the notes had assumed an articulate shape: long before their emotional character was defined.

". . . Then shall be brought to pass the saying that is written, Death is swallowed up in victory. O Death, where is thy sting? O grave, where is thy victory?"

The volume swelled and the pitch rose and the whole church was filled with a kind of laughter.

Faulkner's head went up, his eyes blinked with horrified astonishment. Trying to finish the lesson with all seemly speed, he missed a line and began to stumble amidst unrelated words. The congregation stared at one another, then quite openly sought the cause of the disturbance. Some of them even looked under their seats.

And indeed it was not easy to say where the laughter came from. It had an uncanny, homeless echo, as though it were wandering between roof and floor, seeking a mouth to sponsor it. Gorchow church had never had a reputation for peculiar acoustics.

Nina Hassett, whose wits were seldom distracted by imaginative flights, first noticed the suppressed consternation in the foremost pew.

"The little fool's got hysterics!" she said.

She had no need to whisper it. The laughter drowned ordinary conversation.

Delia looked. Olive's shoulders were once more rising and falling in those long, ambiguous, strangely mechanical shudders. They might have been under the compulsion of some forcible respiratory engine—an iron lung.

Surely it was a strange hysteria which produced mirth so apparently controlled, so purposeful. These were no wild, fitful peals breaking out through shattered barriers of the mind; they rang like calculated expressions of mockery: harsh, satirical, instinct with a brutal disillusionment which, yet, had not escaped the last vanity of seeking to convert others to its own inhuman creed. It was the laughter of a gargoyle, proselytizing for hatred and contempt of all noble inspiration. Even physically the sounds were displeasing, inasmuch as they did not belong to the natural range of the feminine voice. Only by a bizarre contortion of her vocal cords could a woman have compassed the dissonant quasi bass of the dying paroxysm.

Eva pushed Olive out of the pew and, gripping her elbow, began to march her toward the door. She kept a stiff upper lip, but the waggling of her lower jaw registered the violence of the outrage to her propriety. She was wearing an almost medieval hat, decorated with a bunch of black cherries: one of them dropped off and went bouncing down the aisle in front of her until it fell through a heat register.

Olive was still laughing. As she passed, Delia once again looked her full in the face. Her muscles, even those of her mouth, were amazingly little disturbed by the production of this unholy, cataclysmic din. A deaf lip-reader would have supposed that she was merely suffering from a mild attack of giggles. When she winked—a deliberate, sardonic wink—Delia had no doubt for whom the gesture was intended. But Nina Hassett, being in the direct line, arrogated the message to herself.

"Olive wants me," she announced in a stage whisper.

"Why?" said Delia.

"I can tell. At school we always used to wink at each other when either of us needed help. Of course, it was usually her."

Small, perky, superbly self-assured, she bounced out of the pew, thoroughly enjoying her role of devoted friend. Delia thought: This is my chance, too: people are so stunned that I could go out in a series of somersaults without attracting much attention. But whether the moment had been favorable or not, she would have followed Olive.

She saw Roger looking over his shoulder toward the door. His face was a ghastly color, the gray-white of sifted ashes. It was not the face of a man embarrassed by being left to brazen out the aftermath of a scene, nor of one suddenly alarmed. It was the taut mask of Cassandra watching her long-anticipated fears translate themselves into reality. He knows something, thought Delia: it's my right, it's my duty, to share his knowledge.

The service had been temporarily suspended. Faulkner still stood at the lectern, his eyes downcast, his hands twitching at the hem of his surplice, like some hermit refusing to notice the challenges of a visiting fiend. Olive and Eva had taken an unconscionably long time to reach the door. Olive's gait was the only thing in her conduct which might have been judged seemly to a funeral. She did not forcibly hang back, she simply refused to respond to the pressure of Eva's hand.

All the time she continued to laugh without the slightest appearance of effort, fatigue, or shame. The congregation reacted according to type. The county followed its immemorial habit of ignoring the "unnecessary" and began to read the Thirty-Nine Articles with great absorption: the medical delegates scarcely attempted to conceal their professional interest in such an extraordinary hysterical typhoon. Several of them, however, began to fidget uneasily, as men of science will when they notice something imperfectly consistent with their own laws.

So soon as Olive crossed the threshold separating the body of the church from the roofed porch, silence fell. She did not laugh any more. This instantaneous abatement gave the ear no time to adjust itself. The harsh peals still rang through the brain with undiminished violence. There could have been nobody present in the church but was instinctively prepared for a gradual recession of the sounds and a slow dissipation of their volume in the open air.

Delia and Nina Hassett made a so much brisker exit that, by

the time they emerged, the other pair were only a few yards down the churchyard path. There was nobody outside the gates, for the weather had driven off that curious fringe of onlookers which likes to see a hearse arrive, but will not endure the half-hour prohibition on smoking and spitting which attendance at the grave involves.

Cloud-shapes of a light, evasive gray flitted across the sky, now interlocked, now seceding like the petals in a ragged potpourri. From their trailing, tasseled edges dropped flurries of crisp, starry flakes. It was good snow, the kind that lies, but it fell too thin to shut out the pitiless heaven or the bleak, lunar landscape. The air was harsh with seventeen days of unremitting, cumulative frost. The temperature had sunk so low that metal was sticky to the bare fingers.

Eva was talking in a furious undertone. From the sharp sawlike movements of her arm on Olive's elbow it was obvious that she could scarcely restrain herself from giving the culprit a good shaking.

Nina ran forward, buttoning up her gloves.

"Olive," she said, "you poor child, you were awful! Worse than I was, that time Miss Harris fell off her bicycle and broke her leg. . . . Olive, what's the matter?"

"I wish somebody could tell me," cut in Eva bitterly. "I can understand money making people too big for their boots, but not why it should make them behave like maniacs!"

"Olive," Nina repeated, "you're looking through me as though I were a ghost."

Suddenly Olive's face broke into a charming, shy smile. She walked straight past her friend and up to Delia.

"Good afternoon," she said, speaking as if to a slight but valued acquaintance; "I'm so glad you've arrived."

"Who's this?" said Eva. Then, without waiting for an answer: "Madam, if you've been sent by one of the local papers to report my brother's funeral, I must ask you, out of regard for our feelings, not to mention the incident you've witnessed."

"But, Miss Marshall," Nina protested, "she's not a woman journalist. I mean, does she look like one? In a mink coat and perfectly sober."

"I'm sorry. But I don't think you both need have called attention to our departure by following us out."

"This is Lady Pond," persisted Nina. "We thought that Olive's hysterics would go on and that we might be useful to slap her hands and burn feathers and that kind of thing."

For a moment Eva searched her memory for some elusive link in the train of association. At last she said:

"If you want to make any inquiries about my brother's will, the proper people to approach are his solicitors in Ely."

Her tone was distinctly unpleasant: but not so unpleasant as it would have been if she had felt that she could look down on Delia as well from the social as the moral point of view.

Delia replied: "I had a letter from a Mr. Marten who said that he thought he'd identified me by my husband's name. I wrote back that I was the person mentioned in the will. But I'm afraid I did not come here for reasons that could properly be discussed through a solicitor."

"Well, you can't expect us to make any concessions beyond your strict rights. These bequests outside the family have left us with very limited resources."

Delia controlled her temper with a considerable effort. There is nothing more insulting than to be accused of demanding the charity you are about to offer.

"It was precisely your family's position that I had in mind. I have no particular wish or need to take any benefit from your brother. I came here to say that I should be quite prepared to renounce my legacy in favor of any relation who could show that he or she was inadequately provided for. Perhaps you'll forgive me for saying it, but my knowledge of James led me to suspect that he might have distributed his money in a rather capricious fashion."

"I say," interrupted Nina, "they'll all be coming out soon. It won't look too good if we're still standing here dividing up the spoils."

They moved in a body toward the gate. To her amazement Delia found that Olive had taken her arm. Miss Marshall was apparently too wrapped in the process of mental readjustment to notice this singular gesture.

If Eva had been a more intelligent woman she would not have

illustrated the maxim "Circumstances alter cases" in the form "Circumstances alter manners." She became almost uncomfortably confiding.

"Well, it's very clever of you to have thought of such a thing. As a matter of fact, dear James did not always consider the future of those on whose attention he was dependent for his comforts. You probably know what these scientists are! At any rate, I feel that you and I might have a private chat about the subject. Perhaps you'll come back with us and have tea at the Manor?"

Delia agreed, although she had seldom met anybody who inspired her with less eagerness to abandon her rights.

"Perhaps we had better take my taxi," she said. "There are others of your family to return."

Percy disengaged himself from talk with the chauffeur of a large black Daimler hired out by the undertaker. If he had made one of his half-baked comments on their untimely departure, Delia felt that she would have slapped his face.

The two older women sat on the back seat and the girls faced them. They covered the first quarter of a mile in silence, though Nina Hassett's tongue was obviously straining at the leash. Finally it broke loose.

"I mean," she said, addressing Eva, "it's positively amazing, isn't it?" When she received only a blank, uncomprehending stare, she protested: "Don't tell me you've not noticed it! Talk about two peas!"

Not since she left the church had Eva paid much attention to anything going on outside her own mind. That had been deeply occupied with two vital questions: How am I going to face people after the scene in church? How am I going to get some more money? Nina interrupted her on the point of concluding that the answer to the first was inherent in a successful solution of the second. With another £4,000 in her account she would be fortified to face the whole world.

But when she looked up, she immediately found herself confronted with a horrible choice between her pocket and her propriety. There was the woman whose goodwill she must court, blandly sitting opposite to the evidence of her own scarlet sin.

Eva, though prone to take the lowest view of human conduct,

had little deductive imagination, even in the matter of scandal. Once she scented something discreditable, she could be trusted to ferret it out down to the smallest detail, but she was slow to pick up fundamental clues.

She could clearly recollect the occasion, just after the war, when she and Roger had lunched with James. She had known comparatively little of him in those days, and his suggestion that the family should return united to the home of their childhood had seemed quite attractive. She remembered, too, how, leaving early, he had stood for a moment by the table looking down on them with a peculiar smile.

"By the way, my adopted daughter will be sharing our roof. She should cheer our withered age, eh, Eva?"

Even if he had given them the chance they would not have dared to press him with questions. Of course, she and Roger had discussed the matter at length. In the glorious relief of the Armistice charitable thoughts flew about like butterflies, and it had not seemed unreasonable to suppose that James, softened by age but still a confirmed bachelor, was striking a compromise which would give him the interest of parenthood without the inconvenience of marriage. As Eva herself had pointed out: "It's not for us to complain. Supposing he had decided to find a wife, there would be no place for us at the Manor." Roger had not said much: but then he seldom did.

And Olive, a little less than a year old, had duly appeared. With the lapse of time it became increasingly difficult to go into her antecedents. Eva quite genuinely believed that James had probably walked into Dr. Barnardo's Homes, or the equivalent, and said, "I want a child." Why he should have done anything so unlike himself, she did not seriously speculate. Possibly it was a whim, possibly it had occurred to him as an amusing way of disconcerting his relations. Unconsciously Eva had confirmed herself in her acceptance of the official version by her habit, in moments of temper, of muttering about ingratitude, foundlings, and the dangers of an unknown heredity.

Even now an aggrieved feeling was rising in her heart. To show displeasure with Lady Pond would have been tactless and unsafe: with Olive completely illogical. Nevertheless, she was secretly as angry with one as the other. Delia's attitude seemed to her the zenith of shamelessness. And as for Olive . . . sitting staring at the woman with that look of schoolgirl devotion . . . almost as though she *knew*. Suddenly Eva wondered what, if anything, Olive did know or assume or guess. Sly, she thought, I've often felt that girl was sly. In the muddled chaos of her mind she counted it as part of Olive's slyness that she should have deceitfully suppressed all paternal characteristics. Everything was the mother's. The small-boned face, the pointed chin, the black, liquescent eyes—they all combined in a striking picture of unilateral heredity. Yet it was possible at first glance to miss the likeness—not on account of any structural variation between the two faces, but because they were attuned to such widely different expressions. Even when one had made allowance for the hardening, strengthening effect of years, it was quite obvious that Olive would never achieve the older woman's calm, balanced resolution. There was the same difference between them as there is between a millpond which drives a wheel and a little ornamental lake.

Though, thought Eva, it seems scarcely appropriate to dwell on the meekness and ineffectuality of somebody who has lately shown herself to be capable of the most ruthless, inconsiderate and cynical conduct. Thereby she impliedly recognized for the first time a distinction between the natural and the counterfeit Olive.

Indeed, her reflections brought to Eva only a single, rather venomous scrap of consolation. How furious it must have made James, with his lust for power, to find that he had failed to impose on his child a single physical sign of his share in her creation! He must have felt no better than a cuckold husband.

"Yes," she said, "I can see what you mean, my dear Nina. These likenesses crop up all over the place, and they can be most embarrassing."

Nina tittered.

Dusk was gathering as they drove up to the front door. Inside the lounge tea things had been laid, and the firelight flickered over the hanging kettle and the heavy silver tray, relics of Orsett Marshall's solid Victorian opulence.

Of the four, Olive alone seemed to find her company entirely congenial: perhaps because she continued to treat the party as a tête-à-tête between Delia and herself. She ventured few original remarks, but she was keyed to a mute expectancy, an eagerness for someone else to take the initiative so that she might respond. Presently, under this subtle coercion, Delia found herself monopolized and caught up in a duologue which she felt to be both unwise and impolite. Yet a kind of uneasy curiosity forbade her to break free. Underneath the exchange of smiling trivialities, she felt that she was being subjected to a wordless appeal. Faint, elusive, borne by the channels of telepathy, came the cry for help in great distress. Then with sudden impatience she rebuked herself: Good God, if I carry on in this way I shall become like those idiotic women who go round telling everybody that they're a mass of psychic intuition, and they "sense" things, and they simply "knew" when one of their friends was killed a thousand miles away.

It took a great deal to offend Nina Hassett, but Olive had almost managed it. Their friendship dated from their schooldays and was founded on complementary qualities. Nina was an inveterate gossip; Olive, an ideal repository for confidences, inasmuch as she was always interested enough to take them in, but never sufficiently so to indulge in dangerous repetition. Only a person of plastic temperament could possibly have shown an adequate response to each one of Nina's endless series of enthusiasms. At one time and another Olive had listened sympathetically to the praise of Dramatic Art, Social Work, Theosophy, and Anglo-Israel. Nina had quite naturally considered her as fair target for the new panacea—communism. Consequently it was more than a little irritating to find that her faithful audience had suddenly branched out into an independent, exclusive preoccupation. She felt that Olive had allowed herself to be seduced by the brilliance of a rapid, evanescent meteor. It had never before occurred to her that Olive was capable of the positive preference involved in disloyalty.

"Olive thinks she's found a soul affinity," she said acidly. "I'm sure Lady Pond doesn't like being gooped at."

Just then Roger came in. He accepted Delia with the air of a man who is past being surprised at anything.

"The Wrights and Laura said they wouldn't come back to tea, after all. I didn't press them."

"A very good thing," agreed Eva. "I could hardly have brought myself to entertain them."

"Now, now, there's no need to take it too hardly, just because Olive happens to have a fit of hysterics at an inappropriate moment."

"It certainly doesn't worry the person most concerned."

He glanced quickly at Olive, whose face now radiated a gentle contentment, very like the expression of a good placid little cat which has come in out of the storm and found a warm spot beside the hearth. The sight wrung his heart.

"Tea?" asked Eva.

Roger shook his head. He liked tea and seldom refused it, unless he had recently happened to read something about the disastrous effects of tannin on the stomach. This time he had a different reason. His nerves were in such a state that he could not trust himself to keep the cup on its saucer.

Nina suddenly announced that the last train would be leaving Haines for Ely in half an hour.

"I can easily walk it," she added meaningly.

Delia got up, but before she could say anything Eva had intervened.

"Lady Pond has come all this way to talk about an important business matter. It would be a pity if she had to go off without saying a word."

"Oh?" said Roger rather blankly.

"Yes," pursued Eva with some firmness, "she wants to discuss the position under James's will."

In her experience people were liable to repent of their generous impulses, and, much as she disapproved of Delia, she did not intend to let her out of the house before some arrangement had been reached.

A kind of slow, speculative light was kindling behind Roger's pince-nez.

"Lady Pond," he said abruptly, "will you let me speak to you for a moment in private?"

"Certainly," said Delia, "if your sister will excuse us."

Eva's jaw wobbled in a manner which might have been taken to signify assent. For a moment she had an absurd fear lest Roger was trying to steal a march on her and cash in on the fairy godmother. Delia was inclined to doubt whether anybody whom she had met within the past three hours was completely sane. Not that she much blamed them, for they seemed to exist amid a tangled conspiracy of shadows.

As soon as he had closed the door Roger spoke in desperate, urgent tones.

"Madam," he said. "I want to ask you a question which you may either fail to understand or think grossly impertinent. Have you any interest in Olive?"

In the secret darkness of the hall Delia heard herself levelly replying:

"I have every reason to suppose that I am her mother."

"But do you feel any obligation toward her?"

"You may well ask," said Delia. "You probably take a low view of a woman who disregards her child for twenty years, but I have never even known that she was alive; still less where to find her."

"I'm sure that there's no cause for reproaches about the past. It is now that the test will come."

"What do you mean?"

"I believe," he said, "that you have appeared at the moment in Olive's life when she most needs assistance."

"Mr. Marshall," said Delia, "what *is* wrong?"

"If I were merely to tell you what I thought without explanation, you would laugh in my face."

"Is—is she losing her mind?"

"I suppose you might put it that way—unless you draw a distinction between the mind and the soul."

"But what can I do?"

"You can put yourself to the inconvenience of remaining twenty-four hours in this house."

"I haven't got any things," said Delia automatically. Her life had always taken her by delicate ways. In common with many other women of her class, she had no true proportion in her regard for small amenities. The process of staying was inseparable in her mind from trunks and hat boxes and a dressing case full of silver-stoppered bottles. If she had been seized by Chinese bandits, she would not have been much more upset by the prospect of execution than by the absence of lavatories and soap.

Roger sighed.

"I'm afraid this isn't a pleasant social invitation. I'm anxious to have the opinion of somebody unprejudiced by previous knowledge of Olive, but interested enough to observe her closely."

"But I've been talking to her for some time, and she has appeared quite normal."

"Quite exceptionally normal." Roger brought out the paradox with fierce emphasis. "I'm only afraid that you may have such a good influence on her that you will see no signs of trouble and consider that your time had been wasted."

Delia shook her head.

"I may be mystified but I can recognize sincerity when I see it, Mr. Marshall, and I know you're not frightening me for nothing. The least I can do is to stay and be grateful for the chance of canceling some little part of my debt to Olive."

So dark was it that Delia could only just see Roger incline his head in acknowledgment. With bent neck he was no taller than herself. She felt a sudden affectionate admiration for this little retiring man who staggered on so valiantly under a burden of obscure responsibility. Even if his troubles were nine-tenths imaginary, he deserved credit for the manner in which he had braced an obviously reluctant nature to meet them.

As they were re-entering the lounge he said rather pathetically: "You know, Lady Pond, I don't usually behave like this. You must think that I have no regard for propriety."

Delia saw again in her mind's eye the little cony: it had come from its burrow into the open, because the shadow of a hawk's wing lay dark over a young creature of its own breed.

Nina Hassett took the taxi back alone. She had more room to move, but less scope to express herself. She was very peeved. Who had discovered Lady Pond, anyhow? Who had entertained her and interested her in these Marshalls? It was sheer snobbery and robbery to have grabbed her in that ridiculous way. "Bourgeois," said Nina aloud in venomous tones. She repeated the word several times with greater conviction of hatred than she had ever been able to muster since first she saw the Red Light. Finally she said it so loudly that Percy turned round from the wheel and tapped on the glass partition and favored her with one of his choicest leers.

CHAPTER SIX

ROGER had been talking for nearly three-quarters of an hour. As he stopped, the door opened and the maid Dora came in. Her entry was so exactly timed that he could not help wondering whether she had been at the keyhole.

"Please, m'm. I've locked up the back. Will you be wanting me again?"

Eva looked at the clock and dismissed her. It was half past eleven. Their conference had been delayed until it could reasonably be suggested to Olive, without exciting her suspicion, that she should go to bed.

There was a heavy silence.

"Well," said Roger, at length, "is this a polite way of telling me that I'm the person whose condition wants looking into?"

Faulkner took the dead pipe out of his mouth.

"Personally I believe every word you say. I saw the operation on that child."

"By the way, how is it?" asked Roger.

"On the road to recovery. They got Mailey in. At first he wouldn't believe that it was the work of an unskilled person. He said that, in a young child, the chances against anyone but an expert making a correct incision were thousands to one. He had a great admiration for Olive's pluck. He said he was going to write to some medical journal about the case."

"Nobody tells me anything," said Eva. "Why didn't I hear about this when it happened?"

"I didn't want to worry you," said Roger lamely.

"And then this business of finding the girl in James's room doing some sort of nasty ventriloquy and scaring your wits out . . . !"

"Miss Marshall," said Delia, "you sound as though you thought it was all a horrible practical joke on the part of Olive."

"I wasn't aware that I'd expressed any view," said Eva. In her heart she added: Why don't you give us our money and go away—and take your child of sin, if you want to?

"That's exactly the trouble," said Roger wearily. "Nobody seems to dare to express a definite view. After all, there can be no remedy without diagnosis."

Faulkner said gently: "You haven't told us what you think yourself. It looks as though everything were being left to you, but, the fact remains, you're the person who has had the best opportunity of forming a conclusion."

"Oh, very well," said Roger. "Between these four walls and without prejudice to my reputation for sanity, I think that Olive is possessed."

"By what?" said Eva unsympathetically.

"By some survival of the personality of her . . ."

He stopped short.

"Her father," said Delia quietly.

"I suppose," continued Roger, "that if you want to go into refinements of the supernatural, you can contend that the force at work is not the same entity as James, but some wandering influence of evil which chooses to attack in his guise."

"What I want to know," said Eva, "is whether we are in twentieth century England or in superstitious, heathen Rome!"

"There is nothing essentially heathen in the idea of demoniac possession," said Faulkner. "Until comparatively recent days the Christian Church would probably have considered you a heretic if you had denied its occurrence. A deacon, for instance, was primarily invested with the power of casting out devils."

"Yes," said Eva, "but surely the devils were just diseases which people didn't understand?"

"Epilepsy and depressive mania? Possibly. That is the comforting modern theory. But if you were to examine the innumerable cases cited by both pagan and Christian writers, you would either have to assume that there had been gross exaggeration or else that the illnesses in question were formerly far more terrible and uncanny things than they are today."

"Faulkner's an authority on Early Christian literature," Roger explained to Delia in parenthesis.

"I dare say he is," said Eva. "But does he, or does he not, as a priest of the Church of England, solemnly assure me that it is possible for the spirit of a dead man to enter into another person's body?"

"My dear Miss Marshall," said Faulkner, "you sound as though you were on the point of reporting me to my bishop! As a priest of the Church of England, I naturally hedge. I'll simply say that, in my official capacity, I would exhaust all other explanations before I believed such a thing."

"And what," pursued Eva with comical intensity, "is James doing ... well, loose, at this time? Oughtn't he to be safely in—in one place or the other?"

"Heaven or hell? I suppose he should, but our Protestant eschatology is very hazy. We tend to pass quickly over the uncomfortable gap between death and the universal resurrection. Unfortunately, Miss Marshall, we have no purgatory to keep your brother in his place."

"Well," said Eva, "you sound very cynical about it. Just as if it were all a game, and you couldn't be bothered to look up the rules."

Faulkner favored her with a beautiful, pathetic spaniel look from his brown eyes. It completely melted most fractious women: they thought it was so spiritual; as a matter of fact, it came over his face whenever he met with stupidity so appalling that he felt the hopelessness of argument.

Roger said: "You've spoken of exhausting all other explanations. What others do you suggest?"

"I merely know that psychotherapists are only just beginning to expose the enormous range of purely subjective phenomena."

"That theory was put up to me several days ago," said Roger dryly. "In my view the only thing it has to commend it is a certain pseudo-scientific ring. It involves discarding a coherent, though improbable, explanation in favor of the mere nebulous supposition that another cause might exist elsewhere if we only knew how to look for it."

"I'm sure that's the sort of argument which would sound very well in a law court," said Eva sarcastically.

"It's a pity we can't discuss this terribly urgent matter without quarreling," Roger replied.

"Or appearing to treat it as an academic problem," said Faulkner, tactfully diverting censure to himself. "I know the unfortunate effect my own manner often produces. But I don't think there's any real doubt that at heart we're all extremely concerned."

Roger turned to Delia. "What do you think, Lady Pond?"

"In any matter where James was concerned," said Delia, "I should expect the worst."

By force of contrast, the laconic indictment was utterly damning. Drawn up from a secret, inner well of suffering, it floated stark and factual on the calm surface of her self-possession.

"I don't think that's a suitable remark to make about a dead person, whatever his failings," said Eva.

On the occasions when she said something of whose hypocrisy even she herself was conscious, her voice took on a peculiar bleating note, as if the ninety and nine Biblical sheep were trying to lament the one that had gone astray, while busily consuming its ration of green fodder.

"I'm not venting a private feud," said Delia sadly. "Nor even a personal idiosyncrasy of judgment. Do you remember the Annamese servant that was attached to James in the last war? He was a nice, silent, little yellow man. I always thought of him as 'inscrutable' and 'sphinxlike'—the things that Orientals are popularly supposed to be. Until once when I was waiting alone in James's flat, and he came up to me and said in his funny, hissing French: 'Lui, il est méchant, méchant. Même l'herbe meurt en dessous de ses pieds.'"

Roger nodded. "Everything withered under James's touch—except, for some curious reason, the human body. The longer you live with most people the more you appreciate their redeeming qualities. With James, the progress was reversed toward absolute disillusionment."

"Nobody would think," said Eva, "that three of us had managed to endure association with this monster, for various periods, and in various degrees of intimacy."

"I saw comparatively little of him," said Faulkner. "He never concealed his dislike for me. In fact, he showed it in very clever and malicious ways. All the same I could not escape a feeling of fascination in his company. He was—well—exciting."

"He had talent—genius almost—and even greater personal courage," said Delia. "I always laugh to myself when I hear it said that bullies are invariably cowards and without sensibility."

"Neither of the qualities you mention makes it less shocking that he should be in control of a young girl's mind," said Roger.

Delia asked: "Had he a great influence on Olive while he was alive?"

"No," Roger admitted doubtfully. "At least I think not. He didn't appear to bother. Certainly she wasn't given to imitating his manner or his tricks of speech."

"Ah," said Delia, "it was never James's way to exert himself on other people's account until they could be of immediate use to him. Then he could make the most surprising captures in a very short time."

Eva began to gather up her work and pack it away in a round wicker basket. She seldom moved without her knitting, but the articles which she was making progressed slowly, remaining for weeks in an amorphous state, looking like pieces of stewed tripe.

"We've let the fire die down," she said, "and I'm not going to sit here freezing any longer. I expect Lady Pond is tired too."

Delia glanced at Roger and Faulkner and saw that they showed no signs of moving.

"I think," she said, "I'll stay a little longer. There are still some points . . ."

"Oh, very well. You know your room. I hope you find everything there that you want." She reserved her parting shot ostensibly for Roger. "Don't sit up too late, or you'll be saying a lot more things that you'll regret in the cold light of tomorrow morning."

Roger closed the door behind her and returned to his place, shaking his head.

"I'm afraid my sister is not very open to new conceptions," he said. "She doesn't rate my theory any higher than the fantasy of Dracula."

"I don't believe she has any definite opinion," said Delia. "And she doesn't want to be compelled to form one. I could tell that she was deliberately shutting her mind. So long as she can pretend that this is no more than a ridiculous fuss about a neurotic girl she doesn't feel lost or out of her own depth. I hope you don't think I'm being impertinent?"

"No," said Roger, "I think you're being very accurate. Though God knows why Eva, who really hated James—and with good cause—should affect to be outraged by a few mild truths!"

"Ah," said Delia with a faint smile, which made her face look for a moment almost Japanese, "but he's dead, you see. Women have a great sense of the fitness of things."

Roger pondered over this. It was a relief to him to be able to relax his mind on the sidetrack of a perfectly harmless generalization.

"Have you thought of getting Olive out of this place for a while?" asked Faulkner.

"Eh?" said Roger. "Yes, of course. In fact, I'm in favor of it, with one or two reservations."

"Whatever theory you adopt, there'd probably be considerable advantages in a change of scene."

"Change to where? Somebody must keep a close eye on her."

"Well, for instance . . . weren't there some cousins from London at the funeral?"

"Laura's family. One of the daughters is just getting married. In any case they're not the kind of people with whom Olive would be very happy. They live in a kind of competitive social whirl, always trying to get into range of the *Sketch* photographer. I shouldn't like to have the task of explaining to Laura why Olive needed her care and hospitality. She'd think she was being used as deputy for a mental home. You know how suspicious people are of the words 'breakdown' or 'eccentric.'"

"Well," said Faulkner, "well . . . if relatives are out of the question, what about Miss Hassett?"

"Same difficulty. You could only tell the colonel and his wife a pack of half-truths. Supposing Olive had an outburst in their house! It wouldn't be fair to them, and it would damn her throughout the neighborhood. Besides, would Ely be, so to speak, outside the radius of the influence?"

"Come to that," said Faulkner, "I don't see why it should have any spatial limits at all."

"Except that in tales and legends of the supernatural it is almost always assumed that the power of the spirit is restricted to the locality of death, and particularly burial."

Delia nodded. "Even the living can express themselves more freely in their own familiar place."

Roger said: "It's up to us to find a suitable refuge."

Both men with one impulse turned to Delia. When she became conscious of their regard, she said, with something like petulance:

"My dear men, be reasonable! I'm supposed to be a respectable, married woman. You wouldn't seriously suggest that I should import Olive into my own home, to share it with a husband completely ignorant of her existence, and certainly not elastic in his moral views, two daughters who're quite old enough to take notice, and a lot of inquisitive servants? You surely recognize the difference between accepting the consequences of folly and flaunting them like an Oxford Grouper!"

"H'm," said Roger, "quite! I must admit I had not properly considered . . ."

"If you want to know," continued Delia, "Olive was not even born out of wedlock—by somebody other than her father: which scarcely improves the situation."

Roger felt that this was the point at which he might well say something soothing and complimentary about Lady Pond's frank co-operation in circumstances which must cause her considerable pain. He began to frame the rounded phrases, trying to make them sound neither patronizing nor reminiscent of the kind of political speech in which somebody explores every avenue.

Then came a loud scream from the upper part of the house.

For a moment they were all paralyzed by the shock. Sudden alarm bears less hardly on the completely unprepared than on those who are steeled to expect trouble, but not so soon, not yet.

"Eva," said Roger, answering the others' unspoken question. "We ought never to have let her go upstairs alone."

He made for the door.

They followed one another up the stairs. On the second landing Roger was panting from the unaccustomed speed of their ascent. As they paused to listen again, he muttered jerkily:

"Eva was only safe with James alive, because he wouldn't risk his neck for her. . . . Now he's got a free hand. I shall never forgive myself. . . ."

A hinge creaked loudly on the floor above.

"Is that you, Roger?" said Eva's voice.

It was unsteady and quavering, but it obviously did not come from a throat which had been cut or wrung.

"What's wrong?" they chorused.

Charging forward, Roger caught his foot on one of the stair rods, blundered into the wall and dislodged Hope from her sustaining nails. The picture fell on one corner and began to bounce downstairs, shedding fragments of glass with every impact.

"There's no need to smash the house up," said Eva. Then: "I think she's had a fit. I can't revive her."

"Does she mean Olive?" said Delia.

"Who do you think, you fool!" snapped Eva hysterically. "The cat?"

Eva was leaning against the angle of the balustrade. The pins had fallen out of her hair on one side, and long gray strands were escaping down her cheek. Directly behind her the door of Olive's room swung gently to and fro, creaking in the slight draft.

"In there?" said Faulkner.

Without waiting for an answer he pushed past Roger and vanished into the room.

The white nursery furniture, decorated with little floral sprays, had never been changed. Some of the paint had peeled off, but there still remained enough to catch the light and reflect it with a cool, even brilliance. It was a reassuring room: in it a child would have felt as secure by the glimmer of a night light as in open day.

There were fifty-four elephants on the mantelpiece: bronze, wood, ivory, and two rather inferior pieces of jade. Olive had begun to collect them at ten and she had been remarkably faithful to her choice, never going astray after any other animal or even postage stamps. She was still attached to her elephants and occasionally added to their number.

Olive lay on her back halfway between her bed and the dressing table. Her frock was crumpled and rucked above her knees. Every muscle of her body seemed to be relaxed in profound unconsciousness. But for her heavy breathing and the red flush which suffused her face and neck, she might have flung herself down in a stupor of exhaustion.

Faulkner was kneeling by her, trying to find her heart.

Eva's invincible propriety gave her a twinge.

"There's no necessity, Mr. Faulkner. It's going. I saw to that myself."

Faulkner paid no attention. Gently he lifted one of Olive's eyelids. She did not stir, but the surrounding muscles offered that slight resistance which is absent in the deepest anesthesia. The pupil beneath was faintly bloodshot. When he straightened himself up, he said:

"I can't make this out. I hope to heaven it's not some form of stroke."

"I suppose," said Delia hesitantly, "that the flu doesn't ever start this way?"

"It might make you faint. But I'm sure she hasn't just fainted."

Meanwhile, from sheer distaste at his own helplessness, Roger was allowing his glance to wander round the room. On the third circuit it was suddenly arrested by something which lay glittering beside the bedstead, half concealed by the trailing valance. He stepped forward and picked it up. It was a crystal goblet about six inches tall, carved with an unusual design of depressed bands intersecting between raised facets. James had brought it back from India. It was supposed to be valuable. Roger put it automatically to his nose.

"It's all right," he said to Faulkner, almost brusquely.

So soon as she saw the little vessel, two expressions chased each other across Eva's face: first complete astonishment, then nauseated comprehension.

"The d-disgusting little . . ." she began.

Roger handed the glass to Faulkner, pointing to a few drops which clung and slid about the bottom. He turned to Eva.

"Now," he said, "are you still skeptical?"

"She may have thought she'd try what it tasted like," said Eva, fencing weakly with a growing conviction.

"You know perfectly well she's always loathed even the smell of the stuff. And what about her choice of cups?"

Faulkner handed back the goblet.

"Of course, you're quite right," he said. "When one knows what to look for, one can smell it on her lips."

"I wish you wouldn't go on exchanging cryptic phrases like a pair of detectives in a thriller," said Delia. "I don't know what you've discovered."

Roger replied tersely:

"James was in the habit of sitting up to all hours of the morning. Shortly after midnight he invariably went downstairs and helped himself to a nightcap of whisky, which he brought back, either to his room or the laboratory, in this glass. He was not a continual drinker, or in any sense an alcoholic, but he had an amazing head for liquor, and at regular intervals he swallowed doses of it that would have stupefied any ordinary grown man. His measure was always the full capacity of this glass and he took it neat."

Only its serious corroborative implications prevented Delia from regarding the incident in its essentially ludicrous aspect. She could not help seeing the funny side of James's attempt to pour whisky into Olive's body on his own Gargantuan scale. Of course, he might have done it on purpose, but it seemed more probable that he had been caught out in a genuine miscalculation. Her amusement quickly changed to uneasiness as she realized that this was one of the few occasions when the culprit would not have to pay for his own excesses.

"Do you think there's any danger of alcoholic poisoning?" she asked anxiously.

Faulkner shook his head.

"Not much. Though, of course, her system's completely unused to the stuff. I'm trying to make her sick."

He was performing a series of operations on Olive which he remembered from a course of artificial respiration for the apparently drowned: on the sensible assumption that what got rid of water would probably be equally effective against other liquids. He rolled her about and worked her limbs until his face began to glisten with perspiration. Finally her eyes blinked open for a moment, and she gave a little choking cough.

"Here we are," he said. "Somebody hurry and get that basin."

You're a queer, cool fellow, thought Delia. Quite an admirable one, I'm sure—kindly without sentimentality, virtuous without priggishness. I like you. But your temperature is just a little subnormal. That equable detachment is rather disconcerting. It doesn't fit in with your ingenuous, sympathetic appearance. You look as if you would be most in your element running a boys' club in the slums and being very jolly with the younger members. In point of fact you'd probably rather be in hell. I believe the cloisters are your proper milieu; with a library full of old manuscripts in the background.

All the same, her thought went on, I bet there is a cardboard plate somewhere in your armor. If anything were to pierce it, you'd take the wound pretty hard.

Olive was very sick. The process seemed to be a mere reflex, for during it she did not show any signs of active consciousness. Afterwards she continued in her comatose state for another five minutes, then her eyes suddenly opened and her lips moved.

"Can't take it," came the thick, gruff whisper. "Years since my bloody stomach went back on me."

She relapsed.

"Well!" said Roger, breaking a long pause. "You all heard!"

"It was only a whisper," protested Eva tremulously.

"Yes, but *whose?*"

"I don't see how you can judge. James never whispered. He always roared and shouted."

She had obviously not the least faith in her increasingly puerile arguments. She was simply fighting a desperate rear-guard action to retain her comfortable skepticism in face of an encroaching dismay. Roger was sorry for her, but he could not afford to be content with anything less than an open admission. Remorselessly he pressed home his point.

"Supposing that the whisper had been amplified to the volume of ordinary speech . . . ?"

Delia grew impatient.

"That was the voice of someone whom I knew as James Marshall. Even after twenty years, I could almost swear to it."

"The interval in my case is only a few hours," said Roger dryly. "So I think I'm entitled to be equally positive."

"Oh, if it's true!" cried Eva. "How horrible! How horrible! Such things can't happen—not nowadays."

She began to sob. The last of her defenses was down. Fear swept in, more gruesome and ferocious for having been so long denied. She was in a pitiable state of mental panic.

Faulkner felt that he was called upon to administer a spiritual tonic. Unfortunately, his idea of consolation—which is certainly not everybody's—consisted in lecturing on the trouble in its general philosophic aspect.

"We live in a world," he said, "where terrible and apparently meaningless catastrophes still occur. In the physical sense that is a platitude. Everybody recognizes that he is a potential victim of high explosive or a powerful motor-car. But spiritually we are inclined to assume that the advance of civilization has put us beyond the range of capricious forces. We refer, rather patronizingly, to the 'age of miracles,' meaning the age of indiscriminate credulity. People do not sufficiently consider the implications of their own professed beliefs. If a man is an orthodox Christian he is, even today, bound by the authorities who tell him that Satan and his agents roam the earth, wantonly, and sometimes irresistibly, attacking the good for no other cause than to be revenged upon their virtue."

He stopped. Roger waited, expecting him to draw some practical inference from his principles. As the seconds ticked on, he began to suspect that Faulkner was perfectly satisfied to have stated the problem in a lucid form, without attempting a solution.

"And that's where the Church steps in to protect its children?" he suggested hopefully.

"She's beginning to get hiccoughs now," said Faulkner, observing Olive's prostrate form. "That's a very good sign. The muscles of the diaphragm are reacting."

Roger's cheeks puffed out with indignation, so that he looked like one of Queen Elizabeth's seraphim destroying the Armada.

"Haven't you any ideas beyond her immediate bodily health?"

"My dear chap," said Faulkner, much embarrassed, "anyone would think you wanted me to exorcise her!"

"I won't have any papist tricks," said Eva.

Faulkner smiled.

"Miss Marshall's quite correct. Our church has abandoned the rite of exorcism."

"We've no time to waste on sectarian distinctions," said Roger. "I know it seems ludicrous to resort to incantations, but on your own showing, Mr. Faulkner, cases may occur in which no other remedy is available."

"One can always begin by giving the doctors a trial," said Faulkner.

Roger made a gesture of despair.

"You just toy with the idea of possession, as an intellectual curio. You may accept its theoretical possibility, but in your heart you don't for an instant believe that you're confronted with it as a fact."

"At any rate, I keep an open mind on the question. Not everybody would go as far as that."

Eva was rearranging her hair in front of the mirror. Her mouth was half open in a yawn when an owl hooted just outside the window. She bit her tongue. Delia jumped, too. Owls had notorious associations. Nevertheless, she would greatly have preferred that the supernatural, if it must impinge on her life, should do so in the familiar, old-fashioned style, dressed in a white shroud and accompanied by clanking chains. An invasion of headless specters would not have been so demoralizing as these skirmishes on the borderland of the mind.

Faulkner was agreeing, without enthusiasm, that perhaps he ought to do something. He might start by having a talk with Olive and trying to find out a little more about her reactions. Would he kindly take a stronger line and invoke protection on her behalf? Well, he supposed he might pray for her, if occasion offered. In Delia's opinion, he was as likely to produce a cure by sacrificing two black kids under the full moon. She knew that he also distrusted his powers of intervention, though for a different reason. Whereas she herself was fundamentally skeptical, he was simply afraid of putting any part of his faith to so violently practical a test. He dreaded the repercussion of failure on himself.

CHAPTER SEVEN

"YOU'RE not paying the least attention," he said. "If you were, it wouldn't take you five minutes to answer a simple question."

"Ah! but my dear Dick, you don't understand, which is not your fault, because I don't think I understand myself. If I could only explain—but it would sound too silly—as though I were suffering from delusions, which I may be. Sometimes it quite frightens me, the way my memory has started going blank. Not that it was ever good, not even at school. 'The Assyrians came down like a wolf on the fold, their noses were gleaming with booze and the cold.' That was Nina. The trouble she got me into, when I recited it like that before Miss Harris. But, of course, nobody can say that a person isn't all there because she's bad at school-work. It's when it comes to forgetting, no, not just forgetting, having no idea at all what you were doing an hour ago and whether you had your bath this morning. . . . Black-out. Like that awful undergraduate in Derek's party who was so drunk, the time I went to May Week, and he kept on saying, 'She's spinning already, sister, kiss me farewell, because there's a black-out coming,' every time we turned or took a corner . . . most embarrassing, and no pleasure dancing with a man in that state. Not to mention his behavior afterwards. I was terrified in that car, all squashed up together. I would have screamed or slapped his face, only people despise a girl who makes a fuss. I don't suppose I should ever learn to cope with men. I don't know that I want to. I don't like the sort that need coping with . . . always having to push their hands away and turn your face. I like quiet ones, Dick's sort, and he's getting furious with me, though he won't show it . . . because of his cloth. What a ridiculous phrase, when it's really his ideals making him forgive everybody! But I can't help it if it takes me five minutes or ten minutes or a week to answer questions. Because I've run out of answers, or else I'm not allowed to invent them for myself. Does a person's brain ever split up and start working in separate departments? One-half receives your inquiry, dear sir, and will submit it to the proper quarter for immediate attention. . . . But by the time they've been passed up to the head office, and somebody has dictated a reply, an unavoidable delay has occurred, and if the customer has to wait, it's not my fault, it's the system's."

"Surely," he said, "there's nothing unreasonable or difficult to understand about my suggestion? You can say yes or no."

"I can't," said Olive vehemently.

"You mean you refuse to go away for a little?"

"No. I don't mean that. I mean I can't tell you whether I will or not."

"But is it so hard to make up your mind? Your family and I simply think that you're rather run down and would be better for a change. After the strain of a death in the household, it's quite usual to take a holiday."

"Oh, for heaven's sake, don't go through all that again," said Olive, on the verge of tears. She leaned forward and pressed her aching forehead against the stiff brocaded arm of the sofa. He came over to her and began to pat her gently on the back, and presently to touch the nape of her neck and the soft, springy borders of her hair.

I'm a bad liar, he thought. I do protest too much. Too much talk about a little trip for the health's sake. On the third or fourth repetition, a phrase like that excites anybody's distrust. It's the kind of ineffectual bromide which conjures up nightmares. Let her once think that she is being spied on and humored, and the normal part of her mind may easily collapse under the shock. Nothing, they say, makes lunatics so quickly as the fear of lunacy. And yet somehow this probing must be carried out. Until we discover how far, if at all, she is aware of her own misfortune, we are fighting blindfolded. With that handicap we should stand no chance, even against a tangible enemy.

With each hour which had elapsed since Roger first outlined his theory, the balance of Dick Faulkner's mind had tilted farther away from a purely supernatural explanation. He still accepted James Marshall as the causative agent: but rather as a corrupt example, whose strength and pervasion—like those of certain cancers—were only ascertainable after death, than as a demoniac intelligence, continuing to operate in defiance of established laws.

He had not come to this conclusion without a struggle, in the course of which he had had to throw overboard several long-standing beliefs. It had always seemed to him that the writings of the Early Church, considered simply as evidence, made out a strong case for admitting that in certain instances men were ravaged by creatures subordinate to the power of Evil. In his opinion the subjective explanation often raised more difficulties than it solved. Now his views had suddenly ceased to be academic: a thousand years no longer separated him from their practical application. The agent of the personal fiend had appeared on his own doorstep, clamoring to be recognized.

When it came to the point, he could not do it. He could not believe that his God, who, like himself, was a quietist, would subject human beings to a trial so terrible and apparently capricious. The value of the most acute temptation he could understand. But where was the profit or the justice in allowing the victim's soul to be undermined, depriving him of his power of resistance so that he no longer exercised any free choice between good and evil? He neither would nor could contemplate that doom for Olive.

He had too much intellectual honesty to fall back on the feeble and arbitrary compromise that a phenomenon, possible a millennium ago, might no longer be capable of occurring today. For the forces with which he was dealing were, *ex hypothesi*, timeless, undying, invariable in their characteristics. There was no middle way. His former belief had to go. It went, because, in the last resort, it had become too painful to be endured.

Olive raised her face. The corners of her eyes were whitened with the salt of half-shed tears. Her glance wandered aimlessly round the room, then came to rest on a bracket nailed against the wall, supporting an ornamental plate, of the kind which became popular during the "blue-china" craze of the eighties. Its general style showed the influence of willow pattern, but the details were the original work of some unknown Victorian designer. A stream flowed through the center of the picture between two little pavilions: in front of one a man in Japanese dress was waiting, looking over at a girl on the opposite bank; she had handed a scroll to a messenger, and he was just about to convey it across the steep, arched bridge which spanned the river.

From her childhood Olive had always been fascinated by the scene on the plate, and bewildered by the problem of its true interpretation. Why, for instance, did not one of the lovers (and they were surely lovers) cross the bridge so that they could talk together, instead of writing letters? What was the obstacle? As a small girl Olive, remembering Grandpa Orsett, had decided that the bridge was probably unsafe, and therefore the parties preferred not to risk their lives on it. But even so, it seemed as though it should have been quite simple to converse across such a narrow expanse of water. Lastly, was the messenger a man or a woman? He or she was curiously indeterminate in dress and indistinct about the face. One thing Olive had never questioned—all the actors in the drama were unhappy, they bore themselves as persons in great dejection.

And suddenly the plate gave up part of its mystery. The sequence of events which had led to the tableau remained obscure, but she understood the most important thing. She knew beyond doubt what troubled the girl-lover. She blessed the old curio that it should have come to her aid when she most needed some simple concrete representation by which to interpret herself.

"Look, Dick," she said, pointing with her finger.

"Yes?" he said. "Very nice. But what about it?"

"That's me—the girl in the blue dress by the river."

Faulkner thought that this was even worse than he had supposed. He dreaded to hear her tell him with the next breath that she was the Empress of Japan.

"What a funny notion!" he said, carefully schooling his voice to an amused unconcern. "Whatever put it into your head?"

"I don't mean that it is really me. I only want you to imagine that it is, because that's how I feel. There is only a little distance between the girl and the man in the picture, and yet they can't talk to each other directly. When the man speaks to her she doesn't answer him: she goes back into the little summerhouse which you see behind her, and she asks somebody who is hidden inside it what she must reply. Even when she has been told, she can only send word by that funny-looking messenger; she is not allowed to go near the man on the other bank, though there is nothing in the world she wants so much as to be able to cross over to his side."

She was in earnest. It was impossible to suspect her of indulging a whim for fantastic monologue.

"How do you know all this?"

"It's just come to me."

"Aren't you making up a rather elaborate story to explain quite a conventional little scene?"

"I didn't suppose you'd understand," she said almost bitterly.

"But I do. All but one thing. Who's this person in the summerhouse? The artist seems to have left him out."

Olive smiled a faint, secret smile, which curved up the corners of her mouth without any parting of her lips.

"Of course, he's not shown. But he's there. He's the most important person of all."

"What's he like?"

"Oh," said Olive, still smiling, ". . . very strong . . . but not nice to know."

Both her language and her demeanor were becoming more cheerful—almost slyly flippant, it seemed to him. Nevertheless, he was determined to pursue her weird outburst to its source in the hope that it might yield some valuable clue to her obsession.

"And the girl has to do whatever he says?"

Olive assented. She was just about to add something when the door opened and Delia came in.

"Excuse me," she said. "I'm just trying to find an envelope."

On her way out she paused in front of Olive, anxious to assure herself that all was well.

"I hope I haven't disturbed you."

Olive never even looked at her.

After a few more attempts at questioning, Faulkner regretfully concluded that Lady Pond had been wrong in her hope. Once interrupted, the trickle of communication refused to flow again. Sometimes Olive languidly evaded his queries, sometimes she received them with indifferent silence. A rather unpleasant and totally foreign self-possession was creeping over her manner. She had thrown herself back on the cushions of the sofa in a pose of studied carelessness. In other circumstances he might have lost his temper and told her not to behave like a film producer's conception of a beautiful spy.

Suddenly she sat up. "I expect you think I'm being very foolish, Dick," she said.

Never before had he heard her voice so soft, a kind of wistful purring.

"Of course, I don't. You're not quite yourself, that's all."

"Which self?" she asked.

He was momentarily taken aback. She had hit the nail so neatly on the head. He hoped that she had done so by mistake.

"I should be careful," he said, "how you indulge in introspection. Too much of it may be dangerous. It sometimes leads to . . . well . . . undesirable things."

"I suppose you mean hysteria," said Olive.

"Well, if you like to put it that way."

"I think I *am* in rather a hysterical state," she announced.

He seized eagerly on the admission, imagining that he was about to carry his point.

"I've been telling you that you needed a holiday."

"That seems to be your cure for everything."

"Surely it's worth a trial?"

She shrugged her shoulders.

"If you knew you'd got acute appendicitis, you wouldn't see much point in trying a pill."

"This is quite beyond me," he said despairingly. "A minute ago you had hysteria, now it's appendicitis."

"Silly! Appendicitis was just an example. I meant that what was a good remedy for one complaint might be useless for another."

"Well, if you can prescribe for yourself, by all means do so!"

"I shouldn't dare," she answered, suddenly sinking her voice, like a child which stops abashed on the verge of a broad hint for sweets.

Faulkner made another effort, which he promised himself would be the last one.

"When you talked about hysteria, I suppose you were in earnest. What did you mean?—that your nerves were on edge, that you might be heading for a breakdown?"

"There's more than one cause of hysteria," replied Olive evasively. But though she had produced the impasse, she apparently did not wish him to stop trying to find a way round it. She seemed equally unwilling either to give him a straight answer or to let the conversation drop.

"Dick," she said, "have you ever noticed cows?"

"Of course."

"They get very funny sometimes, don't they?"

"On the contrary, they always seem to me to behave most sensibly."

"Then you've never seen a young heifer in her second season. Don't you know why she's restless?"

"Probably wants the bull," said Faulkner.

The instant the words left his mouth he realized that he had not made a facetious wisecrack, but the very response for which she had been angling. He was deeply shocked by this revelation of violent, long-concealed desire. Yet it was contagious, it set up an answering excitement in his own body.

"But, Olive," he began, "I had no idea . . . I didn't know that you thought much about these things."

"Sometimes," said Olive, "I get so desperate that I could have a plowboy."

"You wouldn't . . . you haven't, have you?"

"No, Dick, sweet Dick. No, I haven't. I'm not really abandoned except in my thoughts—and even then, it's only with one person."

"You've got no right to talk like this."

"Didn't you drag it out of me? Didn't you pester me to tell you why I called myself hysterical? Now you've got the truth, you draw away in righteous horror."

"I'm sorry, I didn't mean that," he mumbled. "I was . . . I just wasn't expecting . . ."

"And yet only a few days ago you were asking me to marry you!"

"I still am," he answered, because he could not answer anything else.

"I wouldn't take advantage of you, Dick. You wouldn't be getting what you obviously bargained for. You wanted a nice, cool, bloodless little snowdrop, not a woman. I shouldn't be equal to the strain of living as brother and sister. And you'd be better employed reforming Magdalens. They wouldn't get any change out of *you!*"

She seemed to be almost distraught. The raillery tumbled from her lips with a grotesque eloquence. His reason, which faintly protested that neither the matter nor the manner belonged to Olive, was being swamped by a rising flood of anger. There was either great luck or great subtlety in her choice of gibes. Faulkner was far from wishing to be accounted a conqueror of women: he would have been rather flattered by a comment on his self-restraint; but he could not endure the insinuation that he was lacking in normal instincts. He had heard too many jokes on that line. The clergyman who did not know what to do on his marriage night, so he asked another clergyman. . . . The old witticism, in its many variations, trailed back to his undergraduate days. Always behind it lay the galling picture of the priest as a half-man, a skirted epicene, partially castrated by his calling. The affront was harder to endure from females: it became an intolerable slander on the lips of the woman one had chosen out of all others. A man lost his self-respect, passively listening while she cast her physical dissatisfaction in his teeth.

Faulkner took hold of Olive by the shoulders and shook her to and fro.

"You little bitch!" he said, panting. "You've brought this on yourself."

He began to kiss her roughly. He cut his lip against one of her front teeth, and the blood left smudgy imprints on her mouth, her cheeks, her throat. Presently, thawed by the warmth of her response, his cold anger melted, passing into a simple voluptuary delight. His caresses became gentler, more protracted.

He dropped his head toward her breast, so that her face was uncovered and stared out over his shoulder into the darkening room. Under the stipple of blood it was waxy pale, and it wore an expression of extraordinary composure: not the boredom of a harlot suffering her thousandth experience of commercial passion, but the speculative calm of a scientist noting the reactions of an animal subject. Slowly her eyes opened into an opaque stare, behind which lurked a faint, frosty glitter.

"Ah!" she said. "Ah! Dear Dick, do that, do that!"

2

Delia rearranged all the pens and pencils in the tray, graduating them in order of size. She lit a match and dissolved an unsightly blob on the stick of sealing wax. She had always worshiped neatness, and whenever she was upset or at a loss she resorted to tidying as others might to sedatives. The sheet of note paper before her still presented the same fashionable quarter-clothed aspect.

Dear Joseph . . .
I feel that I owe you at least an explanation why I have turned an afternoon's absence into one which has already lasted two days and is likely to last considerably longer.

She automatically addressed her husband in his own somewhat inflated diction. Indeed, it was to be doubted whether, after thirty years in the courts, he would have understood the ordinary Anglo-Saxon brevities. Unfortunately this same training had made him very quick to detect fallacies and inconsistencies amidst a three-ply mass of verbiage. Delia disliked telling any lies except the stereotyped social ones, which she regarded as a necessary form of civilized politeness. She felt the indignity of deceiving her husband almost as acutely as the difficulty of doing so with success. But it was hopeless in the circumstances even to consider telling him the truth. It would be cruelty. She visualized the words on paper—

"I have just run across an illegitimate daughter of mine down here, and as the poor girl is not at all well, I have decided to remain with her for a short while. You would scarcely believe that a mother's sense of responsibility could revive so strongly, so painfully, after a separation dating from birth."

No. However she decked out the news, Joseph would read it as a stark, impudent confession of bygone adultery. And when, as would be inevitable, it came to supplying what the lawyers called "further and better particulars . . ." She shuddered physically at the prospect. The legacy alone had put her in a sufficiently unpleasant position—as James had doubtless realized that it would. Her original motive in visiting Gorchow had been to get rid of every penny without her husband's knowledge.

And then the business of explaining why Olive required her presence!

". . . I found the girl possessed by the spirit of her late father: or the devil; we aren't quite sure which."

It became so preposterous as to verge on farce. To say that Joseph would not believe one word would be an understatement: he would not even realize that he was *meant* to believe such nonsense. He would treat it as deliberate insult to his intelligence.

Joseph was naturally opposed to the two essential elements in the story—the immoral and the fantastic. His watchwords were decency and probability. Respect for the latter was not, perhaps, surprising in a man whose achievements were built on the capacity to sift and test a mass of contradictory evidence. But one might have supposed that his work, carried on so often amidst the sewage and wreck of other people's lives, would have taught him a certain broad tolerance toward human folly. But not at all! Vice, to him, was a thing which came to light before judges, and which it was his business to denounce or minimize according to his client's interest. In its proper place he could treat it quite impersonally. But the very approach of scandal to his own hearth would send him into a paroxysm of glum, bewildered rage. What had he done to deserve such afflictions! Fortunately, up to the present, his trials had not been severe, nor had they touched him very intimately. There was that wastrel cousin whom he had had to rescue from the consequences of his unrestrained use of a checkbook—Joan, the maid, who had nearly died in the house as a result of her efforts to get rid of an unwanted baby—the occasion when Angela had been caught reading (with very little understanding) a popular work of sexual instruction. Trifles: but Joseph's reception of them did not encourage Delia to put him to any higher strain.

Suppose, she thought, I were to have been taken ill down here. Nothing unlikely in that. This flu comes on so quickly. By the law of averages our household can't escape forever.

But it wouldn't do. It would be too unfair to delude Joseph into worrying miserably about her safety. She knew that he would suffer torments of anxiety. To her he had given all the love of which he was capable. If he lacked passion, he made up for it by an unwavering, single-minded constancy. Her instinct told her that in twenty-five years of married life the bare idea of infidelity had never once crossed his mind. She was exceptionally lucky to have a man who stood so far above temptation that he had no need to resist it.

Delia was grateful to her husband—for his devotion, for Angela and Joyce, for the position and leisured existence which his industry and his razorlike brain had given her. But she did not love him. So far as she could remember she had ceased to do so within a year of their marriage. Their physical relations had never been a great success. Delia knew it, and sometimes reproached herself. In fact, she was less at fault than Joseph, whose ruthless efficiency became rather sordid when applied to love-making. He had a logical, ingenious method of shaving himself whereby he obtained excellent results and saved several seconds daily; he was quite capable of inventing a parallel system for use in bed. Delia had needed a tact and tenderness which were not in his character. She was not naturally frigid, but she suffered, in sexual matters, from the psychological repercussions of one disastrous, horrifying experiment with fire.

It was really remarkable how much damage James had caused in seventy-five years. Given equal opportunities, he would have put Genghis Khan in the shade.

A tap sounded on the door, and Dora entered.

"There's a gentleman on the phone for you, m'm," she said.

"What name did he give?"

"I didn't think to ask."

A slight frown gathered on Delia's forehead. Then she remembered that she was not in her own home and had no right to teach other people's servants their job.

As she followed Dora downstairs she reflected that, at any rate, she would not have to complete that letter. The caller could only be Joseph, to whom she had already sent a telegram. Nobody else knew her whereabouts ... unless that voracious Miss Marshall had been spurring on her solicitor to badger her guest into signing something irrevocable. Delia's lips set in a tight line. She did not intend to hand over those four thousand pounds in a hurry. They were still too valuable as a counter. Once the goose had laid its golden egg, it was likely to find a drop in the temperature of its welcome.

The telephone stood in a little cupboardlike cloakroom, opening off the hall. She picked up the receiver. The formal preliminary cough at the other end of the line confirmed her original guess. This, she thought, is going to be very, very difficult, but perhaps I shall do better extempore.

"Hallo, Joseph. So you got my wire?"

"I did, my dear."

"I hope you don't think I'm behaving very eccentrically!"

"Eh? No. But you might have given me some warning. Who are these people you've suddenly decided to stay with?"

"They're called Marshall," replied Delia evasively.

"I suppose they're connected with your organization. If that trouble with your Eastern Counties branch has come to a head, I shall be pleased to help on any legal issue."

What a man! Quite spontaneously he threw off the very lie which she had spent two ineffectual hours in trying to invent. His mind moved so rapidly that, like the owner of a powerful car, he sometimes threw dust in his own eyes.

"Things have got into rather a mess in this area," she said guardedly.

Delia belonged to a large charitable society which ran homes for destitute old women, and temporary shelters for young ones who were stranded or had nowhere to go. The society's work extended all over England and involved considerable problems of management. The governing committee, which was entirely female, included, in Delia's opinion, too many people with titles but no talent for anything except self-advertisement. She was about the only one of them who had the slightest grasp of business principles. They were quite content that she should do most of the chores, while they frisked round getting up an endless series of balls and matinees out of which the charity seldom received anything more substantial than the mention of its name on the posters. The arrangement suited Delia. She was very competent and enjoyed evolving order out of chaos.

Lately a difficult situation had arisen in the subcenter for the Eastern Counties. Its treasurer, a woman of hitherto irreproachable character, steadfastly refused to furnish any accounts. Nobody knew whether she had embezzled the funds or was merely having a fit of sulks. Since she gave her time voluntarily, the society did not like to employ the more stringent forms of investigation. Delia had been very worried, otherwise she would never have spoken about the matter to Joseph. Now she congratulated herself on the lucky reference. Whatever she might have done, the woman should go free. Delia could not have borne to jail anybody who had been so useful to her in a crisis.

"Are you managing all right without me?" she asked. "I should hate to feel you were uncomfortable."

Joseph cleared his throat again.

"The staff has not yet forgotten your excellent training."

"How are the children? Does Joyce think I'm neglecting her in her holidays?"

"Joyce," he said dryly, "appears to be quite happy and more or less self-sufficient. As for Angela . . . she went out to a cocktail party yesterday evening. I understand that her attack of nausea at breakfast this morning was not due to any serious cause!"

"The little pig! Joseph, I haven't gone away without good reason, but if you need me I'll come straight back."

"My dear Dee, you know how much averse I am to interfering with your work."

Joseph profoundly believed that everybody should have a job, paid or unpaid, by which to justify his share in the blessings of modern society. He despised people who simply lived on unearned incomes: presumably he would have liked to see them all sweating away to take the bread out of the mouths of their less fortunate contemporaries. But in his company no one dared to pursue the argument to its logical conclusion, for Joseph was not good at differentiating between intellectual disagreement and personal insult.

"Of course," she began to repeat, "if you should need me—"

He interrupted: "We seem to be at cross-purposes. I rang up to apologize for my own plans, not to complain about yours."

"What do you mean?" She could never, after all these years, entirely disabuse herself of the idea that his formal phraseology might conceal some inner irony.

"I received an invitation last night to join the McDonough Commission. We sail tomorrow."

"Oh, Joseph, how splendid!"

"I flatter myself that this will be another, and perhaps a final, step toward the bench."

There had been rioting in the British West Indies—a state of affairs which always causes shocked surprise in circles ignorant of the disgraceful conditions which prevail among the Negroes. This time an unusual amount of damage had been done to life and property. The grievances disclosed had been so serious that the government had felt bound to call in that most pretentious and long-lived of amateur detectives, the Royal Commission. Its personnel, as originally announced, had included one well-known K.C., selected because he happened also to be a sitting member of the House. Unfortunately, in the interval between appointment and sailing, the influenza had picked him off. Joseph—not without a little dignified angling—had stepped into the post which many people felt he should have occupied from the first. And he would have, too, Delia thought, if he had only been able to suffer fools with less obvious agony.

"I shall probably be away until the end of January," he pursued. "I shall miss the opening of the Easter Term, but I have made all arrangements with my clerk, and I think there will be ample compensations for any financial loss."

Those were the last words which Delia properly distinguished. The line was still clear, but a penetrating racket from somewhere in the house was confusing her ears. It was like the slaughter of a pig or a party of children left to their own devices.

Delia made him repeat his last remark twice, then gave it up. She could not concentrate on what was coming over the wire because her brain insisted on trying to locate the outside noises.

"Yes," she said at random, "yes. Very nice!"

In the lounge. Somebody frightened, somebody hurt. Somebody shouting for help!

"Joseph, Joseph, quickly! I must hang up now. No, nothing wrong. Just . . . just someone calling me. I haven't time to explain. Good-bye and God bless you. Give the children my love."

She dropped the receiver, cutting off his indignant questions. "O

God," she thought, "what is it this time? We sit and wait for each new outbreak, always expecting it, yet always taken off our guard."

The door of the lounge was flung open and Olive rushed out. She was in a state of wild disarray. Her skirt had come undone at the fastening and was wrenched round on her hips so that it hung almost back to front. A great rent in her blouse completely revealed one breast, across which ran a long bloodstained scratch. Her face was daubed with a crimson pattern. Only when they came into actual collision did she seem to realize Delia's presence.

"Keep him away!" she panted. "Don't let him touch me!"

Delia took her firmly by the shoulders.

"Now tell me what's the matter," she said in a cool, crisp voice, which was far from representing her state of mind.

"He . . . Oh, the beast, the beast! He pulled my clothes down. He tried to do the most filthy things to me. I never knew . . ."

Very slowly, still looking like a spaniel, but a spaniel conscious of gross misdoing, Dick Faulkner slunk into the hall. His face was gray-white. There was a thick coat of sweat on his forehead. He gave Delia a look of dumb, agonized appeal.

"Do you mean that he tried to rape you?" she said deliberately.

Olive nodded, choking down a sob.

"Is this true, Mr. Faulkner?"

Faulkner twice passed his tongue over his lips, but no reply would come.

"Look!" said Olive. She pointed to her lacerated breast.

"You've told your story," said Delia sharply. "I'm waiting for his."

She did not know what made her speak so sharply—except that she disliked a certain shamelessness in the victim's attitude. Olive seemed to treat the indecent state of her dress simply as a trump card, valuable for confirming her version of events.

At last Faulkner said: "I think I have behaved in a way which leaves me no right to defend myself."

"If you don't," said Delia, "this is likely to be a most disastrous matter for you."

Olive chimed in: "A clergyman! And I thought you were so good and kind. You beastly, immoral satyr!"

She began to sob again. But not quite punctually enough. In

one brief instant between the closing of her lips on that last angry word and the fresh contortion of weeping, Delia saw her face. It was not at all the face of a girl who has been brutally assaulted. It was a far worse face. In it was something akin to triumph.

Delia's nebulous suspicions crystallized into a black, malignant certainty. With a movement of surprising speed and violence she reached out and seized Olive by the wrists, jerking her hands forward and upward to the level of her own eyes. Olive's fingernails were pretty, pink, undyed: on one hand they were fastidiously clean; on the other, the nail of the index finger was soiled with red spots, and a long strand of skin had lodged against the cuticle. Delia glanced again at the scratch on Olive's breast. Then she smacked her face as hard as she could.

"You despicable little liar!" she said, too indignant to distinguish between the master and his helpless tool.

Olive had been fighting furiously to release her hands. When she saw that the game was up she ceased her struggles. A bitter philosophic amusement overspread her face, as of an old ex-convict tripped up in a promising perjury.

This time she had James's voice to perfection:

"Well, well, and what do we learn from this distressing incident? We learn that it is never too late to mend. Delia Pond exhibits signs of almost human intelligence. The maxim 'Once a bloody fool, always a bloody fool' is now discredited."

As soon as she definitely departed from her own personality, Delia's anger was stilled, chilled, replaced by a tragic pity.

"Olive," she said, "Olive, you're talking to your mother. . . . She wants to help you. . . . Mr. Faulkner, for God's sake, can't you *do* something instead of looking like a stuffed scapegoat?"

There was no need for action. Olive gave a deep, rending gasp, as though the spirit were leaving her body, forcibly breaking an exit in its anger and its haste to escape. She slumped back, and though she was still conscious, only the wall prevented her from falling. Her eyes stared blankly. Even the luster seemed to have gone out of her hair.

3

If he had remained in the garage it would have affected him very differently. Instead of self-disgust he would have felt the righteous fury of the defrauded. Talk at street corners and experiments in dark lanes would have taught him a harsh name for girls who promised and then withheld fulfillment. If he had for a moment questioned his own conduct, it would merely have been to doubt whether he had asserted his rights with enough full-blooded masculine vigor.

Or perhaps he would have scotched the whole problem by committing a justifiable rape.

Intensive education did not show to its best advantage in Dick Faulkner as he sat back in an armchair (he would not again go near the sofa), his body shivering like a seismograph in sympathy with the collapse of a cherished ideal.

Faulkner could utter the parrot cry of the modern clergy, "I flatter myself I'm as broad-minded as anyone," with more than the usual amount of truth. He *was* broad-minded about other people's sins, they hardly ever shocked him, because, in spite of his profession, he took little notice of them. He had a certain affinity with Cain—not as a homicide but as a philosopher who doubted whether he was his brother's keeper. The common reason why a man disclaims responsibility for his fellows is moral apathy. Occasionally, however, intense moral preoccupation produces the same result. Here and there a man has it in him to be a good gardener, but is too busy cultivating his own plot to concern himself with his neighbor's weeds. Dick Faulkner really cared about what he believed to be the Good Life. It was so important to him that he dared not interrupt for a moment his efforts to achieve it in himself. And since he would be satisfied with nothing short of complete success, his zeal as a reformer began at home and stayed there.

The same spirit once drove men out into the terrible Nitrian solitudes and peopled the monasteries of Europe and Asia with selfish, fanatical, heroic refugees. Faulkner, living in a less drastic age, was content with a hermitage of the mind, and canons of moderation rather than asceticism. But though the severity of the rules was relaxed, the standard of obedience was not. He would worry for days over even the most trifling lapses from his code.

The repeated doses of Early Christian propaganda which he had originally absorbed in the cause of scholarship had taught him many admirable aspirations; but they had also infected him with several of the more unbalanced obsessions of the third and fourth centuries A.D. He set an excessive price on chastity. Instead of keeping it in line with the other virtues, he had allowed it to usurp a cardinal position. The holy desert fathers, whose nights were so disturbed by the insistence of alluring female demons, had passed on to him their afflictions in the less concrete shape of a neurosis. It could not be called prudery; it did not reflect itself in his speech; it was simply a disproportionate horror of casual sexual contacts. It was only the thought of immorality in himself which so repelled him. Once again, he had a different criterion for other people. He often read divorce proceedings and newspaper accounts of a certain offense against a certain girl with mild anthropological curiosity.

At one time he had thought that he believed in celibacy. Later he had changed his mind, but not so far as to make a difference in his views on any relationship short of marriage. Toward even marriage his attitude was rather Pauline. He could not quite rid himself of the idea that it was a concession to the morally C.3.

On the whole, it was just as well that he and Olive would never now enter into a bond for which one of them had so little fundamental respect.

Delia re-entered quietly. In the moment before she switched up the light he mistook her for Olive, and started defensively to his feet.

Delia's cheeks were faintly flushed, but she took a cigarette and lit it quite coolly.

"Pull yourself together," she said.

"God knows what you think of me, but it can't be worse than I think of myself."

"My dear Mr. Faulkner, Olive didn't deceive me. By good luck I caught her out in one little detail. I didn't know I had the instincts of a stage detective!"

She gave a dry, strained, little laugh.

Faulkner shook his head.

"She wasn't just lying. What she said was half true. But she made it sound worse . . . as though I—"

"As though you'd attacked her like a wild beast instead of having merely responded to an invitation?"

"Well . . . yes. But that's no excuse."

"It was good enough for Adam. 'The woman tempted me.' "

"What's the use of a man in my position if he loses control of himself every time a girl makes a thoughtless advance to him?"

"Every time!" repeated Delia, a little scornfully. "You'll never do it again as long as you live, Mr. Faulkner."

"No," he said, "perhaps not. But you can learn a lesson too dearly. Now that I know myself, it would be mockery to go on preaching to others."

"Don't be a fool. You're the one that's really been outraged. Can't you see that you've had a very malicious trick played on you? It's not even a new one: women blackmailers have been working it in railway carriages for years." Then she added defensively: "Not that poor Olive knew what she was doing."

"That makes my behavior actually criminal. Aren't there severe penalties for taking advantage of a person whose mind . . ."

Delia interrupted: "Oh, well, if you want to wallow in it!"

She was exasperated by his paroxysm of self-abasement. One would have imagined that he had at least founded Sodom and Gomorrah! She felt that he was demanding a pity which properly belonged to Olive. And yet she sincerely wanted to help him and to repair his damaged self-respect.

"Of course," he burst out suddenly, "you mustn't think that I actually—"

"Actually what? Oh, I see. No, I quite believe you. That's partly why it's so silly to make a fuss."

"I was only saying that to reassure you about Olive. From my point of view, an . . . an indecent attempt is as bad as . . . the other thing."

Delia said: "You stand up before a congregation and regularly proclaim that all men are very sinful. Why are you so shattered when you find it's true?"

"There's a limit," he said naïvely. "Apart from religion, decent people aren't capable of doing some things. You're decent yourself. You couldn't act as I have."

"I'm a woman," said Delia, smiling in spite of herself.

"I mean you couldn't sink so low."

"If you talk much more like that I shall begin to agree that you're not fit for your work. Don't you understand that virtue isn't an inborn quality of the ordinary man or woman? It's one that has to be acquired by bitter experience. If we do right now, in most cases it's because we've done wrong in the past and learned either from our suffering or from our remorse."

"Sin in order that you may repent?" he inquired. "Rasputin was the last celebrated exponent of that doctrine. It isn't highly thought of in my church."

But Delia was not attending to him. She stood looking at her own reflection in the darkened windowpane, clenching and unclenching her hands.

"Listen," she said. "I am going to disabuse you of this idea that you're the only black object in a snow-white world. You picked me out as one of the 'decent people' who don't make disgraceful mistakes. If you'll listen to me for a little I'll tell you a story from which you can draw your own conclusions. I warn you it's not one that makes either pleasant hearing or telling, but at any rate it isn't stale. You'll be its second audience in more than twenty years."

She sat down opposite him on the sofa. Like the Wedding Guest in *The Ancient Mariner*, he wavered between fascination and a strong desire to beat his breast.

"Yes," said Delia, speaking to herself, "I think this will be good for me, too."

She paused for a moment like a bather hesitating on the brink of a cold sea. Then in a firm, brisk voice she plunged into her story.

"When I was young, in the days before the war," she said, "I was a public menace. I hope that to you, seeing me now, that statement sounds unlikely. Perhaps I should have said a public nuisance. I could learn things like a parrot, and I had a rather gratifying record at Somerville. Of course, I was under the impression that I had won my certificates and prizes by stern original thinking. I was so certain of my ability to manage my own life that I already had plans for interfering with other people's. By sheer genius I was going to reform almost everything. Quite dispassionately, you understand."

Her faint, measured irony was having a tonic effect on Faulkner. He perked up, and said:

"In fact, you followed ordinary lines of undergraduate development."

"Up to a point," said Delia. "But I'm afraid—though it didn't come out till later—that I had less than my share of youthful disinterestedness. At first I took it for granted that, after quite a brief period of probation in the outer world, I should automatically become celebrated, a national figure. But time went on and I didn't seem to be getting any nearer to the public eye. At that age a few months without tangible success are proof of a wasted lifetime. I began to notice that many persons whom, rightly or wrongly, I considered my inferiors, managed to achieve results, not by their own talent, but by clambering up on the backs of friends who were already prominent. In other words, I discovered the practice of lion-hunting—the commercial kind of hunt. I don't know whether it's better or worse than a mere snobbish passion for trophies. It comes to much the same thing in the end: one breeds the other. When I think of the way I behaved I blush. Alternately back-scratching and backbiting, according to whether I thought I had anything to gain from a person or not."

"Aren't you rather surrendering to the lure of confession?" suggested Faulkner, in almost normal tones.

"I haven't any Oxford Group principles and I'm not exaggerating. My parents were quite rich, so I had little difficulty in making contacts with well-known people. Actually I think my intended victims got more out of me than they ever gave. Still I wasn't discouraged. It was practically impossible to discourage the New Woman. Perhaps I should have said that my chosen line of self-advancement was social work. I succeeded in getting on to a lot of committees.

"Then I married. At the risk of sounding unfair to my husband, I must admit that Joseph was no corrective to my falling. He was the type of keen, resolute young man with a mapped career who sees life, almost literally, as a succession of rungs. You may know him now as a barrister. If you'd seen the ghastly, grumpy old men we entertained, just because they were senior partners in some solicitors' firm. . . .

"Soon the war came. During the first two and a half years Joseph was pressed, strongly pressed to stay at home. They wanted him in the attorney general's office. People have said things about his war record, but I know nobody has a stronger, more personal sense of civic obligation. You can see how strong it is, because, when I talk about it, I instinctively use his own phrase."

"I can see that you have a great respect for him," said Faulkner.

"You remember that when the Russians started to collapse we tried to stem the tide—rather like Mrs. Partington—by sending out bevies of technicians and advisers. I forget exactly how Joseph got himself included, but I know the reason—he couldn't stand the sight of fee checks any longer. He was away from the beginning of 'seventeen to the spring of 'nineteen. I believe he had some remarkable experiences. He seldom talks about them. Anyhow, I was left with my munitions. I had quite a high administrative post in a factory. I pity the people under me. I developed a steely glare. Under cover of an unapproachable efficiency I received ten pounds' worth of raw material and triumphantly handed out the value of a fiver in finished products. I thought mostly about the decorations I should soon receive. In case you think I'm painting myself too black, I'll add that I was also genuinely keen to make the world safe for democracy.

"I met James Marshall when we were both on leave in London. He had a terrible reputation, even then. But it was pretty heavily overlaid with recent glamour. Silly women used to talk about him as though he were a reincarnation of an Elizabethan hero-buccaneer."

"A degenerate reincarnation," said Faulkner. "That wouldn't sound silly."

"He had just performed one of his most typical and notorious feats. He had been put in charge of an advanced clearing hospital only a short distance behind the firing line. The French had given him the job because they were using a large number of colored troops—Senegalese and Moroccans—in that sector. He had great experience of African races and I suppose that was an advantage, even at a time when they were being riddled with bullets instead of tropical disease. Anyhow, the Germans made a big attack, and the line was terribly knocked about—actually broken in one place, I believe. James heard of the danger and immediately collected every man in the hospital who was still capable of walking and forcibly drove them up to the front. You can probably picture how he persuaded them to go into action. Poor devils, they only had the Germans in front, but there was James Marshall behind! They fought all night in the trenches—such of them as survived so long. He told me himself that sixty per cent died from either exposure or additional wounds. But they saved the situation until regular reinforcements could arrive. In fairness, I should say that James remained with them during the whole of their operations, showing the most reckless courage."

"I'm sure his conduct was strategically excellent," said Faulkner, "but I shouldn't have thought it was the kind that would appeal to women."

"I never said it did," agreed Delia crisply. "In fact, generally speaking, it roused less enthusiasm in England than in France, where the national logic fastened on the fact that the line had been saved, and dismissed the wretched wounded Senegalese with a commiserating shrug and 'Que voulez-vous? C'est la guerre!' I wasn't dazzled by James Marshall's heroism. What attracted me was his celebrity value. I was flattered by the attention he paid me. Though he was even then well past his youth, he had the good looks which would have enabled him to take his choice of dozens of women far prettier than myself. I've no doubt he did, but, when I think of the time he wasted on me, I can only conclude that I must have possessed some curious and uncommon attraction for him.

"I never really liked him. I remember thinking that he wanted taking down a peg or two and taught—don't laugh!—more respect for women. I determined that, since he had chosen to force his company on me, I was justified in making use of him. I don't mean I went in for crude gold digging. But I did pester him to pull strings on behalf of my munition works. He knew all the medical hierarchy, and a few words in the right quarter got me little advantages over other factories—such as apparatus and a couple of attached nurses to deal with the common cases of fume poisoning among the workers. It was effort well spent from the point of view of the national interest. And I honestly had the country at heart. It tied for first place with myself. At the back of my mind was always the realization that the better my fuses and detonators the higher my name would stand with those in power."

Faulkner interrupted: "It doesn't strike me as particularly discreditable to do public service knowing that some personal reward is likely to result from it. Otherwise there would be a violent falling off in everything, from charity subscriptions to the number of candidates for Parliament."

"It's all a matter of degree," said Delia. "There's an indefinable point at which consciousness of one's deserts turns into a cold-blooded determination to grab them at all costs. Only the individual knows when she has overstepped the dividing line."

She lit a cigarette and paused, blowing out the first cloud of smoke. With the nostrils thus distended, her delicate face hardened and she looked for a moment like the woman in her own story.

"In consideration of his services James was allowed to take me out to all the then fashionable and expensive restaurants. We used often to go to the old Piccadilly. I remember best the night when I walked out halfway through dinner. He had been talking about the war, gibing at everything I and others thought we were fighting for, proclaiming that within a decade or two we should find ourselves squaring up again to the same old futile struggle. Of course, what he said was terribly accurate, terribly far-sighted. If he had gone the right way about it, he might, even then, have convinced me against my will. But he took such obvious pleasure in his theory of the incurable baseness and stupidity of mankind that the truth of his predictions became irrelevant. I was instinctively revolted. You probably can't understand, because you must have been too young for the war to affect you. But it was a terrible thing to listen to him there, in that bright, warm room, full of ninety-six-hour-leave men—young officers with the brass shining on their Sam Browne belts and their faces either twitching with strain or empty and noble with untried courage.

"So I got up and walked out, and if I'd kept the promise I made to myself then I shouldn't be here now. But, of course, I did see him again. I'd let his dangerous fascination get a grip on me. I don't mean that I was the least in love. I just felt that there must be a next meeting, because next time I'd show him, I'd teach him, I'd bring out all those crushing answers that I'd somehow missed at our previous meeting. And next time, of course . . . well, I went away with the same feeling of inferiority. I was used to keeping up my end in any company—probably because clever people had always been kind to me. It was left for James Marshall to teach me that one can be as badly outweighed intellectually as in a boxing match. But I wouldn't give in. I was a very determined young woman. In those days I should have done well on a Burning Deck.

"I made my worst mistake when I let myself be drawn into a barefaced conspiracy to push my own interests. Being more or less indefinitely on leave from France, James managed to get himself appointed to a committee which was investigating the conditions of health among war workers. They came round to all the munition plants. When their findings were published I need hardly tell you which factory showed up to the best advantage. He must have rammed that report down his colleagues' throats by sheer force of personality. I admit I thought he had gone a bit too far—particularly as he and I had been about so much together. However, nobody noticed anything—or else I never happened to overhear any gossip. The press, always on the lookout for Gallant Little Women, gave me several write-ups which would have been fulsome if applied to Florence Nightingale. Shortly afterwards I got a decoration—which my husband thinks is still in the bank, and I know has long been in the fire.

"As far as I recollect, I showed myself decently outraged when James suggested that it was now my turn to raise the stakes and become his mistress. You may ask why I didn't seize the chance to clear out with my ill-gotten profits? I'd become disinterested in my desire to take it out of James. So long as he wanted me and I was sure of my capacity to withhold myself, I believed I should possess the whip hand.

"And yet I have never been a sadistic woman, nor one who habitually traded on sexual attraction. I can only say that this man had the extraordinary knack of reducing the morality of those that dealt with him to his own level.

"You must make allowances, too, for the prevailing spirit of those days. A lot of young wives whose husbands, like mine, were compulsorily absent for months slipped into a round of eating, drinking, and being merry. Some of them put it on patriotic grounds —the duty of giving returned heroes a good time. The vast majority started out with purely platonic intentions and a lot of innocent talk about 'fun.' But it's not easy, particularly when one's nerves are on edge, to keep a tight rein on 'fun': once it gets out of hand, it goes downhill surprisingly fast.

"So I spent the next few weeks in being baffling and mysterious toward James, allowing him to hope, but giving him no real grounds for doing so. Theoretically, I was in a very strong position, because in a crisis I could always turn round and accuse him of presuming on imaginary encouragement. All the same it wasn't long before I began to feel rather frightened. James seemed to be perfectly well aware of my little game. He let me see so. He joked about it. If you went fishing and a large, experienced salmon came cruising round your fly and then took it with a leer of cynical understanding, you'd perhaps feel a bit uneasy about your catch. You might even imagine that it was plotting to get you into a deep pool where your waders would fill with water and you would miserably drown. Not that James had anything in common with salmon—which are said to be rather stupid—except cold-bloodedness.

"But I still wouldn't be ruled by my better instinct. It needed a practical warning to make me ready to give in. Several of my own and Joseph's friends began to cut me in marked fashion. Cutting was still effective in nineteen-eighteen: nowadays the outcasts merely observe charitably that one really shouldn't be shy of wearing spectacles in middle age. Anyhow, I was worried enough to look discreetly for a reason. I found that almost everybody with any interest in the question took it for granted that I was having an affair with James. Some offered no comment, others were inclined to congratulate me on a lover of such appearance and distinction, still others solemnly catalogued the known facts about James's previous amours, and begged me to beware of homebreakers. I didn't mind about their private reactions. What worried me was the knowledge that people were pawing over my reputation, that I was losing my social status without even the satisfaction of having really broken the code. The final straw was my discovery that, without committing himself, James had used his best endeavors to confirm the rumor.

"I tried to write him a scathing letter which would leave me with all the honors of war. Unfortunately, my literary abilities fell far short of my imagination. So I tore it up and conceived the brilliant idea of a final, smashing tête-à-tête. In it I was going to explain to him exactly how far I had been from surrendering to his charms. I quite forgot that a woman doesn't bother to denounce the suitors for whom she has a genuine contempt.

"I did my denouncing all through dinner. James listened with an extraordinary humility. He only took his surprised, penitent gaze off my face to order more champagne—which I drank with an abstracted, prophetic fury. I've never been very good with alcohol, it isn't palatable to me in the majority of its forms or my moods. But when one has worked up to a certain emotional pitch one will do anything to avoid a gradual depressing fall of temperature. I must have been mildly drunk by the time we left, because I can clearly recollect giving the attendant in the cloakroom half a crown and murmuring: 'Poor James, poor James. La belle dame sans merci!' It was a pity the stuff didn't make me feel sick.

"I floated out into a taxi without inquiring its destination. However, I was a bit staggered when we pulled up near Marble Arch at the entrance to James's flat. In spite of my broad mind I still belonged to an age in which the finding of a lady's glove in a man's rooms supplied all the tensest dramatic situations. James explained that I had drawn up a curtain on the darker places of his personality, my penetrating invective had given him the first glimpse of his own nature as it appeared to other people. In my right senses I don't believe I should have swallowed his suggestion that he only needed a little more encouragement to set seriously about the process of reform. But my passion for high-principled interference was badly inflamed. I went in.

"I'm not going to dwell upon the next part of the story because I think that already we have both had an overdose of the revolting.

"I could feel my inspiration flagging. So I accepted my first brandy-and-soda. I don't know what was in it, besides the obvious ingredients. I can't even swear that anything was added. If I did, the word of a person in my admittedly hazy state wouldn't have much value. But this I do tell you—and if I wanted to preserve my good name I could do it more effectually by silence than excuses—I believe that I was deliberately given a powerful drug."

"Don't worry," said Faulkner, "I'm not skeptical. Every brute has its characteristic form of attack. Your story rings psychologically true. James was capable of worse than Tarquin."

Then he blushed, because he remembered that he also was numbered among the ravishers.

Delia went rapidly on: "It may have been something which caused real unconsciousness: or again it may merely have destroyed my sense of responsibility, together with all subsequent memory of what I did while I was in that state. In other words, I don't know whether my downfall was due to absolute or modified rape."

"Now your lip's bleeding," said Faulkner. "You've bitten right into it. Don't you think it would be a good idea to call a halt? I already know so much that I can imagine the rest."

"No," said Delia in a hard, dry voice. "I began this story for your benefit, I'm going to finish it for my own. It's doing both of us good. I left James Marshall's flat at six o'clock the next morning. I'm glad to be able to report a dry mouth and a splitting headache—the detective story signs of dope. If you ask me why I didn't go to the police, I shall probably scream."

"If you think I'm such a fool," said Faulkner, "you'd better stick to words of one syllable."

"I'm sorry. Just nerves! James was asleep when I left. I didn't wake him. Any recriminations would have been hopelessly inadequate to express my feelings. Besides, I was still in such a daze that I could hardly put a sentence together. I was just a half-thawed block of cold misery. I took to my bed for nearly a week. During that time I shut my eyes tightly every time I had to expose my body so that I might have seen it. Does that sound absurd? I was so utterly disgusted with its self-betrayal.

"Almost as soon as I had pulled myself together sufficiently to get up and go about my work, I learned—accidentally, not by inquiry—that James had gone back to France. I believe he'd only put off his return for so long in order to complete my seduction. After a while I began to take a saner, wrier view: until I discovered that

I was pregnant. I'd weathered the first shock by telling myself that this beastly affair was only an incident—something transitory and disconnected from my real life. Now I could see the shame of it stretching out indefinitely and filling the whole future. Though I'd listened to a lot of earnest talk about unmarried mothers, I wasn't the type of woman who knew complaisant doctors or possessed friends that could direct her. I'd queered my own pitch in advance by the lofty, quasi-biological pose I'd adopted toward sexual errors. The people I knew could have imagined me meting out advice to sinners, but not demanding it for myself. There I was. If you're having a baby, you become terribly conscious of the advance of time. At the end of a few months of sickness and nervous strain your pride is pretty well dead, and you need the moral support of your marriage lines. Joseph had been away for too long to leave me with the least shred of virtuous pretension. My marriage might not have fulfilled all my first romantic expectations, but it meant a great deal to me and I was terrified by the thought of its approaching wreck.

"So I wrote to James. I told him what had happened. I suggested to him that, whatever might be our opinions of each other, this was a matter in which we both had a common interest. Of course, that wasn't true. If James had any interest at all, it was purely in observing my discomfiture. I got my reply nearly a month later, written on a half-sheet of notepaper. It said: 'Won't it be frightful if it's twins!'

"That finally broke me. I couldn't go on alone, unsupported, any longer. Fortunately, I chose to unburden myself to a very sane, broad-minded woman who'd had plenty of experience. She was much older than I and I didn't know her particularly well. I can't think why she took such pains to help me. I've never ceased to be grateful to her. She was the only other person to hear what I'm telling you tonight. She's dead now and in heaven, if there is such a place. She made me see that there was no more use in wringing my hands over the disgrace of my position: I was in a jam and my best course was to concentrate on getting out of it with the least possible damage to myself and the people I cared about. She made arrangements for me to retire to North Wales and spend the last months before my child's birth in the cottage of an elderly ex-nurse—another nice woman, but, for some obscure reason, she was always convinced that I had been seduced by royalty or one of the more important peers, and insisted on regarding my condition as a sort of left-handed honor.

"I was still worried as to what I was going to do with the baby. I didn't want it: it was impossible for me to bring it up; on the other hand, I couldn't be completely callous. My friend tried hard to arrange for its adoption into a decent family, but the war made everything doubly difficult. It seemed as though, after all, the only solution would be to write, telling Joseph the whole truth, and begging him to divorce me quietly so that I could disappear and devote myself to the child. I'm sure he would have done as I asked; but I'm equally sure that he wouldn't have gone further and forgiven me. I don't blame him.

"I was just on the point of throwing in my hand, when, to my amazement, I received a letter from James. He simply said that he had been considering my previous information and that, although he did not for a moment admit paternity of the child, still, as an act of charity and in order to save me embarrassment, he would undertake the entire responsibility for its upbringing, on condition that it was taken from me immediately after birth and that I solemnly renounced all my rights, even to see it or discover its whereabouts in the future.

"You may think that I was very selfish to abandon my child to a man whom I knew to be quite unfit to have control of it. After the first relief, I saw it in that light, too. But I was ill and frightened and my friend—who naturally couldn't be expected to regard the offer as anything but a God-sent opportunity—persuaded me. So Olive was born, but I never saw her. (James sent down a rather bewildered medical acquaintance to attend me and enforce that part of the agreement.) I registered her under my maiden name, Father Unknown, which was probably very illegal. Much I cared!

"Three months later the war ended. Five months later my husband came home. Six months later I started my legitimate Angela."

Delia got up and poked the fire. She poked it at the end which did not need poking. Then she took another cigarette.

"So you see, Mr. Faulkner," she said, "you are not the only person with a disfigured youth. In fact, by comparison, I should say your record was scarcely even piebald."

4

She had distracted his mind from his own troubles, but she was far from having set it at rest. Faulkner went home that evening a sad and uncertain man. He had seen life in one of its unguarded moments and he did not at all like its appearance. He regretted that he knew nothing about cylinders or gear boxes or any of the other devices for stopping men from thinking.

Delia went to bed as soon after dinner as she decently could. Finding herself unable to sleep, she took some notepaper from the bureau and began to write. This was not a new departure. Since the war she had kept a full and faithful record of every day's events, however trivial. She had developed the habit through sitting up for Joseph, who worked very late: after midnight she felt the need of some mental effort to keep her awake. Besides, she rather enjoyed writing. A diary which preserved in black and white her past actions and reactions helped her toward her ideal of an orderly, consistent life. She could express herself quite well on paper. In earlier days, before deciding that she had no real gift, she had twice tried to write a novel. And that at any rate is one more than the average number of attempts at literature.

CHAPTER EIGHT

*D*ECEMBER 16th. No developments. Took turns keeping observation on O. A very unpleasant phrase and a very unpleasant task. We are agreed that she cannot safely be left alone for any period of the night or day. Someone must always happen to be with her. It is a great strain making one's presence in the room just *happen*: the only alternatives are uncomfortable silence and uncomfortable conversation. One's guilty conscience tells one that a child could see through either. Miss M. really will give the game away if she does not improve. She was officially "on duty" this morning. I went in, and she was asking the poor child whether she always remembered to say her prayers since she had grown up. She is probably toying with the idea that the present state of affairs is a judgment on O. She would like to discover something which absolved her from making any more calls on her deficient stock of sympathy. That is probably unjust, but I dislike Miss M. very much. She has no sense of proportion whatever. She doesn't even possess the compensating domestic virtues of most narrow women. This house is badly run, even allowing for shortage of staff. That maid slops about in a dirty overall until teatime, and if I shake a cushion in my bedroom it raises a dust storm.

R. makes my stay here bearable. He is very sweet. After breakfast he took four tablespoonfuls of some awful glucose mixture, two little glasses of pink liquid and a lump of sugar. He saw me watching and said apologetically that he thought the worry had upset his carbohydrate balance. I did not realize before that he had been a barrister. Joseph, of course, he knew by reputation, and had met once or twice. Said he had a great respect for him. I am afraid the compliment would not be returned, which is a pity. J. is still inclined to regard nonsuccess as proof of essential inferiority. That is a fallacy which I have managed to discard. R. is the rarest kind of born failure—he has every qualification for getting on except motive power. Like a well-constructed car with a permanently empty fuel tank. Obviously it is only by the strongest effort that he can bring himself to cross wills with another person on even the most trivial point. I admire his recent conduct all the more.

There was no hot-water bottle in my bed last night, and in this weather I felt justified in speaking about it. This evening I have been given one, but it has no cover and tends to leak.

December 17th. We are still hindered by the absence of any clue to what goes on in O.'s mind. Not that it's easy to find out, because direct questioning is barred. Decided that I was best placed for detective work, being a stranger. Anybody naturally grows suspicious if her own family begins to take an interest in the state of her mind. This afternoon I insisted on O. accompanying me for a long walk. Mostly through untidy-looking farmyards, petrified seas of mud, only passable because of the frost. One heel off the suède brogues.

O. is a sweet girl. If she were not, it wouldn't be such an intense, shameful pain to know that I am her mother. She has had very little of the things she deserves—love, fun, companionship, and a good education. When I think of serving a twenty years' sentence in this household! The kindest thing one can say about Miss M. is that she would probably take the trouble to instruct a child in the more obsolete refinements of etiquette. R., with all his good points and his obvious affection, suffers from this rather contagious defeatism, which is not healthy for the young. I prefer not to think of her having lived in the same house as her late father. Thank God that, in her true self, she took nothing, nothing, nothing from him. She is not difficult to interest, but she seems to take it for granted that conversation consists in listening attentively to somebody else's monologue. I don't think this is mental laziness, I think it's the ripe fruit of association with these blasted Marshalls: on one side, a sort of human rogue elephant, stamping out the slightest vestige of independence; on the other, a soured and browbeaten spinster, with a mind like a ruined suburb.

I am getting very venomous, and I feel it. I hope it is all righteous indignation and not Change of Life affecting my glands.

My tactics with O. were rather subtle—borrowed from that psychologist-man who took me in to dinner at Mary's. Told her about two fictitious dreams and emphasized that their illusion tended to persist in the waking mind. One was supposed to be about tramcars, I can't think why. Response very poor at first and I pressed rather undiplomatically, but just as we were going through another frozen swamp she came out with a question I thought v. significant: "Do you ever have dreams which seem to last several days?" I asked if she meant continuously, and she replied no, not all of one piece, but mixing themselves up with your daily life so that you were never sure whether you were asleep or not. By way of promoting confidence I then produced the astounding untruth that such a state of affairs was not uncommon in people of her age. She murmured something about the embarrassment of being uncertain whether your actions were real or imaginary. I said, with an agonized smile of badinage: "Do you do such embarrassing things in your dreams?" I think I caught her off her guard. "Yes," she said, "I do frightful things."

I imagine that I have learned something which approximates to the truth. Though it is foolish to be too confident when one is uncertain how far the answers are coerced or represent a personality entirely different from her own.

Coming back we met Mr. Faulkner. Thought at first he was going to do the Levite on us. However, he rallied nobly, and we had quite a chat by the roadside. Poor man, he looked most uncomfortable. Like a lobster which has suddenly realized that water may be hot as well as cold. I don't think he will ever quite recover from his scalding. I suppose it was almost his first intimation that the "terrible accidents" of which he spoke so impressively the other night are not exclusively reserved for parishioners. I have not altered my mind about him, he is nice, and if he still wanted to marry O. I believe she might go much farther up the social register and do far worse. But I fear that the wedding bells are irretrievably cracked. No girl can expose a man to himself without paying for it.

Dressing case arrived today—very late. Scent bottle and soap container broken owing to ineffective padding. *Must remember to speak to Bristowe severely.*

December 18th. Phoned home this morning. Spoke to the girls in turn. Joyce very full of her appointment as a prefect for next term. Told me quite seriously she was planning to "clean up" No. 4 Dormitory—which might disturb me as to the moral tone of the school, if I didn't know it meant stopping illicit bananas and sardines. Joyce has the typical Pond sense of the magnitude of the trust reposed in her. At present it is rather endearing to see her staggering like Atlas under her responsibilities. But am afraid that a period of priggery looms on the near horizon. Real concern with Angela, who will repeat my mistakes in life (just as J. will repeat Joseph's). Saturday, A. was apparently taken backstage of the musical comedy, *Love in a Rocket*, by Jean O'Hara, whom I have never liked—more money than morals. Floods of naïve appreciation from A. of the marvelous people she met: the zenith being a young man called Tony who comes on for ten minutes dressed as an airman and sings a song. His full talent is, of course, unrecognized. A. assures me that he is a genius and like Bing Crosby—a quaint pair of synonyms. I suppose I am lucky to have daughters who are so confiding. All the same, shall keep my eyes open for Tony. She had lunch with him yesterday. In spite of a certain doubt about their virility, I distrust these chorus boys and am not going to take any chances.

Proverb "It never rains but it pours" is one of few which I have found a reliable guide. If I am depressed about private matters, the world situation always matches up to an equally somber shade. Probably subjective, but really the newspapers just now make appalling reading. People dying like flies all over Europe. No sign of abatement in the epidemic, no sign even that more localized horrors are vanishing in the general disaster. In Germany flu is now known as the Jewish Corruption, and quite a promising pogrom has already been inspired by Dr. Goebbels's theory of pestiferous non-Aryans. Japan also is keen on the germ's Chinese origin.

Still there is one very bright spot. O. has once more passed a perfectly normal day. Miss M. is now referring lightly to passing nerve storms and the tonic effects of cod-liver oil. Fancy that R. and myself have a truer appreciation of the adversary's subtle and tenacious quality, his delight in an ambush for its own sake. R. did, however, suggest one hopeful line of reasoning. He drew a parallel with the vibrations of a gong. If the instrument is very powerful and raucous, it may still deafen one for some time after it has ceased to be struck. But provided it doesn't receive any new stimulus from outside, the volume is bound to decrease progressively until it becomes too faint to affect our senses. James is dead and therefore cannot be renewing the energy which he so charmingly expends. I wish I had more faith in that kind of analogy.

Something else R. said awoke me to the extraordinary apathy with which O. has accepted the arrival of myself, an unheard-of stranger. I made a point of suggesting that she must have wondered what I was doing in the house. But no! I am here to give Auntie Eva back some money which I owe her! This is very choice. It is the first thing that has made me regret the demise of James. I suppose Attila was the only person who could deal adequately with a few of his contemporaries.

December 19th. There was somebody who rolled a rock time after time toward the top of a steep mountain, but just before the summit it always slipped back, and all his hope and labor were wasted. I can't remember his name, but whoever he was, I feel like him.

I really did think that we'd helped O. to weather the storm. God knows we've all tried hard enough, even Miss M. Perhaps we wanted to go too fast. But she had been perfectly normal for three days, and it seemed a good moment to consolidate our advantage by getting her out of the immediate neighborhood. I always suspected that we might be banking on a fallacy, because there's no reason why the corrupting influence should be limited in space. But I didn't see that, at the worst, it could do any harm. Miss M. and I tried our joint powers of persuasion this morning, in the course of an expedition to the village store. We talked like travel agents all the way down to the shop. Miss M. even managed to remind O. without bitterness that she was now quite a rich girl and could take her holidays abroad. O. silent but not discouraging. I expected her to agree, not because she was particularly enthusiastic, but because she's the almost extinct type which will allow older people to know best. Shopping interrupted the campaign. Miss M. bought several dusters and some cleaning things, most of which, to judge from the state of the shelves in the store, came to the customer second-hand from the rats and mice.

We had walked back nearly as far as the Lord Harvey when Miss M. rather foolishly tried to force the issue. Assuming the chief point in her own favor, she began to make up O.'s mind for her about details—where she should go and when she should start, etc. O. ceased even to answer in monosyllables. I thought she might be getting sulky—not without justification. We were just opposite the village pub when she suddenly said:

"Auntie, have you got my welfare at heart?"

I didn't care for the tone or the words. Both struck me as being deliberately parodied. But Miss M. was rather gratified. She said, yes, of course she had.

O. had been carrying some of the purchases. She quietly took a long bar of kitchen soap out of its bag and, swinging it back, hit Miss M. hard and accurately across the mouth. She said: "Then perhaps that'll teach you to mind your own bloody business."

The wretched woman was lying on her back in the middle of the roadway before I realized what had happened. That would have been shocking enough in any circumstances. Unfortunately (or by design?) it all happened with the maximum of publicity. Time and place couldn't have been better calculated for giving Gorchow a first-class view—half a dozen laborers already standing outside the Lord Harvey, and not a minute before the whole of the taproom had joined them in the street. All gaping, I helped Miss M. up. Her false teeth had been knocked almost down her throat, and she was groping about in her mouth. I didn't know whether I ought to be succoring her or policing O. Anyhow the decision was soon taken out of my hands. O. was completely amuck, uncontrollable by any means short of a physical grapple. I wasn't going to treat the villagers to that. She turned round and began to abuse me and Miss M., but obviously the crowd was her real audience. She accused us most eloquently of conspiracy to rob her of her inheritance, giving the most scabrous details of our jealousy and underhand maneuvers. She said we wanted to send her away where she couldn't claim what her uncle had left her, also that we'd been keeping her prisoner at the Manor. It wasn't very consistent or logical, but must have sounded horribly specious to simple, slow minds, educated on a mixture of *News of the World* and *Cinderella*. Mutters and clucks of disapproval all round. Saw us being lynched on nearest tree. Felt powerless—the only counterblast being to suggest that O. was hopelessly deranged.

I wasn't going to propose that explanation myself. But was distinctly relieved when somebody else put it forward.

The influence overreached itself. O. began to hold forth in a satirical vein, which was out of character—out of the character, that is, of a simple oppressed maiden. Her master is presumably still experimenting. (I shudder to think what will happen if he ever achieves entire harmony with his medium.) Anyhow, the false note jarred even on the rustics. They started looking at her less like a martyr and more like a circus turn. Finally, just as she paused for breath, the landlord, who was the latest arrival on the scene, observed in tones of pitying scorn: "Poor little bitch, she's cracked as a newt." Some controversy. Landlord referred to a person called Tupp (?) who apparently holds the same view. The crowd began to melt back into the bar. O. immediately relapsed into the state of walking coma which seems to be the invariable aftermath of these exhibitions. It provides a very convenient escape from consequences, and some people might suspect her of faking it, like a naughty child which pretends to be asleep. But I do not think so. Grabbed her and marched her back to the house at the double. Miss M.'s dentures slightly damaged. Their fit is affected and she hasn't been able to say much since.

R. terribly depressed by news. Said that the question had changed from "How long is this going on?" to "Is this ever going to stop?" So much for our delusion that time and mechanical laws were working in our favor! We might have known James better than to suppose that he would ever release a strangle hold or give up a joke while it was still capable of causing pain.

R. and I differ about what is the worst feature of today's relapse. He is v. worried because this is the first occasion on which one of O.'s paroxysms has been accompanied by physical violence. He believes it may indicate a dangerous new tendency, prejudicing our right to leave her at large. I think he exaggerates. She's not strong enough to do serious harm. R. returned the compliment by making light of my anxiety about village gossip. After all, O. lives and is well known in the district. But he takes the view that the damage in that quarter has already been done, once and for all, by these people called Tupp or Thrupp. It was their child on whom O. operated. They seem to have been the only person to profit by her misfortunes, but apparently that hasn't prevented them from "talking."

Feel very tired and more than ever conscious of myself as being ultimately chargeable with this tragedy.

December 20th. Have just drunk a large glass of medicated milk. R. persuaded me, he said it would do my nerves good, and I hope it will, because it certainly doesn't suit my stomach. The electric light in this room is disgraceful—about as powerful as the blue bulb in a sleeping car. Can't think why Miss M. doesn't see to it. She went in to the dentist today and her teeth have been put straight.

Suddenly remembered Christmas presents at breakfast this morning. Wrote orders to every shop where I have an account, and perhaps some of the things will arrive in time. Poor Angela and Joyce, I expect they think they've got a funny mother, anyhow. But so long as they don't feel she's forgotten them entirely . . . ! Have noticed myself getting rather sentimental of late. The children are probably reveling in my absence. Don't suppose J. has given it a thought, and if A. has discussed it with that Jean O'Hara, she is probably convinced that I am spending an illicit fortnight with a dance-band leader or some other figure of romance. I wish one of them would write.

In this house I have not heard anybody mention Christmas at all. Not really surprising, because I don't think they've paid attention to the calendar for many days. Time here doesn't seem to be measured by hours and minutes but by the intervals between one calamity and the next.

Today we had a most peculiar and rather impudent visitation. Soon after lunch a man came staggering up the drive, carrying a load of assorted planks strapped over his back. He asked to see Miss Marshall, but, thinking he might be rough, we all went to the front door. His appearance justified any precaution—a great mass of wild black hair and a face whose bones seemed to be bursting through the skin. It was impossible to tell whether he was young or middle-aged. He looked us all over and then burst out in a voice like a suppressed scream: "Which of you is afflicted? Which of you has felt the breath of the Pit upon her?" Miss M., who has the strength of limited imagination, looked at the contraption on his back and told him that we had quite enough firewood already. He didn't take any notice, but launched into a fantastic rambling oration about sins and God and the Mark of the Beast and blood offerings of propitiation. Our attempts at shutting him up were simply drowned in pseudo-Biblical bombast.

I think I was the first to realize what he was getting at. Something he said about laying-on of hands gave me a clue. He had heard about O., and he was offering to cure her. He was quite mad. If I'd wanted to be cynical, I should have said I didn't believe in homeopathy. Finally, we just banged the door in his face—the only way to get rid of impervious prophets. Afterwards I explained what I thought. Miss M., however, remained convinced that he'd wanted to sell us the timber on his back—until further details were forthcoming from the maid, Dora, who had a complete biography at her finger tips. The creature is apparently well known throughout East Anglia. He is a highly individual kind of revivalist, who tramps from village to village and preaches on a collapsible platform constructed from the various planks which we saw on his back. When properly fitted together they form a little dais in the shape of a cross, resting on two trestles. Everybody agrees that he is insane, but this opinion is qualified by a certain respect. The fervor of his eloquence goes a long way to make up for its incomprehensibility. Also he is known to have "prayed off" a plague of mice at King's Lynn. Sometimes he will disappear for months, but always returns to his eastern circuit. He has told several people that he is a son of Queen Victoria.

This absurd incident has its serious side. I refrained from saying "I told you so" to R., but it is now obvious that O. is getting precisely the publicity I was afraid of. Gossip must be pretty prevalent locally for an itinerant fanatic to get hold of the story. Whatever happens, I very much doubt whether Gorchow still remains on the list of O.'s possible future residences. Not that I think it will be much loss to her.

She has been very quiet all day—too quiet, as if she were still partially stupefied. Previous attacks never had a reaction which lasted so long. They used to leave her rather stunned—as though she were recovering from an overdose of alcohol or some narcotic. Now, by comparison, she might be a confirmed drunkard or morphinomaniac, waiting in an uneasy semiconscious haze for the next dose of poison. This is the refinement of James Marshall's triumph—that he should not only possess her, but also that she should be unable to exist without him. I don't think I exaggerate. I can see logically that continued subjection to a foreign influence—whether chemical or human—must inevitably destroy the mind as an independent entity. It seems to follow that whether or not James's power is on the wane, it may, before its collapse, have irrevocably damaged O.'s intellect. In fact, the best we can hope for is to get her back as a harmless imbecile.

I don't know if it's that milk or my thoughts which are making me feel so sick.

R. and I haven't mentioned it, but I know we're wondering about the same question. Wouldn't it be simpler, wiser, more effective to throw over all pride in appearances, all pretense that things would ultimately right themselves? James (and by now I can only suppose that we really are dealing with him) will continue to take deliberate and cynical advantage of our natural unwillingness to treat O. as an insane person. But suppose we did put her into a private home for a short while? That would at any rate render pointless these exhibitionist tactics. There would be no fun in hitting and abusing trained attendants. They wouldn't be impressed. To them it would all be in the day's work.

But *he* knows, *he* knows, *he* knows! That devil knows we daren't inflict such a handicap on a young girl, unless we're forced to. Poor Nancy's daughters—the eldest went into retirement for a year—she's been all right since, but nobody will look at her or even her sister, though they're pretty and inherit that pile of money. Everybody mutters cryptically about hereditary taints.

Suffering is not distributed in strict accordance with moral laws. That I have always realized. People die of cancer and are drowned swimming. But, outside certain familiar forms of disease and accident, one still instinctively looks for some flaw in the victim's character to explain a tragedy. Now it is brought home to me very vividly that there is no connection whatsoever between innocence and immunity. One is driven to believe either that the world is governed by blind chance or (which is an even more repellent idea) that the children's teeth can be set on edge because their parents have eaten sour grapes. I haven't much doubt whom an Old Testament prophet would have held responsible for O.'s misfortunes.

December 23rd. I have missed two entries, because I simply haven't dared to tempt fate. Now I'm sure enough to commit myself. These have been three good, three wonderful days. I do not mind that Dora has distributed my powder over my dressing table and even my underclothes. I do not mind Miss M.'s untimely pressure for settlement of what she calls "a certain business matter between us." She shall have her dole, and I hope it doesn't choke her for some years. In my relief, which is perhaps purer and less selfish than any I have felt before, I would give away my last sixpence. When I talk about altruism, I don't forget the load lifted from my own conscience; but ninety-nine per cent of my thankfulness is on O.'s behalf. I suppose that in this brief hectic time I have come to love her as my own child. This must be biological, because (poor O.!) she certainly hasn't had much chance to endear herself to me in any ordinary way.

Have often wondered why women who'd led lives of misery with their husbands and ultimately divorced them should be so eager to keep the children begotten by men they hated. Now I understand that it's a thing about which you can't reason.

On Wednesday O. came down to breakfast rather late. She said good morning brightly and naturally. The alteration in her manner threw us all out of our stride, and we sat like stuck pigs. She must have noticed because she said:

"I feel quite different today. Not like I've felt since Uncle died."

Then she went on:

"I know my behavior has been very queer of late. Quite dotty. I can't exactly remember what I've said or done, but I'm sure it's upset everybody."

She blushed bright scarlet. I thought there was something pathetic and noble in her apology—pathetic because it was so unwittingly inadequate to the terror and anxiety she has caused, and noble because she was no more bound to say she was sorry than a baby which has been sick over its blankets. Her character—if not her intelligence—promises better than her mother's did at the same age.

Seeing that R. and Miss M. were both completely flummoxed, I took it upon myself to make a tactful answer—very dégagé, hardly looking up from the bacon. I said that, of course, the doctors themselves admit that these inoculations may have extraordinary effects. The best lies are the ones which don't explain too much to start with, and are so outrageous that it's impossible to believe anybody would dare to invent them.

O. asked me what I meant. Surely she remembered that they'd all had anti-influenza injections after her uncle's death? No, she didn't remember at all. Well, there she was . . . that just showed how badly some people took!

R. luckily caught on. He has quite an imagination and he evolved a most convincing story how, after his own dose, he had spent twenty-four hours under the impression that the war was still on and they had given him anti-typhus, preparatory to shipping him out to Salonica. O. showed no sign of skepticism, in fact her simple faith led her to drop a fair-sized brick. She said: "It seems to have funny effects on everyone—Auntie Eva, too. Didn't it make her think she was going to get a lot of money?"

Great subsequent difficulty in persuading Miss M. that O., far from being malicious, was quite unable to see her own recent actions in their true light—much less those of other people. Pointed out that it would be just as unfair to blame somebody for her opinion of your looks, when she'd only seen you through a distorting mirror. But it was cash she wanted, not reason. For the sake of peace I let myself be blackmailed into promising I'd make over the legacy in legal form at the first opportunity. But she's damned well going shares with R. I'd give him the lot only it'd let him in for the same pestering. Miss M. is not really grateful for benefits—I suppose because she is firmly convinced that she has never received her deserts from the world, and regards any windfall as an overdue debt whose payment is the reward of her own conscientious dunning.

The thought of that woman always produces a rush of acid to my pen—which is unsuitable for a day of rejoicing.

Incidentally, why did James leave his money to Olive instead of to some really useless institution? The obvious motive—to stir up bad blood in the family—doesn't seem quite adequate. Surely there was more fun to be got out of their efforts to cope with sudden poverty. Can it be that James, believing at the time that death would close his relationship with O., felt some flicker of casual benevolence toward her, some impulse to take a graceful farewell? This is a rather improbable flight of fancy, but at any rate it more than atones for my previous "cattiness."

The improvement in O. has been even more marked yesterday and today. If the phrase weren't so nauseating, I should say she'd acted like a normal, healthy English girl. Told R. so, but he was rather inclined to croak and remarked that being healthy and English wasn't normal to everyone. I chose the wrong moment to talk to him, because he was upset by a most unfortunate accident. Miss M., who'd been tidying drawers in the lounge, had asked O. to help her in tearing up and burning a lot of old receipts, etc. Apparently R. often works at the escritoire and uses it to store the current section of his MS. Poor O., flinging herself into the task with renewed vitality, found what she thought was merely a pile of old gardening catalogues, which she straightway tossed onto the fire. Unfortunately there was only one catalogue, the rest of the stuff consisting of parts of R.'s notes and script, wrapped up in similar colored cardboard folders. About a hundred pages and six months' groundwork went up in smoke. Nobody could blame an author, who'd suffered such a loss, for being depressed and annoyed. But it's no good attributing one's misfortunes to persecution. Not that R. specifically did so, but he looked as if, for the moment, he was tempted to draw inferences from O.'s past deliberate mischief-making. Which I feel is most misguided. It was a pure mistake.

Perhaps I sound overconfident. But I'm not falling into stupid optimism, just because O. has stopped acting abnormally. After all, we've had lulls before—but they were just lulls, negative patches, during which there was no recovery, only an abeyance of evil. Now I believe that her mind has not merely cast out the influence, but also developed a positive strength—a sort of antibody—which will resist its return.

The post brought a note from little Miss Hassett asking O. to a party tomorrow, Christmas Eve. Am afraid Miss Hassett must have been hearing a few things and hesitated about this invitation, otherwise she wouldn't have left it so late. If for no other reason than to stop gossip, O. should go. That was my view. But Miss M. and R. were discouraging. Both nervous of allowing her about in public. They must at all costs be prevented from making this incident in O.'s life an excuse for treating her as a sort of permanent convalescent who wastes her youth in semi-seclusion. When I succeeded in getting them alone for a minute, I tried to din this into their heads. R., of course, saw my point, but Miss M. went on bleating that "she couldn't take the responsibility" for so long that in desperation I said that I took it, every atom of it, fully, completely, and entirely. Fear I am rather a managing woman, and have incidentally reaped my reward in the prospect of an evening's mild boredom. O. ringing up to accept let out that I was still here, and Miss H., with large-hearted hospitality, immediately insisted that I should come too—saying that though the party would be mostly young, she had an old uncle who would just suit me. After my remarks about responsibility I couldn't very well refuse.

I'm not going to bury my head in the sand as regards the future. When I go back—which will be immediately after Christmas—I shall arrange for O. to come up to London and be looked at by a tactfully disguised mental specialist. Quite how I'm to give him the data without making him think I'm the patient, God only knows! But it's a precaution that mustn't be neglected. This has been a thing such as cannot be endured more than once in a lifetime, either by O. or by those around her. It could only recur in a world that was not worth living in.

CHAPTER NINE

"DELIGHTFUL!" said Roger. "Delightful! Turn round again. It reminds me of the old days in May Week."

Olive pirouetted.

"It must be badly rucked at the back, if it reminds Uncle of his youth," she said. "They wore bustles then."

"No, no, nothing so antique as that. The naughty nineties was my time."

"I somehow can't imagine you at the May Week Balls."

Roger coughed deprecatingly.

"I did not actually attend them. But I know about the dresses they used to wear because one year I watched the ladies from my rooms."

Delia smiled sadly into the fire. Poor starveling! He watched the ladies!

"I hope you had a nice strong pair of field-glasses," said Olive.

"What do you mean?" asked Eva.

"Oh, nothing. Only that when I went to Derek's party in May Week all the town boys were posted behind bushes along the river, looking for a bit of slap-and-tickle in the punts."

"Good heavens!" said Eva. "How dare you suggest that your uncle . . ."

"My dear child," observed Roger mildly, "in my day everybody wasn't either a Casanova or a Peeping Tom."

"I thought it was a little warmer outside this afternoon," said Delia.

"About time," replied Eva, expending her accumulated indignation on the weather. "The frost has been most unnatural. We're not built in this country to stand a month of it before Christmas. It gets into the blood."

"It gets into the brain," said Olive.

"What d'you mean?" asked Delia sharply.

"Oh . . . just nothing."

"We had dinner early," said Eva, "so that you and Lady Pond could be in time for your entertainment."

"My God, auntie," said Olive, "you make the party sound so repulsively clean! Your entertainment . . . as though it would consist of lemonade and lantern slides in the church hall!"

"We'd better be starting," said Delia.

Olive went lightly out, humming to herself.

There was an uncomfortable silence: broken, at last, by Eva.

"Roger," she said, "just tell me—do you ever remember Olive, as we used to know her, speaking in that loose, indecent way?"

"No," said Roger shortly.

Delia was as much averse to a certain kind of humor as anybody, particularly when it came from the wrong lips. But stronger than her distaste was the impulse to defend Olive.

"My dear Miss Marshall," she said, "the younger generation have a way of talking that doesn't always appeal to ours."

"I suppose you're referring to London and the so-called Smart Set," said Eva.

Roger cleared his throat. He said:

"No doubt, Lady Pond, the young are sensible to discard outworn conventions. But that, to my mind, misses the present point. However common such behavior may be, it doesn't tally with Olive's character. She has always been reticent—prudish, I suppose, according to modern notions."

Delia felt the stubborn resentment of a person whom confusion of issues has seduced into championing an unworthy cause.

"Perhaps," she said, "Olive is merely displaying a little more contemporary sophistication."

"For myself, I don't believe she's at all normal yet," proclaimed Eva.

"What, simply because she makes a couple of jokes in doubtful taste?"

"No, Lady Pond. You're willfully trying to misunderstand me. My brother and I, in our peculiar way, have cared for Olive since she was an infant. We may not have been very successful in your opinion, but we have learned to know her in all her moods. Believe me, everything about this present one rings false—the self-possession, the outspokenness, even the high spirits. Olive is a quiet girl, not one of your Mayfair debutantes."

Delia gave an exasperated shrug of her shoulders.

"Very well, don't let's quarrel about it. I only wanted to warn you against the old mistake of giving a dog a bad name. If you're going to pounce on the least word or action which doesn't fit in with your preconceptions of her character, neither you nor she will ever know any peace. Surely you can distinguish between the real Olive, even if she has used a phrase you don't like, and the ghastly, dispossessed creature which passed for a while under her shape?"

Olive's voice sounded outside the door.

"Lady Pond," she called, "Lady Pond, are you ready? I'm just going to take the rug off the radiator."

Roger absent-mindedly flicked his thumb over the depleted pile of his manuscript.

"You're going through with this party?" he said interrogatively.

"Of course," replied Delia. "The more chance Olive gets to mix with other people the better for her. You don't want her to become a hopeless introvert?"

The two Marshalls sat in silence, listening, while the front door banged and the engine of the Rover warmed up through spasmodic rattling to a steady purr. Then the gravel crunched and the headlights swept for an instant over the blind.

"We don't count for much in this house now," said Eva. "That woman is altogether too sure of herself. That's probably how she came by Olive. And others, too, for all we know."

"Now, now, my dear," said Roger, "nothing to be gained by bitterness. After all, it's only means, not ends, we disagree about. Lady Pond has Olive's welfare as much at heart as ourselves. Besides, she's a very intelligent woman."

Eva resumed her embroidery. She was working the neck of a very upper-class swan, which appeared to be floating down a bright blue river. The swan had a haughty, cynical look in its small stitched eye. At the corners of the piece hovered four pink lozenges of no discernible function.

Roger also addressed himself to his studies. But once more he found his mood to be recapitulatory rather than creative. He was discouraged by the loss of several weeks' laborious research, and his concentration flickered under the inrush of disturbing speculations. He began to skip his way through what he had long since written—that barren relaxation of dilatory authors. Mr. Justice Combe had conversed in Latin at the age of four . . . Mr. Justice Harrandine had been appointed "without regard for God or Man"—a bit of rather tactless jobbery, it would appear, because the learned judge was stigmatized by one contemporary as having "not so much law as an ass hath or a sheep, no, not so much as to confess *ignoramus* in his own behalf." Somebody else, however, had praised his "neat, spruce, clean aire." The world, to be sure, was full of a number of curious things. What a pity that all the most interesting ones seemed to have happened several hundred years ago!

2

"My dear girl!" said Delia, in accents of mild protest.

"Why, what's the matter?"

"Oh, I suppose it's quite usual at your age, but somehow I never suspected you of speed mania."

"This old car won't go really fast," said Olive.

"You were doing your best with it round that corner. I can't forget that we've got six feet of water on one side of us."

"More," said Olive cheerfully. "And then there's the mud. These dikes have no proper bottom. I once saw men dredging a mainlode and they brought up masses and masses of thick, black slime."

"Well," said Delia, "I don't want to make its close acquaintance."

"Oh, you'll be all right. I wish I had a sports car."

"You never told me you were keen on motoring."

"I'm not, really. But tonight I feel that I'd like to go tearing round the countryside, making people jump into the hedges and bobbies pull out their notebooks."

"Wouldn't the last part prove rather expensive?"

"No," said Olive. "Because, you see, I should be carrying false number plates."

Delia laughed, a little uncertainly.

"We all toy with the idea of a gorgeous, extravagant burst of lawlessness. I used to fill in sleepless hours by imagining how I'd set about burgling my friends' houses. Crime is great fun in theory, but I suspect that most of its romantic charm would evaporate in practice."

The white warning posts followed one another in endless succession along the bank. Their inset reflectors caught the beam of the headlights and threw back a series of briefly twinkling reddish stars. Occasionally the sheeted ice in the dike was lit up; it still presented the same appearance of a solid, unbroken pavement: but the bright, diamond-like refulgence of its upper surface was faintly misted. The topmost particles were already in process of slow dissolution. As yet there was no real thaw, only a relaxation of the frosty grip. The moon, suddenly emerging, revealed a similar indecision among the clouds. Their billowy volutes threatened snow, but the gray color and the woolly texture which accompany snowstorms had given place to the darker, more definite outlines of suspended rain.

"Aunt Eva told me you would be going away soon," said Olive apropos of nothing.

"Yes."

"For good?"

"Well, I expect so, because I'm only a business acquaintance. The will, you know . . . ! But, Olive, I do hope you'll sometimes come up and see me in London."

"Where? At your house?" Then she laughed.

"Why does the idea amuse you?" asked Delia.

"I don't really know. I just thought it might look funny, if I suddenly turned up at the door."

Delia did not answer immediately. Is Olive, she wondered, trying to tell me that she's guessed? It would be nothing strange if she had. But surely she would not show her knowledge in the form of sly little digs? Perhaps she is very embarrassed. Embarrassment often vents itself in inappropriate humor. And, anyhow, she makes a very good point, one that I hadn't properly considered. Of course, she can't come home. That likeness would start gossip even among the servants. No, once you have put a skeleton in your cupboard, you can never open the door by so much as a chink; in fact, as time goes on, you have to double and treble the locks. Olive may understand that, and yet feel aggrieved. It must seem a sordid and clandestine business to her, that a child mayn't cross her mother's threshold. Probably she will think hole-and-corner secrecy too high a price to pay for meetings. But, God knows, I don't want to lose her!

"Olive," she said, taking a sudden decision, "before I go I should like to have a private talk with you about certain important but rather unpleasant things."

"I know them already."

"What do you know?"

"The facts of life."

"Don't be silly. Anyhow, why should you suppose that I was the person to tell you about such things?"

"Sorry," said Olive. "Just a joke. We used to say that at school whenever anybody got very confidential."

"I see," said Delia. But she didn't. For all the rest of the journey she was trying to reconcile two inconsistent pictures. On one side was the dreamy, innocent, unpractical girl, vouched for by her aunt and uncle; on the other, a self-possessed, rather "flip" young thing with a distinct edge to her tongue, who gave every sign of being able to hold her own in the world. The latter was the resuscitated Olive, the one who had returned from haunted twilight to make her mother's acquaintance.

Delia could produce no synthesis. Naturally, therefore, she believed her own experience in contradiction to other people's. Eva and Roger were very old-fashioned, and belonged spiritually to an age when wilting little snowdrops were still in vogue. Their view of Olive was no doubt colored by their obsolete ideal of maidenhood. She might well—and small blame to her!—have played up to them for the sake of domestic peace.

Ely has comparatively little suburban development. The semi-detached villas on its outskirts are limited to a few rows, even in the most prolific direction. Delia did not realize how close they were to the town, until Olive said:

"Now we're nearly there."

"Good. By the way, what are we going to do at the party?"

"Oh, I expect Nina will have collected some enterprising men."

"I shall watch you cope with them," said Delia lightly.

"I like that!" said Olive. "You're not past the age for active service. I feel this show has come at the right moment."

"How do you mean?"

"Well, just before you go back. I should like your visit to end up with a bang."

She repeated the words "with a bang," meditatively, as though turning them over in her mind.

For a moment Delia found something humorous in the suggestion that she was being treated to a grand climax of revelry. Then quite suddenly she ceased to be amused at all. Shivering, she put a hand to the back of her neck to make a bridge with the collar of her coat and ward off the draft which was sending goose flesh down her spine.

They swung through the streets. The roadway was still thick with gravel, but now, instead of bouncing up like tiddlywinks, it submitted to the wheels and was crushed into the softening layer of ice.

The Hassetts lived in a solemn, faded Georgian house, bordering on the large green which faces the cathedral. It would not have satisfied everybody's requirements. It did not really satisfy the Hassetts', but they lived in it perfectly cheerfully, despite its endless passages and medieval plumbing, because they all knew that it was only a temporary place of refuge. Mrs. Hassett believed that one day those cads, the Russians, would be forced to pay up on prewar bonds: then she would be able to buy back her ancestral mansion in County Wicklow and live like an Irish gentlewoman amidst a peace only punctuated by the shotguns of outraged tenants and the belling of hounds. Colonel Hassett did not mind, because he was a genuine pessimist, and thought himself lucky that he still had any sort of roof above his head. He never bored the younger members at the local golf club by telling them that the country was going to the dogs: he regarded its decline as too self-evident for comment. He had caused several bricks to be removed from behind the hearth in his wife's bedroom, leaving a hole in which he had hidden a pearl necklace and a diamond ring. He argued that when the Red Hand of Moscow triumphed, and the revolution arrived, and the currency was worthless, a cache of jewelry might make all the difference between starvation and black bread.

Nina was even less inclined to complain about her home. Her happy knack of losing herself in the idea of the moment made her more or less indifferent to her surroundings. Indeed, there were only three things she really noticed: what she put on her body, what went on inside her head, and men.

A maid showed them up to a first-floor bedroom.

"You might be a dear and lend me your lipstick," said Olive from in front of the mirror.

"I've never noticed that you used the stuff," said Delia.

"Oh, yes, I do. At parties anyhow. But I happen to have left it behind."

Delia fished out the container from her bag and unscrewed it.

"Fortunately, we have the same coloring," she said.

She began to adjust her hair before a second mirror. When she again turned round Olive was ready waiting for her.

Delia's violent start was completely unaffected.

"My dear girl," she said, "what *have* you managed to do with your mouth? That shade needs handling with discretion."

"People have different styles of make-up. I don't know why you should suggest that mine's ridiculous."

"Not ridiculous," said Delia. "Bizarre. If you intended that effect you've been very clever. But I still think it's repellent."

Olive's mouth was neither a smear nor a slash. The coloring had been heavily applied in the center: it toned down toward the corners, then, at the junction of the lips, once more rioted out into a scarlet angle. It produced a curious distortion, as if her features were fixed in a vivid but not altogether wholesome smile. With a few strokes she had utterly changed her superficial personality.

Delia had a great horror of mothers who bullied their daughters in matters of adornment. She had seen, in her own circle, how interference with individual taste could produce either spineless frumps or defiant imitations of Bond Street tarts.

"Oh, well!" she said. "Different generations, different ideas. My own grandmother once seriously informed me that she would rather see me dead than rouged."

Olive smiled as pleasantly as the shape of her mouth would permit.

They went downstairs together. A babble of voices came from the big room on the first landing. They were hesitating in front of the open door when Nina suddenly detached herself from a group inside, and bounced out to greet them.

"We'd almost given you up!" she exclaimed.

"I'm afraid we started rather late," said Delia.

"I bet it was Olive's driving really. She rips along at twenty-five on the straight, but it sinks to ten on bends and corners, and anyhow the times she stops the engine would spoil anybody's average. I know her."

No, you don't, replied Delia mentally. Olive merely smiled. The act of itself called attention to her.

"My God!" said Nina. "The ewe lamb has blossomed out. I always said you could make yourself interesting."

"I told her that her appearance was rather sensational," observed Delia.

"I only wish I could get that sinister effect," said Nina with obvious sincerity. "Men love it. But however hard I try, my face still looks like a pink puffball."

They moved into the drawing room. It had been practically stripped of furniture, partly in order to allow more space for dancing, and partly because Mrs. Hassett was convinced that various pieces of furniture which she had inherited were extremely valuable—a common belief among elderly women, which they do not usually live to see exploded by public auction. Several couples were dancing to radio music. Some of the other guests stood about by the walls, but the majority were drinking hot punch in a large recess which ran back at right angles to the main body of the room, like the small arm of the letter L. Nina led them toward the table. On the way she said to Delia:

"I'm so glad to see you again, Lady Pond. I was thrilled when I heard you'd come. I'm afraid this party won't be quite up to your standard. I don't mind admitting it between ourselves, because we're neither of us snobs."

3

The faces repeated themselves punctually like the hours on a clock. Half-round, opposite the second window . . . and there were the redhead and her partner coasting up on the inside, still wearing the remains of the grin which had begun at the same point on the previous circuit. There, diagonally across the room, was Olive, still dancing with the attractive, peevish Pan, whose ears stuck out a little too far. Somebody had said he was an R.A.F. officer from Mildenhall. He had a hard, reckless, dissatisfied look, but one which nevertheless subtly suggested that a little sympathy would cause it to melt in the most naïve and charming manner. Delia had seen his type before: she could appreciate his appeal to women and docket it under the heading—"He's just a sulky little boy: some girl ought to take him in hand." Few girls could resist that kind of self-appointed task. But Olive was choosing the wrong approach. Imitation may be the sincerest flattery, but it is not the one which is most successful between the sexes. No man likes to see his own salient characteristics mirrored, exaggerated, flung back in his face by his female companions: he instinctively suspects a hidden irony. The dégagé manner of the young officer paled beside Olive's expression of callous, world-weary indifference. He danced quite well but negligently: she sloped round the room after him like a tired puma. She must have some lessons, thought Delia. This ridiculous style is just put on to cover her very natural incompetence. In fact, her whole attitude tonight is one long revelation of inferiority complex. Her social education has been disgustingly neglected, she's uncertain of herself, she falls back on third-rate films and novelettes for her conception of how a sophisticated woman should behave. I'm not annoyed. I sympathize.

Delia had to tell herself several times that she was not annoyed. What really mollified her was a certain pride in her own insight and breadth of outlook.

As if to recall her thoughts, her partner kicked her briskly on the ankle. He was the promised uncle, a tall, red-faced man, recently retired from the consular service. He had apparently been in many of the world's most interesting and remote spots, but that was a thing which one only discovered at second hand. His own conversation was restricted to gardening; not from modesty, but choice. For the past five minutes he had been ranging contentedly about the vegetable world. Delia had not been listening for so long that when she again gave him her attention she felt quite embarrassed, as though she were eavesdropping.

". . . I thought that would do the trick. But not a bit of it! This year they were just as bad as ever. Overgrown and tough like bits of wood."

"I beg your pardon!"

"Eh? My rhubarb, of course."

"How frightful!" said Delia. Then, feeling that she owed him something: "I've had exactly the same trouble with mine."

Nina passed, looking back over her shoulder, smiling and saying something to Olive's partner. She did not seem to notice that she had one of her own. After all, it was rather creditable that Olive should have annexed the jeune premier of the party.

"Really?" said the uncle. "Tricky stuff, rhubarb. Where did you say you lived?"

"Eaton Square," said Delia.

4

"Your father wouldn't have been putting any of the clues out of doors in this weather?" asked Mrs. Hassett.

"I don't know," said Nina, "I left it all to him."

"Because it's no time for a guest to be rummaging in the cold and dark after little scraps of paper."

"Now, mother, calm down and don't go all Irish on me. I've got this Treasure Hunt in hand."

She rushed off. They could see her going from group to group, organizing furiously.

Mrs. Hassett turned to Delia.

"I don't know what my daughter would do, if she weren't doing something," she said. "But you and I are of an age to content ourselves with quiet, decent games. Do you play bridge now?"

Though she played quite well, Delia did not always admit even to knowing the rules. Bridge with strangers, particularly if keen, was often too like a free pass to their family quarrels. On this occasion, however, it was distinctly the preferable alternative.

The party was well under way. Several of the men had been reinforcing their spirits with the colonel's whisky. This would be a very hearty, jolly, dress-destroying Treasure Hunt.

A table had been set out with cards and markers in the small arm of the drawing room. Delia began to play with the uncle against Mrs. Hassett and a Cambridge don. She did not find it easy to concentrate on the cards because of the noise which still went on in the other section of the room. The hunters were apparently pairing off by lot. Colonel Hassett held a bowl from which each girl picked a screw of paper, bearing the name of a man. When the process was finished they were asked to read out the results. Olive was called on quite early.

"Jack Morris," she read.

The young R.A.F. man looked up with more than the usual sulkiness in his expression. He made it clear that he was not particularly grateful for his luck. At that moment Nina interrupted:

"There's been a mistake somewhere. I've got Jack on my slip."

"Then," observed Colonel Hassett reasonably, "I should say, Nina, that when you made out the slips, you copied down the same name twice. If you've done it more often, we shall be here all night."

Nina treated the suggestion as beneath contempt. Going briskly over to Olive she took the paper out of her hand.

"My dear girl," she said, "you want a pair of reading glasses. H-a-r-r-i-s. Jack Harris, that's your partner."

Olive looked at Nina. Not a muscle in her face moved.

"How stupid of me!" she said at last. "I can't read some writing. I once tried to help our schoolmistress at Gorchow with the children's exercise books, but I couldn't manage it at all."

"Well, I like that!" began Nina indignantly. "My writing . . ."

Mr. Jack Harris himself intervened with a facetious remark, which the company acclaimed less as a piece of wit than an opportunity to relieve the sudden inexplicable tension.

The couples dispersed about the hunt.

Delia was so seated that she had had a clear view of the incident. She did not doubt that Olive had been deliberately trying to bounce her hostess out of her legitimate partner. It worried her. She began to hedge from her former opinion. Olive was not yet perfectly normal, only convalescent. In bodily disease, certain weaknesses persisted long after the cure. Why should not an attack of acute wickedness leave in the mind a similar tendency to deceit and crooked dealing? She began to understand that, though happiness and well-being can dissolve in a flash, their converse is of a more stubborn character.

"You to play."

As the hand came to an end, she caught Mrs. Hassett's eye fixed on her with a speculative gaze. The question came as no surprise.

"You must excuse me asking, Lady Pond, but are you any relation to the Marshalls?"

"No," said Delia.

Let them talk. But thank God for Olive's indiscretions with the lipstick! They at least did something to lard over the damning details of resemblance.

Colonel Hassett had returned. When the rubber came to an end, he cut in. Delia's partner made way for him, hunting out odd coppers from his trouser pocket.

"There you are," he said. "One and threepence."

It was chiefly his fault that they had lost. His bridge was a game played almost entirely with the hands, like throwing cards into a hat.

Delia said: "I've left my money in the bedroom. I'll just get it."

"Oh, settle up afterwards."

"No, I'd rather do it now, if we're changing the four."

Going upstairs quietly, she heard voices on the half-landing between the first and second floors. Two people were sitting in the recessed window seat. The curtains were half-drawn, but did not conceal them from certain points on the staircase.

Jack Morris was saying:

"Of course, there was a bloody row at home. After that I decided that the air was the only place where I had a chance of being left alone."

He snapped his fingers, dismissing care and responsibility together. Delia thought that he sounded curiously genuine—a somber young desperado who had probably made many places too hot to hold him. Nina, however, looked to be enjoying his company. To Delia this seemed just as well for Olive's sake. One could not regret that one's daughter had lost a tug of war, when the prize was a full-grown boa constrictor.

As she came down again she heard footsteps mounting from below her. Her arrival on the half-landing coincided with Olive's. The tête-à-tête behind the curtains had ignored an odd passer, but it could not continue in a public meeting place. Nina and Morris sat decorously upright, and dissociated themselves with edging movements.

"Hallo!" said Olive. "Why aren't you hunting?"

Nina replied good-temperedly:

"Daddy hid the clues, but I can pretty well guess where he put some of them, so I should have rather an unfair advantage."

"I wonder you thought it worth while to get a partner."

"Oh, Jack's just sacrificing his chances of a prize to amuse me."

Morris scowled at Olive.

"Anyhow," Nina continued, "if you're so keen on the hunt, what have you done with your own man?"

"I sent him to search the scullery, and ran away. He was too exciting. Did you know he has a motorcycle of I forget how many horsepower, and he plays hockey for the bank on Saturdays?"

The sneer was more cutting for its toneless, dispassionate utterance. The wretched Harris was simply dismissed as unfit for human consumption. Nina, who resented irony more than abuse, attacks on her friends more than personal criticism, sprang to arms at once.

"I don't know what's wrong with Jack Harris," she said. "He's good enough for most people. He's not exactly intellectual, but it's never struck me that you'd be very comfortable with anybody who was."

She bounded out of the recess in her indignation.

"You've forgotten to pull up your shoulder strap," said Olive.

She stared for a moment at Morris, then passed on upstairs.

"Nina," said Delia, speaking low, "you mustn't take any notice of what Olive says tonight. She's not been well and her nerves are still on edge."

Nina's face cleared.

"Of course, I understand, Lady Pond. I'd heard that she'd been . . . sort of queer ever since the funeral. Only she and I have always been such friends that it's a bit of a shock when she tries to bite my head off at my own party."

"I know," agreed Delia soothingly. "I'll take her home early."

"Oh, you mustn't! It would look as if we'd really quarreled. Besides," Nina added candidly, "I'm more surprised than hurt. In the old days, if either of us was going to be bloody, it was always me. I didn't know Olive had it in her."

Jack Morris suddenly threw in a staccato comment. He said: "That girl reminds me of a woman I knew in Paris who used to take drugs. She was a devil when she'd had a few shots."

Delia went back to the table and played the worst bridge of her life.

5

It really was extraordinarily decent of her—a noble experiment in applied communism. Hard it might be for a woman to share her inanimate possessions, but far harder to relinquish the exclusive property in a man. Yet beyond doubt Nina was doing it deliberately. As soon as she had come into the dining room with Morris she had made for the corner of the buffet where Olive was already eating her supper. There they stood, the three of them, laughing and talking, on the best of terms. Or rather Nina was on the best of terms with the other two, and working energetically to produce a friendly compromise between Olive's still obvious hankering after Morris and his indifference to her. Not without success. The hard, predatory look had faded from Olive's face. Even her mouth had lost its startling venomous quality and become merely the mouth of a young girl wearing too much lipstick. For the first time in the evening she had the appearance of enjoying herself.

Morris, too, was responding, but more warily. As she watched him, Delia could believe that he had taken a genuine, though probably transient, fancy to Nina Hassett. Men had unlikely tastes. One would have expected him to find the perky, garrulous type boring to the last degree. Perhaps he merely had an easy seduction in view. Delia very much hoped not, because Nina deserved better. Unfortunately, she gave the impression that it would be extremely easy to trade on her confidence. She was the type to whom one could always sell a gold brick.

Morris took a glass of beer from the maid behind the buffet. As he turned round holding it, either he was bumped from behind or his hand slipped. A stream of liquid shot over the front of Nina's dress.

"Blast you, Jack!" she said.

"Frightfully sorry!" he protested. "Does it stain?"

"Stain! This frock'll look like a bar counter unless I do something quick."

Olive said: "Haven't you got any stuff you can dab it with immediately?"

"Have we, Rose?" Nina asked the maid.

"I'll see, miss." She went out of the room.

"I don't suppose you'll forgive me in a hurry," muttered Jack.

"I shouldn't," said Olive lightly.

"Maybe not. But I was asking Nina."

In the circumstances Nina was probably glad of the chance to send up her stock by displaying a little magnanimity.

"Oh, I don't know," she said. "You can't help it. You were born strong and silent and clumsy."

Mrs. Hassett's voice could be heard from the other side of the room, saying:

"I hope we don't have any more upsets tonight. There might be some real damage next time."

The maid returned carrying a bottle and a wad of cotton wool.

"This is all I could find, Miss Nina."

"What is it?"

"Ammonia. It's supposed to take out anything."

Nina withdrew the stopper and screwed up her face as the fumes seeped out.

"It smells pretty drastic. How much does one put on?"

"I couldn't really say, miss. I've always used that patent stuff of your mother's, but we've run out."

"I've cleaned things with ammonia," said Olive. "Uncle . . . Uncle James used to keep it."

"Well, I wish you'd try on me," said Nina.

"Are you sure you really want me to?"

"What do you mean? I shan't hold you responsible if it doesn't act or eats a hole in the material."

"All right," said Olive. "You'd better come over to the fireplace where there's more light."

Nina followed her. Almost immediately the brief distraction was forgotten, and the guests reverted to their food and conversation. Delia happened to be alone for the moment. Or, more accurately, she had moved herself to an inconspicuous position by the wall. She felt tired, too tired to be sociable. In the same idle way as people watch roadmenders, she watched the cleaning of Nina's dress.

Olive poured a few drops on to the cotton wool and passed it delicately over the stained surface. Then she returned to the bottle, which rested on the mantelpiece, to recharge her swab. Delia was near enough to catch fragments of their conversation.

". . . terribly attractive, but quite unprincipled. Someone ought to make a real effort with him."

"Yes," said Olive thoughtfully. She looked round. Jack Morris was the second person watching. "I can't quite get at this bit near the neck. Could you kneel down for a moment and put your head back."

Nina knelt down by the fireplace. Without looking round, Olive stretched back her hand to take up the ammonia. Her fingers passed above the top of the bottle, all but the little one which caught against its neck and toppled it forward, spilling a stream of caustic, vaporous chemical.

In the endless instant before the scream, before the general pandemonium, Delia's sound eyes darted away from those scorched ones, not in squeamishness, but hopelessly seeking denial of her unspeakable knowledge. Jack Morris's head jerked round as though compelled by a magnet. His face was not startled and vacant like that of a man who has seen an accident. It was full of a horrified comprehension.

6

"Do you feel fit to drive?"

"Yes."

Olive backed the car out of the recess by the shrubbery. On their way to the gates they had to edge carefully past the front door, because the doctor had left his car with the lights on in the middle of the gravel. They were the last of the guests to go. An ironic decency demanded it. Oh, those minutes of standing in the empty drawing room while every hushed footstep on the floor above evoked a picture of suffering! Not a word had passed between them. Delia had not been able to trust herself to speak: to sympathize, as though with the unwitting instrument of disaster, would have been nauseating hypocrisy—to accuse useless, perhaps dangerous, anyhow a course on which she could not embark with blurred judgment. Olive had never ceased the rhythmic tapping of her heel against the fender. Nobody could have complained that she looked indifferent to the havoc she had caused. But to Delia's imagination there was something a little too composed about her grief, it resembled too much the tight, prim, pussy-cat face of a young widow at the funeral of her elderly, unprepossessing husband.

If you closed one eye, you could still see quite well. You were not in any sense blind. Not blind, just handicapped.

If your face was scarred you were not necessarily hideous. Plastic surgery was marvelous nowadays. Besides, a face might have other things to recommend it than smooth perfection of skin.

O God, she thought, how easily I console myself for another's misery! "Be good, sweet maid, and let who will be beautiful." Sickening, saccharin dishonesty. Nina is ruined. She has neither the features nor the character to survive such an ordeal. The physical pain will die hard, but the knowledge of her injury will never die. The lack of self-consciousness was her mainspring. She enjoyed life, and she tumbled about investigating it, like a kitten. Now there will not be any more vital silliness or indiscriminate enthusiasm: there will be a crumpled little wreck who wears veils and goes out late so that people may not stare.

And the chain runs back—back to the conceited self-seeking young fool of 1918, who took her tin spoon to sup with the devil. Perhaps Joseph would get me off on that count by pleading that the causation was too remote. But even if it is not my fault that I begot a monster, I still have no defense against the charge of having loosed it on society. Alone, of my own express responsibility, I insisted that Olive should have her chance tonight. I rode down the protests of those who were better able to judge than myself. I wanted to believe that all was well. I wanted it, so everybody had to behave as though the reality would follow from my wishing. The same old folly, the 1918 brand—the smug faith in the infallibility of Delia Pond. I have learned nothing.

For a little while the thoughts ceased to race inside her head. So, it is said, fishermen, having weathered frightful winds and gigantic seas, come occasionally to a stretch of absolute calm, the motionless center of the storm cone. But there is no constancy in the focus of the clouds, and as they move, so the refuge is sucked away and the boat plunges again into confusion.

Strange, she thought bitterly, how small is the capacity of the human mind. Even tragedies are mutually exclusive. That for the moment uppermost has all our concern, our minds are darkened, and no second shadow is visible against the blackness. As though Nina's were the only life wrecked! I hate Olive: not my daughter, but the creature who passes under that name, because we have not dared to invent another. But that is a useless distinction: the child and the fiend go down together because they are inseparable in their common habitation.

Now we have been driven across the last river. Palliatives and pretenses are behind us. There is no more sense in delving for the causes, whether they be natural or beyond the discovery of reason. The unquiet spirit of James or some tiny disturbance in the network of the brain—take your choice, it makes no difference to the outcome. Olive is mad, diabolically mad with a kind of subtle madness which is the more dangerous for being intermittent. It burrows and hides itself for a little while, but its track stands out clear behind it, marked by a succession of ugly upheavals. And it is progressive. At first it was no more than a brutal coarsening of her own spirit; the earliest impact on others was beneficent, the means of saving a baby's life; malice picked its way slowly, step by step, first experimenting on the things that do not show the claw marks—an elderly scholar's peace of mind, a little cleric's tender conscience; now, full-fledged and insatiable, it embarks on a career of open destruction.

Delia was perhaps more impressed than most people would be with the superior heinousness of crimes against the body. It was because the law proscribed them, and she had lived long enough with her husband to imbibe his reverence for the code which represented the accumulated wisdom of society.

She has reached a point, Delia thought, where it is no longer her cure, but the protection of other people which must be considered. Mad dogs are killed, mad people remain nominally alive— in walled forts echoing with the furious protests of the deranged. A bit better if you have money, perhaps; the bed is not so hard, but the bars are still on the window and the time hangs just as heavy. I gave her birth for this—to ignore her for twenty years, and then return to bolt the door on everything of pleasure or freedom that she has known. If only I could believe in hell! I want to pay, it would comfort me to believe that I should pay for what I have brought about.

Though she did not know it, Delia had already achieved her wish in the only form in which it is intelligible to modern opinion. Slow and difficult, the tears trickled down her face, like lava expelled by an intolerable inward pressure.

"Crying?" said Olive abruptly.

Delia fumbled for her handkerchief, staring straight ahead through the windshield.

"If I'm weeping, it's for you, Olive."

"And why, may I ask?"

"Either you know already, or it would be no use my telling you."

"Come, come! You never used to be so shy of attempting the impossible or the unnecessary!"

As the spring of a gramophone runs down, and the high, clear notes of a singing woman drag for a moment and then are distorted to a harsh bellow, so, with each syllable, Olive's voice descended the scale, until two full octaves separated the last word from the first. It was terrible to hear; it was not like the empty booming of a tranced medium: it was a sound monstrous, yet expressive of distinct and individual life. In the last cadence the transition was almost complete. Once more the recognizable utterance of the dead proceeded from borrowed lips.

Delia's skin tingled and her heart tripped in its beating. A kind of claustrophobia aggravated her fear. People are never so much afraid of the uncanny if there is an open door behind them. Boxed up in the little car, moving rapidly down the black ribbon of road, featureless as an orbit in space, she shuddered at each jolt of the car, lest she be thrown into contact with something altogether loathsome. She did not dare to look toward the driving seat. She was afraid her eye might catch the glimmer of a white, silky beard.

But much as she dreaded that ghastly voice, she could not endure to cower in silence, like a mouse, waiting, petrified, for the cat to spring.

"Are you playing the same silly trick on me as you did on your Uncle Roger?"

A rasping, deep-throated chuckle answered her.

"*Olive, is that you?*"

"A nice point, my dear Delia. The materialist would look and answer, yes. The man who exalts spirit over substance might be more doubtful."

The fidelity of reproduction, which at first had terrified her, began gradually to cancel its own effect. The manner and the idiom were so humanly exact that they seemed to transcend illusion and create their own reality: as though she were indeed speaking to the embodied James and had nothing more to fear than the notorious acerbity of his speech. The natural orderliness of her mind reasserted itself. She set about regularizing the situation as she would have some social impasse.

"I always like to deal with the person in control, not subordinates. I'm going to address my remarks to James Marshall, until I have reason to suppose that they are misdirected."

"Very businesslike. Is your time, by any chance, money?"

James had always possessed an aptitude for deflating the competence in which she took a deep, unostentatious pride.

"James," she said, "you were warned once by your brother, you've ignored the warning. You've killed your golden goose."

"If this is a parable, I trust it will be a short one."

"You understand or you soon will. You're not going to have any more fun with your daughter."

"Really? Why is my program to be cut short like this?"

"Because Olive is going to a place where your choicest efforts will be wasted. I shall see to that if I have to move heaven and earth."

"I'm glad you're prepared for a certain opposition."

"Don't imagine that any sentimental horror of Olive's fate will stop me. She has ceased to exist."

The car shot forward at increased speed, as though the accelerator had been stamped down in anger. A cold triumph welled up in Delia's heart. She said:

"I'm going to knock down your fine new residence, James. Get yourself another if you can!"

"So it's to be Bedlam for me and my lady assistant? Have you considered whether they will agree to receive us?"

"What do you mean?" she said.

"Only that I am rather intangible for the purposes of certifying. And who knows but that Olive might put up a very creditable show before a board of mental experts!"

"She'll need to, if she's going to outface the detailed evidence of three or four sane people."

The car was traveling faster still. The beam of the headlights rocked and swayed with the vibration. But somehow it was inconceivable to Delia that this journey should ever come to an end. It had no relation to time.

The harsh, ironic voice of James sounded above the hammering of the engine.

"If my eminent colleagues are all that they were, I should enjoy seeing your attempts to persuade them that Olive suffered from a touch of haunting."

Delia's heart grew cold again. But she answered bravely:

"Maiming—attempted murder—those are things which everybody can believe . . ."

". . . Subject to a little proof. I'm afraid, Delia, that you must have a warped mind to pervert an accident into the likeness of crime. Shame on you! A most unnatural mother that can't take a slip of her own daughter's hand at its face value."

Once more he turned the trick. His frightful perspicacity picked out the flaw which made rubbish of all her agonized heart-searching and the decision to which it had so painfully led. She had steeled herself to sacrifice Olive: and now it was pointed out with inexorable logic that she could not perform the sacrifice because her hands were tied.

"James," she said, "do you think that I am going to wait passively until you commit your next atrocity?"

"I think you're going to wait a lot longer than that. Since when have I been a blunderer? Do you expect our Olive to wander down Piccadilly slaughtering the bystanders?"

In a moment of ghastly apocalypse Delia saw him marching on from one violation of humanity to another—each masked with consummate ingenuity, each a masterpiece of pure diabolism.

She could detect only one weak point in his position, at which to launch a last appeal.

"Once," she said, "you told me that you despised men with small, clever minds, subtle in foreseeing every detail, but without any ultimate horizon. You were wiser in those days. Surely it would be better to die outright than to linger on suffering a kind of posthumous senile decay."

"Well, well, and I thought I was so marvelous for my age!"

"You're not, James. Your actions show the loss of all rational power. It's subhuman to destroy without motive. What conceivable object have you in persecuting those from whom you have no longer anything to fear or gain? Why do you do it?"

"Recreation."

Then Delia knew that the seed sown long ago in the corporeal man had reached its fullest, rankest growth: it had choked out all rivals to its absolute and exclusive possession. James had been a very, an exceptionally bad man, but he had never so far belied his human origin as to be totally lacking in good qualities or periodic flashes of honor. He had undoubtedly performed services to the community which could only have been inspired by a sense of duty. Now all that was gone, gone with the body which imposes its limitations on man's spirit, hindering perfection of virtue and depravity, alike.

The integral James no more existed than the integral Olive. Both were victims, only to be distinguished by the degree in which they had invited their own fates. Both were merged in an elemental evil, which could as little be dissuaded from its ordained function as water from its inherent wetness.

Delia lost the last traces of her fear. She had exhausted its wellspring, which is the anticipation of worse to come. Deliberately she turned her head, stiff-necked from long immobility, toward the driving seat. With a dull surprise she noted how little the figure at the wheel reflected the spirit's inward duress. Olive sat there with the green dress showing under her short fur coat, outwardly unchanged, save for a wooden, doll-like fixity in her attitude. Her face was obscured by shadow.

The dial of the speedometer, too, was invisible. But the little car creaked and groaned under the furious revolution of the engine. From the puddles splintered ice flew up round the mudguards like hail. The wheels slid this way and that on the treacherous surface. Yet there was a kind of nerveless certainty in the driving. It was like the secure progress of a sleepwalker along a high window ledge.

Delia spoke only once more.

"I started this, and now I'm going to stop it."

She was talking to herself, briefly formulating the ancient creed of guilt and expiation.

The red-eyed warning posts that guarded the dike flashed past in a continuous twinkle.

So quickly that all her movements seemed to blend into one, Delia leaned across and wrenched over the steering wheel to the full extent of the lock. Almost the last thing she felt was the cold softness of Olive's hand.

Wood splintered, ice cracked, with a piercing report like the noise of a floe as it splits in the polar sunshine.

ALSO AVAILABLE FROM VALANCOURT BOOKS

Michael Arlen	Hell! said the Duchess
R. C. Ashby (Ruby Ferguson)	He Arrived at Dusk
Frank Baker	The Birds
Walter Baxter	Look Down in Mercy
Charles Beaumont	The Hunger and Other Stories
	The Intruder
	A Touch of the Creature
David Benedictus	The Fourth of June
Paul Binding	Harmonica's Bridegroom
Charles Birkin	The Smell of Evil
John Blackburn	A Scent of New-Mown Hay
	Broken Boy
	Blue Octavo
	A Ring of Roses
	Children of the Night
	Nothing but the Night
	Bury Him Darkly
	Our Lady of Pain
Thomas Blackburn	The Feast of the Wolf
Michael Blumlein	The Brains of Rats
John Braine	Room at the Top
	The Vodi
Jack Cady	The Well
Michael Campbell	Lord Dismiss Us
David Case	Among the Wolves & Other Stories
	Fengriffen & Other Stories
R. Chetwynd-Hayes	The Monster Club
	Looking for Something to Suck
Isabel Colegate	The Blackmailer
Basil Copper	The Great White Space
	Necropolis
	The House of the Wolf
Jennifer Dawson	The Ha-Ha
Frank De Felitta	The Entity
A. E. Ellis	The Rack
Barry England	Figures in a Landscape
Ronald Fraser	Flower Phantoms
Michael Frayn	The Tin Men
	The Russian Interpreter
	Towards the End of the Morning
	A Very Private Life
	Sweet Dreams

GILLIAN FREEMAN	The Liberty Man
	The Leather Boys
	The Leader
RODNEY GARLAND	The Heart in Exile
STEPHEN GILBERT	The Landslide
	The Burnaby Experiments
	Ratman's Notebooks
MARTYN GOFF	The Plaster Fabric
	The Youngest Director
F. L. GREEN	Odd Man Out
STEPHEN GREGORY	The Cormorant
	The Woodwitch
	The Blood of Angels
ALEX HAMILTON	Beam of Malice
JOHN HAMPSON	Saturday Night at the Greyhound
ERNEST G. HENHAM	Tenebrae
THOMAS HINDE	The Day the Call Came
CLAUDE HOUGHTON	Neighbours
	I Am Jonathan Scrivener
	This Was Ivor Trent
FRED HOYLE	The Black Cloud
ALAN JUDD	The Devil's Own Work
JAMES KENNAWAY	The Mind Benders
	The Cost of Living Like This
CYRIL KERSH	The Aggravations of Minnie Ashe
GERALD KERSH	Fowlers End
	Nightshade and Damnations
FRANCIS KING	Never Again
	An Air That Kills
	The Dividing Stream
	The Dark Glasses
C.H.B. KITCHIN	The Sensitive One
	Birthday Party
	Ten Pollitt Place
	The Book of Life
	A Short Walk in Williams Park
HILDA LEWIS	The Witch and the Priest
JOHN LODWICK	Brother Death
ROBERT MARASCO	Burnt Offerings
GABRIEL MARLOWE	I Am Your Brother
KENNETH MARTIN	Aubade
MICHAEL MCDOWELL	The Amulet
	Cold Moon Over Babylon
	The Elementals

Michael Nelson	Knock or Ring
	A Room in Chelsea Square
Beverley Nichols	Crazy Pavements
Oliver Onions	The Hand of Kornelius Voyt
Dennis Parry	Sea of Glass
Christopher Priest	The Affirmation
J.B. Priestley	Benighted
	The Doomsday Men
	The Other Place
	The Magicians
	Saturn Over the Water
	The Thirty-First of June
	The Shapes of Sleep
	Salt Is Leaving
Piers Paul Read	Monk Dawson
Forrest Reid	Following Darkness
	The Spring Song
	Brian Westby
	The Tom Barber Trilogy
	Denis Bracknel
Andrew Sinclair	The Facts in the Case of E.A. Poe
	The Raker
	Gog
David Storey	Radcliffe
	Pasmore
	Saville
Michael Talbot	The Delicate Dependency
Bernard Taylor	The Godsend
	Sweetheart, Sweetheart
Russell Thorndike	The Slype
	The Master of the Macabre
John Wain	Hurry on Down
	The Smaller Sky
	A Winter in the Hills
Hugh Walpole	The Killer and the Slain
Keith Waterhouse	There is a Happy Land
	Billy Liar
	Billy Liar on the Moon
Colin Wilson	Ritual in the Dark
	Man Without a Shadow
	Necessary Doubt
	The Glass Cage
	The Philosopher's Stone
	The God of the Labyrinth

WHAT CRITICS ARE SAYING ABOUT VALANCOURT BOOKS

"Valancourt Books champions neglected but important works of fantastic, occult, decadent and gay literature. The press's Web site not only lists scores of titles but also explains why these often obscure books are still worth reading. . . . So if you're a real reader, one who looks beyond the bestseller list and the touted books of the moment, Valancourt's publications may be just what you're searching for."

Michael Dirda, Washington Post

"Valancourt are doing a magnificent job in making these books not only available but—in many cases—known at all . . . these reprints are well chosen and well designed (often using the original dust jackets), and have excellent introductions."

Times Literary Supplement (London)

"Valancourt Books are fast becoming my favourite publisher. They have made it their business, with considerable taste and integrity, to put back into print a considerable amount of work which has been in serious need of republication. If you ever felt there were gaps in your reading experience or are simply frustrated that you can't find enough good, substantial fiction in the shops or even online, then this is the publisher for you."

Michael Moorcock

"The best resurrectionists since Burke and Hare!"
Andrew Sinclair

TO LEARN MORE AND TO SEE A COMPLETE LIST OF AVAILABLE TITLES, VISIT US AT VALANCOURTBOOKS.COM